WRONGFUL DEATH

WRONGFUL DEATH

a novel in dialogue

Gene Brewer

author of the K-PAX trilogy

Copyright © 2006 by Gene Brewer.
ISBN :   Hardcover   1-4257-1223-1
          Softcover   1-4257-1222-3

All rights reserved. No part of this book may be reproduced or transmitted in any form or by any means, electronic or mechanical, including photocopying, recording, or by any information storage and retrieval system, without permission in writing from the copyright owner.

This is a work of fiction. Names, characters, places and incidents either are the product of the author's imagination or are used fictitiously, and any resemblance to any actual persons, living or dead, events, or locales is entirely coincidental.

This book was printed in the United States of America.

To order additional copies of this book, contact:
Xlibris Corporation
1-888-795-4274
www.Xlibris.com
Orders@Xlibris.com

OTHER BOOKS BY GENE BREWER

K-PAX

K-PAX II: On a Beam of Light

K-PAX III: The Worlds of Prot

K-PAX: the Trilogy, featuring Prot's Report

Creating K-PAX

"Alejandro," in *Twice Told*

Murder on Spruce Island

Contents

The Preliminaries 9

The Case For The Plaintiffs 71

The Case For The Defense 153

The Verdict 217

The Preliminaries 224

Acknowledgments 227

Afterword 229

The Preliminaries

"Hear the one about Tiger Woods and the lawyer?"

"Huh? Oh, it's 'Seinfeld.' Okay, here's a quarter, but I don't have time for a joke today."

"It's your loss."

*

"Please. Sit down."

"Thank you."

"Thank you."

"I'm very sorry about your daughter."

"Thank you. So are we."

"Now what, exactly, did you have in mind?"

"Mr. Allen, we're not out for revenge. We just want to see that what happened to Angela won't ever happen again to someone else's child."

"You want to file a malpractice suit against her doctor."

"If it would put a stop to it, yes. But that would only be scratching the surface. We want to try to stop the company that made the drug that killed her from putting any more unsafe drugs on the market."

"That won't be an easy thing to do, Mr. Calvecchi. The——"

"We don't care."

"Let me finish. The pharmaceutical company that put out the drug your daughter was taking will have a whole battery of lawyers working on the case. They'll try to prove that the company followed strict safety procedures and are not to blame for what happened to her. Of course I haven't had a chance to look at the precedents, but I doubt there have been many successful lawsuits of this kind. On top of that, the judge might consider the case a 'revenge' suit, and throw the whole thing out before it even gets into a courtroom."

"We're willing to take that chance."

"And even if the judge doesn't throw out the case it might take years to resolve it. Expert witnesses, delaying tactics, appeals—it could be very expensive . . . ."

"How expensive?"

"Well, we can do it in one of two ways. Normally we get a third of any settlement we might obtain. No settlement, no fee. Or we could do it on an hourly basis. If you choose the latter and we win, you don't have to pay us a percentage of the award."

"What's your hourly fee?"

"Two fifty."

"How many hours will it take you to prepare the case?"

"Impossible to say, but it would probably be in the hundreds. And that's before we even get to a courtroom."

"We'll take the percentage arrangement."

"We might be able to do that, but I'll have to talk it over with the senior partners in the firm. For now, why don't you tell me exactly what happened to your daughter."

"Here's the newspaper clippings and reports we said we'd bring in."

"Thank you—I'll look these over later. Can you tell me in your own words what happened?"

"Our daughter had diabetes. Her doctor told us there was a new drug out that might help her. In fact, he said it had cured her disease in animals. So we agreed to let him use it."

"A clinical trial."

"Yes, that's what he called it."

"Did he tell you about the risks?"

"He said there might be some side effects."

"Like what?"

"Headaches, nausea, muscle pain, diarrhea—stuff like that."

"Did he tell you what to do if any of this happened?"

"He said to give him a call."

"Did he tell you the treatment could be fatal?"

"Yes, but he said the risk of that was very small. 'Miniscule,' I think he said."

"Did he give you any written information about what you might expect?"

"It's in the folder."

"Did you sign anything? A waiver?"

"Yes."

"Is that in the folder?"

"We didn't get a copy of it."
"You were supposed to get a copy."
"They didn't give us one."
"Who is 'they'?"
"The doctor. The clinic."
"Okay. Now I know this is going to be difficult, and I'm sorry. But could you tell me what happened on the night Angela died?"
"It was only the second day she had been taking the medicine. She didn't feel very good the first day, and we called the doctor, but the nurse told us this was normal and we should go on with the treatment."
"You didn't speak with the doctor?"
"No."
"So you went on with the medication."
"Yes."
"What time did you give her the last—what was it, a pill or a capsule?"
"A bright yellow capsule. Angela thought it looked cheerful . . . ."
"What time did you give her the last capsule?"
"Around seven o'clock."
"In the evening?"
"Yes. Then she went to bed."
"And what did you do?"
"We watched television for a while, then Elmira went to check on her. She came back and said that Angela was asleep."
"And then you went to bed?"
"Yes."
"What time was that?"
"Nine, nine-thirty?"
"It was twenty after nine."
"Okay. And in the morning—"
"She was gone."
"Again, I'm sorry to have to ask you a question like this, but how did you know she was 'gone'?"
"She was cold."
"And she wasn't breathing."
"What did you do then?"
"I stayed with her while Tony called 911."
"But it was too late."
"They said she had been dead for several hours."
"Was there an autopsy?"
"Yes. They said it was required in cases like this."
"What were the results of the autopsy?"

"We only have the preliminary report."

"Her heart had stopped. She had an arrhyth—an arrhym—"

"An arrhythmia."

"That was mentioned as the likely cause of death in the preliminary report?"

"Yes."

"And you didn't hear anything during the night?"

"No."

"How far away from her bedroom were you sleeping?"

"Right across the hall."

"Were the doors open?"

"Yes."

"Do you have the vial, the one that had the capsules in it?"

"No. The police took that."

"Mr. Calvecchi, did your daughter take insulin?"

"Yes, of course. Twice a day."

"Did her doctor say there could be some kind of interaction between that and the new medication?"

"Yes, but she stopped taking the insulin when she started on the medication."

"He told you to do that?"

"Yes."

"Okay. Is there anything else you need to tell me before I look into this matter?"

"Mr. Allen, Angela was our only child. We loved her very much. She was a very smart girl and was already thinking about college and becoming a doctor. Her little life—"

"Take your time, Mrs. Calvecchi."

"She would have been fourteen this month."

"I'm very sorry."

"We hope you'll take the case."

"I'll tell you what I'll do: I'll take a look at the material and talk it over with my partners, then I'll get back to you, probably in three or four days. Would that be all right?"

"That's fine."

"We'll be waiting for your call."

*

"Like to order a dozen roses sent to someone."

"Sure, Mr. Allen. The usual?"

"I guess."
"One dozen . . . long-stemmed . . . red roses."
"Right."
"And who are they going to this time?"
"Nancy Edmondson."
"M-o-n-d?"
"Yes, that's right."
"Address?"
"Eighty-eight West Charles."
"Phone number?"
"664-7660."
"Got it. Cash or charge?"
"Charge."
"Still using Visa?"
"Here."
"Thank you, Mr. Allen."
"Mm-hm."
"Another fight?"
"Not exactly . . . ."
"It's terrible when that happens, isn't it?"
"Mm."
"Red roses are good for that. I ought to know. My housemate and I break up at least once a week."
"And the red roses always work, do they?"
"Every time. I think he's just bitchy sometimes because he likes roses."
"Funny—they don't seem to work too well for me."
"That's what your dad used to say whenever he tried to make up with your mother for something."
"I know."
"How are they doing, your folks?"
"Okay. Divorce seems to agree with them."
"If something went wrong there, it couldn't have been your dad's fault. He's a wonderful man. Did some nice things for us when—well, never mind."
"Really? What?"
"I shouldn't have said that. He made us swear to secrecy. Sign by the X please . . . and Mr. Allen?"
"Yes?"
"You might do better if you send more flowers *before* you break up with your girlfriends . . . ."

*

"You took the case?"

"Well, not in so many words."

"But you encouraged them."

"Not really. I told them it would be a very difficult case. In fact, I intimated that it was practically hopeless."

"It's hopeless, period."

"I couldn't agree more, Sammy. I don't want the damn case. But I told them I'd talk to Bill and Lew about it. And Dad, of course."

"I disagree. No case is hopeless. There are too many unknowns. The judge, the jury, undiscovered evidence . . . ."

"Bill, you know goddamn well it's hopeless. Pass those donuts down, will you?"

"Maybe the parents are right about the drug . . . ."

"Right or wrong has nothing to do with winning, folks."

"There have been more hopeless cases. You've won a couple of them yourself."

"What about *A Civil Action*? That was a hopeless case."

"Yeah, and look what happened to the lawyer. He was—what—selling used cars for a while—something like that?"

"It sounds like a sucker to me."

"A sucker?"

"It sounds like one of those cases that will suck all of us into it. All our resources will get tied up in this damn thing. I'm opposed."

"We haven't asked for a vote yet, Sammy."

"Marc, can you get them to take an hourly arrangement?"

"I doubt it. I don't think they're very well off. But they seem to be pretty dedicated to carrying this thing out, regardless of how—"

"Sorry I'm late, folks. What have I missed?"

"Your son here was telling us about Calvecchi v. Mercer. Says he doesn't want the case. Has he filled you in on that?"

"He mentioned something about it, yes."

"What's your take on that, Marcus?"

"I can see both sides of the question. Anyway, it's up to Bill and Lew. I'm 'semi-retired,' remember?"

"Ladies and gentlemen, we've heard the negatives. Let's look at the positives. We've had some bad publicity lately. Not to mention a couple of other setbacks. I won't name names here, but you all know what I'm talking about. This might be just the kind of case we need right now, win or lose. It's the type of thing that will get us in the papers, on the nightly news. It's something everyone can identify with, even people who don't have children. All of us are at the mercy of their doctors, their medications. There's a lot of concern out there about that, especially in view of the cutbacks and belt tightening going on right now. Stingy HMO's, hurry-up visits, prescription mixups, hospital errors, overpriced drugs—"

"On top of that, it's going to the biggest human interest story going. Did everyone here read about this case? Have you seen the little girl's picture? She was beautiful. Smart. Limitless potential. She's going to have the sympathy of every American who doesn't kick dogs in the streets."

"Is there any more coffee?"

"And the other side of that coin is Mercer & Co. They're going to get the worst publicity in their history."

"And the best lawyers money can buy."

"Marc, have there been any other deaths resulting from the use of the drug?"

"I haven't looked into that yet."

"What's it called, anyway?"

"Mercipine."

"Perfect! They attached their own name to the damn thing."

"No doubt they meant it as a double entendre."

"Obviously."

"They might very well be eager to settle. Get the whole thing behind them."

"Good point. I say we let Marc, Jr. find out how widespread this is. If it's another thalidomide, we go for it. If the girl is the only casualty, it's a waste of time."

"Not if we can get a settlement right off the bat."

"Any volunteers to help Marc on this?"

"It's his case. Let him do some research on it before he takes on a partner."

"What if they can't afford the hourly fee?"

"Ladies and gentlemen, I think we should respect plaintiff's wishes for a percentage arrangement. Any further discussion? Good. Now who wants to help Marc out with this? No takers? Okay, let's look at it the other way. Marc, who would you like for an assistant in this case?"

"Wait a minute! Don't I get a vote on this? I don't have the experience for a medical lawsuit against a giant drug company like Mercer—"

"Marc, you've been with us for six years. When will you be ready to handle something like this?"

"Maybe in another year or two . . . ."

"Perfect. It'll take that long to get it into a courtroom."

"Okay, okay, I'll take it on and I'll do my best. But only if Dad helps me out on it. He's the most experienced lawyer we have in medical malpractice suits."

"What about it, Marcus?"

"Son, right now I've got four cases up my nose and I'm supposed to be phasing out—"

"So have I."

"All right. But only if you're lead attorney. I'll help you in any way I can, but it's your case."

"Any other business, ladies and gentlemen of the bar? Very well, let's go kick some ass!"

*

"You wanted to see me about Calvecchi v. Mercer, Marc?"

"If you have a minute."

"That's exactly what I have, then I'm out of here. What have you got so far?"

"Well, Mercer and company are headquartered in-state, and of course the Calvecchis live here, too, as well as the girl's doctor. The outfit that administered the clinical testing program resides in Illinois, so we'd have to take them to federal court. Then of course we could go after the FDA, but—"

"Hold on, son. Have you looked at all the databases? Figured out who are the top people in the field? Come up with any kind of theory about exactly where the fault lies here?"

"Not yet, no. I'm just getting started, Dad."

"Well, get back to me when you've learned something about clinical testing and looked into all the similar cases you can dig up. Find out who the experts might be on what goes into the making of a pharmaceutical compound and how the doctors are selected to pass out the drug and how the testing is administered. Get some information about the nature of diabetes. But before you do any of that, look into the statutes of limitation. If you're going to sue a governmental body like the FDA you won't have much time to prepare for it."

"'You'? I thought it was 'we.'"

"I said I would help. You're the attorney of record. Got to run, Marc. Have a good weekend."

"But—"

*

"Marcus Allen, Jr.?"

"That's right."

"McBain from the *Post*. How are you?"

"So-so. How'd you know where to find me?"

"I stopped by your office. They said you often come here for a beer when you leave for the day. Though sometimes you don't leave for the day. Buy you another one?"

"Sure. Why not?"

"TWO MORE AMSTELS OVER HERE! I'll get right to the point, Mr. Allen—"

"Marc."

"Marc. I want to do a story on the Mercer case. In fact, I want to do a series of stories. Follow the case as it goes along."

"Why?"

"Lot of reasons. It has a great human interest side to it, with the tragic death of a brave little thirteen-year-old girl and all that. And there's the David and Goliath story. Ordinary people going up against a giant pharmaceutical company, maybe the government. Then there's the price of drugs and what goes into that. Lot of angles . . . ."

"Wait a minute, Mr.—uh—"

"McBain."

"How'd you know about the case, anyway?"

"Off the record?"

"Okay (rrrrp), off the record."

"Can't tell you."

"I see. And you're with the *Post*?"

"That's right. Eight years."

"Then you know I'm not going to tell you a damn thing until we file."

"You misunderstand. I'm not talking about the legal stuff. Not until you're ready for that, anyway."

"What, then?"

"Like I said, I want to focus on the personal side of it. Talk to the Calvecchis. Find out how they live. What they think about all this. Talk to *you*. Maybe talk to the guy who invented the drug, whoever that might be. You know—make it a series about the people involved—up close and personal."

"You don't want to talk to me. I don't have that much of a personal life."

"Everyone has a personal life, even if they don't have one."

"Not me. Anyway, I'd rather keep my personal life personal."

"Then I'll have to write the story from the point of view of the selfless humanitarians who, at great personal sacrifice, developed the drug that might be a miracle cure for diabetes. That makes *you* the 'Goliath.' Or maybe worse. Have a good weekend, Marc."

"All right, goddamn it. I'm thirty-two years old, not married, live with a cat, work seventy-five hours a week, and my sex life is practically nonexistent. What else do you want to know?"

*

"Hi, Mom."

"Do I know you?"

"C'mon, Mom, don't start that. I've been covered up with work."

"It must be genetic."

"No, it's the legal profession."

"No wonder you're not married yet. Who would want to spend their life waiting for you to come home?"

"You married Dad."

"I was young and stupid then."

"You were twenty-five, Mom."

"And your dad was nearly forty. He seemed very worldly then. Oh, I was so naive."

"But you loved him, didn't you?"

"I was crazy about him. Like I said, I was young and stupid. And he pretended he loved me at the time."

"He did love you, Mom. I think he still does."

"He was late for his own wedding."

"Something probably came up at the last minute."

"It always does."

"Anyway, we're working together on a big case now. Did he tell you?"

"When would he tell me? I haven't talked to him in weeks."

"I thought he called you every weekend."

"He did for a while."

"Maybe he's had some big bridge tournaments lately."

"He's always got something going on. But it's never with us."

"He was always good to me, Mom."

"Only because he saw you as his replacement in the world."

"What about Tim? Doesn't he see Tim every couple of weeks?"

"No. He hasn't seen him for a long time."

"Hm. I didn't know that. Want me to ask him about it?"

"What's the point? He won't ever change."

"I'll ask him. Where *is* Tim, anyway?"

"He went off on his bike somewhere. He's got the same genes you and your father do. Never wants to be home."

"Well, you can't blame him. It's the first nice spring day."

"It's a shame, though. He would love to have seen you. Why can't you take him to a ball game or something some time?"

"I will. Soon as I get some free time."

"Uh-huh."

"Mom, I've got to run. I just wanted to stop in and see how you and Timmy were doing."

"We're doing just fine. What did you say your name was?"

"Now, Mom . . . ."

*

"Good morning, Mr. Allen! Have a good weekend?"

"About average."

"For you that's good, Mr. Allen! And how's your dad?"

"Same as always."

"Haven't seen him for a while!"

"He's been pretty busy, Goose. Anyway, the doctor told him he has to watch his diet. No more butter or cream cheese or anything else that tastes good."

"I know how it is! Well, you tell him I said hello!"

"I will, Goose. Can I have a poppyseed bagel and some of that hazelnut coffee?"

"Sure, Mr. Allen! The usual schmeer? With chives?"

"Why not?"

"You got it! Listen, will you tell your dad I could give him a bagel with fat-free, if he wants! Pretty good stuff, and it's even supposed to lower your cholesterol! Use it myself at home!"

"Ah, you don't need to go to all that trouble, Goose. Dad doesn't stop here for a bagel every day, after all."

"For him, it's no trouble, Mr. Allen! He helped me out a couple of times, and I won't forget it!"

"I'll tell him you said that."

"No, no! Don't tell him I said nothing! He said it was just between him and me!"

"Why? How did he help you out?"

"He loaned me money two different times when I was in bad shape! Not too many guys would've done that! But he didn't want nobody else to know about it!"

"That sounds like him."

"But it wasn't because other guys like me would hit on him! He said it just wasn't anybody else's business!"

"Well, that's true, it wasn't."

"Made a big difference to me, I can tell you that! I just thought you might like to know! But don't tell him I said nothing!"

"Okay, Goose. If you say so."

"Thanks, Mr. Allen! Here's your poppyseed and hazelnut! Enjoy 'em!"

"Thanks, Goose."

"Here's your change!"

"Keep it. And thanks for telling me about Dad."

"Thanks, Mr. Allen! And don't tell him I said nothing!"

"I won't."

"Beautiful day!"

"Yes, it is."

"See you later, Mr. Allen!"

"Okay, Goose."

"Say hello to your dad for me! And tell him about the fat-free!"

*

"Hi, Dad. C'mon in."

"Hello, Marc. You ready to talk about Calvecchi now?"

"Almost. How come you never go over to see Tim any more?"

"I was busy last weekend."

"Bridge tournament?"

"No."

"Dad, are you seeing another woman?"

"Are you trying to make me laugh? My woman-chasing days were over a long time ago."

"You worked all weekend?"

"Not the whole weekend, no. If you must know, my back was killing me. I tried to pick up a box of files and it almost went out. My back, I mean, not the box."

"Did you call Mike?"

"What can he do? I've had chronic back pain for years."

"But if it's getting worse . . . ."

"He'd send me to some specialist or other, and I'd end up underneath a knife and a big light. No, thanks."

"It's better today?"

"Some. Enough trivia. What's happening with the Mercer thing?"

"Well, I've searched all the databases and come up short. It's almost impossible to win a lawsuit against a pharmaceutical company. There've been a couple of cases where fraud or incompetence was shown in court, but in both cases someone inside the company testified against them. We'd have to be very lucky to find someone like that at Mercer. I'm still looking into the general procedures the drug people use to show that a new drug is safe, but it's all regulated by the FDA and it's going to be difficult to get at the company on procedural matters. They'll just claim they were following FDA guidelines. But I've already contacted two of the top experts in the field."

"Who are your experts?"

"A guy named McCall. He's a professor of biochemistry at a place called Morgan State University in Montana. He's written a couple of books and testified a lot in similar cases. The other one is a woman. Megan Leonard. Supposed to be brilliant. Heads up a very successful biotech company."

"What are they telling you?"

"Some very interesting things. They think we need to look into Mercer's record—see if there's a pattern of safety problems in the past. They think there is."

"So have you looked into that?"

"I've looked into their history a bit. They've had some problems in the past, but probably not enough to establish a pattern. So it's going to be difficult to bring it into the record. As for Mercipine itself, we'll have to get the information on Discovery."

"So where does all this get us right now?"

"I think we ought to go after the doctor and the drug company. Forget about the FDA and the outfit that administered the clinical trial unless we find some irregularities in the paperwork, something like that. But even if we did, it probably wouldn't be grounds for a federal lawsuit."

"Who administered the clinical trial?"

"A company called Minskoff and O'Rourke."

"A corporate research organization, not a university."

"That's right."

"Have you dug up any dirt on them?"

"Not a speck."

"They did all the right paperwork and so on?"

"Still working on—aren't you listening, Dad? I just told you that."

"Sorry. It's this damn back. Hard to concentrate when it's like this."

"Dad, go see Mike about it, will you?"

"If it's not any better in a couple of days. Who did you say the CRO was?"

"Minskoff and O'Rourke."

"That name tinkles a little bell in my head. Let me see if I've got anything on them in my files."

"Okay, Dad. But after that, go see Mom and Timmy, will you?"

"As soon as I get a few things off my desk."

"And take care of your back from now on, will you? No more lifting. Get someone else to do it."

"There's no one else there, pal. I live alone—remember?"

*

"Hi, Fuzzball, you have a good day? Huh? Have a good day? What a good kitty! WHAT a good kitty! What a GOOD kitty!"

"Yowwwwwwwww."

"Want your dinner? Hmmmmm? Want your dinner, Fuzzy? Oh, you *did* want your dinner! All right. All right. All riiiight."

"Yowwwwwwwww."

"Would you accept Tuna Surprise? Do you find that acceptable? Huh? Tuna Surprise all right with you?"

"Yowwwwwwwww."

"Oh, it *is* all right. Okay, just a minute. Just a MINute. Where's your dish? What have you done with your dish? How'd your dish get way over there? All right. All right . . . . *There* you are. Tuna Surprise!

"Oh, my, you *were* hungry weren't you? WHAT a hungry cat! You still have water? Not much! Did you drink all that water today? I'm impressed—what a thirsty cat!

"Is that good, old lady? You like that? I thought you might . . . .

"What—finished already? Oh, all right. Come on up here in Daddy's lap for a minute. That's a good kitty."

"Rrrrrrrrr."

"Oh, you want me to scratch your ears? Is that it? You want me to scratch your ears, old kitty? You just can't get enough of that, can you? Huh? Can you . . . ?"

"Rrrrrrrrrrrrrr."

"All right, I've got to get to work now. Go on down, Fuzz. Oh, you want to stay here on my lap? Well, all right, but just for a little while, okay? Daddy's got to go to work. Got to go to work . . . ."

"Rrrrrrrrrrrrrrrrrrr."

*

"Hi, Marc. Where's your old man today, do you know? I need to see him about something."

"No, I don't, Sammy. I think he might have gone to see Mike Polidar."

"His doctor? What's the matter with him?"

"Nothing that can't be fixed. Just that chronic back problem of his."

"Well, let's hope he doesn't have to have surgery. Back surgery's a pisser."

"Probably not. He tried to lift something last week and—you know—same old story."

"Yeah. He's had that a long time. By the way, how's the Mercer case coming along?"

"Okay. Dad's been a great help on that."

"Have you developed a theory yet?"

"We both think the only chance we have is to show that either Mercer was lax in determining the safety of the drug, or the doctor was negligent in administering it. We've looked into a lot of precedents, and suing the FDA isn't a viable alternative in a case like this."

"What about the outfit that administered the clinical part of the procedure?"

"Same thing. They had one incident in the past. But as long as they dot their i's and cross their t's, it's hard to pin anything on them."

"That only leaves the doctor and pharmaceutical company itself."

"Yep. That's about it."

"So you'll be filing in state court."

"That's right."

"Marc, there's something I don't understand about a case like this. If Mercer's procedures were approved by the FDA, how can you find grounds to sue them?"

"Well, for example, if the FDA requires that the toxicity of a new drug must be tested on fifty rats, and they only used forty, they can be held liable for reporting incomplete and inaccurate safety information."

"That's not what I meant. If the FDA accepted their data, whether it was complete or not, doesn't that let Mercer off the hook?"

"Not necessarily, Sammy. There was a case about twenty years ago where somebody at the FDA rubberstamped some fictitious data, and the court ruled that the company, not the government, is responsible for producing honest and accurate information. That's a strong precedent that's never been overturned. We're hoping to find some kind of hole like that."

"Sounds like a fishing expedition."

"Not really. Mercer has a mediocre safety record. Up to now they've been lucky and have gotten away with it."

"Marc, if I remember right, the case you just mentioned was overturned on appeal."

"Yes, but for other reasons. And there have been a few cases since then where the precedent was upheld."

"Sounds like you won't be filing for a while."

"Not right away, but we're getting there."

*

"That was a great play, Marc. Thanks for taking me. And for dinner. That was wonderful, too."

"You're welcome."

"Well, goodnight, then."

"Aren't you going to ask me in for a 'nightcap,' like in the play?"

"Not tonight, Marc. Maybe next time."

"I'm not a bit tired."

"I am."

"I'll do all the work."

"Maybe some other time."

"I may be dead then."

"Goodnight, Marc."

"I won't stay long. We could just talk. I was wondering what the playwright meant by 'The times, the times are a'wanderin'.'"

"I think she meant it's time to say goodnight."

"Can I call you?"

"Sure. But I'm booked up for a while."

"All the more reason to—"

[Click]

*

"Hi, Mr. Calvecchi. Mrs. Calvecchi. How are you both?"

"Okay."

"Fine, thank you."

"Please. Sit down."

"Thank you."

"I brought you in here today to go over a few things. First, we finally got the complete autopsy report on Angela. All the microscopical and chemical analyses. I'm going to give you a copy before you leave, but I wanted to discuss it with you first."

"Fine."

"Thank you."

"The good news is that the coroner has ruled that Angela's death was, in fact, caused by drug toxicity. And the only drug she was taking, other than Tylenol, was Mercipine. Those were the only drugs found in her system. That's the good news, if you can call it that."

"What's the bad news?"

"The finding still doesn't legally prove that the drug caused her death, nor that Mercer and company is liable."

"Why not?"

"The laboratory findings are suggestive, but not conclusive. The problem is that there has been very little experience with this drug. It could have been a coincidence. She could have died of unknown causes related to her illness, or to something else altogether."

"Then how can you ever prove anyone died from taking a drug of some kind?"

"Well, in the case of heroin, for example, there's plenty of information on what levels are toxic or fatal. Otherwise, it's difficult. Very difficult . . ."

"So did you bring us in here to tell us you aren't going to proceed with the lawsuit?"

"Not at all. I'm just saying we probably should wait a little longer before we file the suit. We're trying now to find out whether anyone else taking the drug had a—uh—a negative reaction like Angela did. The more such cases we can find, the easier it will be to show that Mercipine was the causative agent in Angela's death."

"How much longer do we have to wait?"

"Not long. Maybe a few more months."

"But it's been four months already."

"Yes, I know. A case like this takes a great deal of research, and that takes a lot of time. I'm sorry."

"Well, okay. We'll wait a little longer."

"What happens when you get everything you need to go to court?"

"As soon as we have everything we need, we'll proceed with the Summons and Complaint. You'll have to sign that, and then we file it with the clerk of the court. That's the first step."

"What happens after that?"

"Dr. Mangan and the Mercer Corporation have thirty days to respond to the Complaint. At that point they'll ask us for certain things like Angela's health records, the coroner's report, and so on. And we would have to tell them who our medical experts are. And they'll probably want a deposition from you folks. Which means we'll have to meet with them at some point and you'll have to tell them all the details you can recall about Angela's medical history and what happened on the night she—uh—passed away. But don't worry about that. We'll meet with you a couple of times before the deposition and go over what you need to say and what you don't need to say. And I'll be with you during the procedure to make sure they don't get out of bounds."

"How long will all of *that* take?"

"Another few months, depending on delays and postponements. And we'll want to get as much information as we can from the defendants—Dr. Mangan and Mercer Pharmaceuticals—detailed reports on the production and testing of the medication."

"Good God. Won't this ever end?"

"I'm sorry, folks. But believe me, when we get into a courtroom we're going to want to be fully prepared for whatever might happen."

"Tony, Mr. Allen is doing the best he can."
"I hope so."

*

"Buy you a beer?"

"McBain, we've got to stop meeting like this."

"I wanted you to take a look at the opening article of the Calvecchi/Mercer series. It's going to press next week."

"What's this—a preview?"

"That's why I'm here."

"Do you always show people previews of articles you write about them?"

"Not always."

"Why now?"

"I'm trying to get a foot in the door."

"I already told you: no press until we file the S & C."

"I heard you. But after you file it'll take awhile to get the case before a jury."

["HEY SARGE, TWO SCOTCH AND WATERS OVER HERE!"]

"Do you always get way out in front on a story like this?"

"Whenever something as interesting or important as this comes along."

"This article: Can I make changes in it if I want?"

"If they're reasonable."

"Who decides if they're reasonable?"

"Me."

"That's what I figured."

"Just read it. See if the thrust sounds right."

"Are you giving the same opportunity to the opposition?"

"They won't let me talk to anybody."

"What if they decide to talk to you later on?"

"I'll listen."

["HA, HA, HA, HA, HA, HA, HA!"]

"What's the first article about?"

"Just introductory. You know—the basics of the case. We'll get to your nonexistent sex life later on."

"I'm not sure I want to read that one."

"You have my number if there are any problems with this one, don't you?"

"I do?"

"You should. I've given it to you twice already. SARGE! TWO MORE AMSTELS! Now tell me why you decided to become a lawyer . . . ."

*

"Hi, Mr. Allen. The usual?"

"Yes and no."

"How's that?"

"I've decided to try your theory: send the flowers *before* something goes wrong."

"Good idea. Still the long-stemmed?"

"Make it medium this time."

"Good choice. Let me know if it works."

"Here's my VISA card."

"Never mind. I'll set you up an account."

*

"Hey, Dad! Look at this!"

"What?"

"I just got this fax from the coroner's office—there have been three more deaths attributed to Mercipine!"

"Did you request the autopsy reports?"

"I'm working on it."

"Are they all from different places?"

"Three different states!"

"Well, that's a start."

"It's just what we've been waiting for, Dad! I think we're ready to file now, don't you?"

"Don't be so impatient, son. Let's take a look at those autopsy reports first. But if that all looks good, sure, go ahead and file the damn thing. Keep one point in mind, though . . . ."

"What's that?"

"You still haven't got a case until you can show that Mercer is liable for a couple of these deaths."

"Well, if a bunch of people are dying, something sure as hell is wrong with the stuff."

"Three is hardly a 'bunch.' Maybe that's normal for an experimental medication like this. Besides, you don't have all your—mmm."

"Dad, are you all right?"

"I don't know."

"What's the matter?"

"It's my damn back. It doesn't seem to want to go away."

"But you saw Mike not long ago, didn't you? What did he say?"

"I never went. Something came up."

"Goddamn it, Dad, will you go see him?"

"Stop nagging me about it! You sound like your mother!"

"Okay, I won't say another word about it."

"In that case maybe I'll give him a call. . . ."

*

"Hi, Elmira, how are you? . . . Good. Listen, I've got some news for you—Tony there, too? . . . No, that's okay, just tell him that we're ready to go. . . . Yes, that's right. I'm going to messenger the papers over to you and all you have to do is sign them where it's indicated and get them back to me. As soon as I have the signed copies, we can go ahead and file the suit . . . . That's right . . . . Well, the doctor and the drug company will respond to our Summons and Complaint with their Answer to our Complaint, and also something called a Bill of Particulars. Particulars. It means they'll want certain questions answered, details of what happened to Angela and a lot of legal stuff . . . . A month, unless they request and are granted an extension . . . . Yes . . . . Yes, that's right. They'll probably request the deposition we talked about . . . . Don't worry—we'll go over all that again when the time comes . . . . All right . . . . You're welcome. Say hello to Tony, and tell him we'll be ready to go as soon as we get the signed copies. . . ."

*

" . . . So I go, 'Well, who do you think you are, like—the *Pope*?' And he goes, 'No, I'm just a simple like—*priest*!'"

"Heh heh heh."

"I thought I'd like—*die*! And then he takes this pen? A regular—you know—like—ball-point pen? And he jabs it into the like—side of this telephone book? And he goes, 'Now, let's see—who we can like—call?' And he shuts his eyes and sort of like—jabs at the page and makes this like—mark? And it says, 'Ziegler's Junk Yard'? And he like—"

[Beep. Beep. Beep . . .]

"Hello? Oh, hi, Jill! . . . Way okay! I'm in this really, really nice seafood restaurant? And— . . . Well, I just finished having a like—shrimp cocktail? And—guess what?—I ordered a lobster! . . . No, not just a tail—a whole like—lobster! . . . Yeah, I know! . . . No, I've only had one in my whole like—life! I remember when I went with my folks to this place in Florida one time and I had . . . You don't know him . . . . Well, he's a lawyer friend? We met in this bar? And he— . . . I told you: You don't know him! . . . Marc . . . I don't know his last name—(What's your last name?)"

"Calvecchi."

"Calvecchi."

"I don't know—I suppose so. Look, Jill, I've got to go? The lobster's like—here? . . . Yeah, I'll talk to you tomorrow. Unless I've got like—something fantastic to tell you about, then I'll call you like—tonight?"

"Tell her you'll call her tomorrow."

*

"Hi, Mom."

"We're very honored by this visit."

"Now, Mom. Hi, kid. How you doin'?"

"Hi, Marc! Want to see my new computer? I'll let you play 'Indy 500' if you want!"

"Not right now, Tim. There's something I have to tell you both."

"You're finally getting married! Oh, I had a feeling—"

"No, Mom. Sit down a minute."

"What—is something wrong? Oh, my God—it's your father, isn't it?"

"Yes, it's Dad. But don't go all to pieces. He's okay."

"What happened?"

"Well, he's in the hospital. But he's fine. They say he's not in any immediate danger."

"Tell me, Marc! Was he in an accident? I told him he should drive more carefully. He's not getting any younger—"

"No, it's not that, Mom. He has some sort of cancer. They think it's in his bones. They're still running some tests. But don't worry—he's going to get the best treatment and it doesn't look so bad right now."

"Is he going to die, Marc?"

"No, Timmy. Of course not. Not for a long time, anyway."

"Why didn't he call us?"

"He did call us, Mom. He called me. He asked me to come over and tell you."

"Well, when did he go in?"

"Yesterday. But he didn't call me until this morning."

"How did he find out? Did he—"

"All right. I'll tell you what happened. He's been having a lot of back pain lately. But you know Dad—he's always had back pain."

"He couldn't sit in one place for very long."

"That's right, Tim. He's always had chronic back trouble. But he didn't want to go see Mike because he was afraid he'd send him to a surgeon, and you know how he feels about back surgery."

"Yes. He's always been afraid of that ever since what happened to his brother."

"That's right. Anyway, he kept putting it off, but finally I guess the pain got so bad he couldn't put it off any longer. So he went in to see Mike, and Mike sent him for some kind of scan, and when he saw the results he sent Dad right into the hospital. They're going to start some chemotherapy on him next week, I think, if the tests confirm it's bone cancer."

"Oh, my God. Has it spread?"

"Not as far as they know. They're going to do some exploratory surgery on him in a day or two to find out."

"Should I bring my 'Indy 500' game when we go to see him, Marc?"

"I don't think he has a computer in the hospital, Tim."

"Do you think he'd even want to see us? Me, anyway. I'm sure he'd like to see Timmy."

"I'm sure he'd want to see you, too, Mom. Anyway, he didn't say he *didn't* want to see you. I've got a phone number here somewhere—"

"Will you call him for me, Marc? I wouldn't want to show up unannounced. You know him—he'd think I had him in a corner or something."

"Well, you would have him in a corner. But I'll call him for you."

"Use the phone in the kitchen. I'll make you some coffee."

"After that, do you want to see my new computer? I'll let you play 'Indy 500' if you want."

"Thanks, kid. Sure, I'd like to see your computer. I'll take a rain check on the game, though. Got a lot of work to do. Next time for sure . . . ."

*

"Ladies and gentlemen, I'd like you to meet the newest member of the firm, Candace White."

"Hello, everyone. I'm looking forward to working with all of you."

"We'll save the introductions for the official reception this afternoon. And Candace's résumé is on file if anyone wants to take a look. Now before we get on to other matters, how's your dad doing, Marc?"

"He's doing okay, under the circumstances. They didn't find anything with the exploratory, and they're about to start him on chemotherapy. He's in good hands, so we're hoping for the best."

"That's good. Keep us posted. And we'll all try to get over and see him before too long."

"He'd appreciate that."

"With Marcus out for an indefinite period, you're going to be up to your eyeballs on the Mercer case. Need any help with that?"

"I'll take all the help I can get. But it better be someone who knows more science and medicine than I do."

"Candace? You want to give Marc a hand with this case?"

"If you say so, Lew."

"Good. Then—"

"Wait a minute! Does she have any experience with this kind of case? Any expertise in pharmacology and the like?"

"Why don't you ask her?"

"I was a pre-med in college before I switched to pre-law. When I was in law school I took some pharmacology courses. As a matter of fact, this is exactly the kind of case I was hoping to specialize in."

"Any problem with that, Marc?"

"Uh—no, not at the moment."

"Well, if you think of one, be sure to let me know, will you? Now, what about Johnson v. Johnson . . . ?"

*

"Marc!"

"Yes, Lew?"

"See you in my office for a minute?"

"Sure."

"Sit down."

"Thanks. What's up?"

"Couple of things. First, what's the real story on your dad? You seemed to be holding something back this morning."

"Well, you're right. It doesn't look good right now, Lew, but he's in an experimental program and you never know. They're using a drug combination that hasn't been tried before. All we can do is hope for the best."

"Don't they normally do that on an outpatient basis?"

"I guess so, but he developed an infection after the surgery and they want to keep an eye on that."

"And how is he taking all of this?"

"He was in denial at first, but I think he's beginning to resign himself to whatever happens. You should go see him—he's motionless for the first time in his life, probably."

"I went to see him when he first went into the hospital—didn't he mention that? Anyway, I'll try to get over there again this weekend."

"He'd like that. And no, he didn't."

"That sounds like him. We go back a long time, Marcus and I. And Bill, too, of course."

"A long time . . . ."

"The other thing I wanted to touch on is our new colleague, Candace White. You didn't seem too enthusiastic about bringing her into the Mercer case."

"Nothing personal, Lew. It's just that she doesn't have much experience."

"It's not because she's black, is it?"

"God, no, Lew. I hadn't even thought about that."

"Did you look at her résumé?"

"Not yet."

"Maybe I ought to tell you something about her. She graduated from the Yale law school near the top of her class—third, I believe. Before that she graduated from college magna cum laude in pre-law, like she said. She has a strong interest in medicine and knows quite a lot of biology and chemistry. Before she came here, she worked for a drug company. Not Mercer, but one of the other giants. As for her color, her father is black and her mother white. They're both Harvard professors. Any questions?"

"Only one. Why did she leave the drug company?"

"She didn't like their motives."

"Meaning . . ."

"Profits over everything else."

"No further questions, counselor."

"One more thing. She's had some personal problems lately. But I'd rather not go into that. In any case, it shouldn't affect her performance."

"Like I said before, no further questions at this time."

*

"Well, I guess it's you and me, kid."

"I guess it is."

"Glad to have you aboard. This is your first litigation since you've been here, isn't it?"

"That's right. I'm looking forward to it."

"By the way, is it 'Candace,' or should I call you 'Candy'?"

"I prefer 'Candace.'"

"Why not 'Candy'?"

"It's a long story."

"Ah. Okay. Now let me see if I've got this right: You were a pre-med major in college, weren't you?"

"You're half right. I was pre-med before I switched to pre-law."

"That's kind of unusual, isn't it?"

"I suppose so. I never thought much about it."

"What happened with the pre-med?"

"I decided to become a lawyer."

"Yes, I know. But why not a doctor?"

"Personal reasons."

"Personal reasons."

"Personal reasons."

"Okay, if that's the way you want it. But we're going to have to work pretty closely together on this. If you're going to wear a chip on your shoulder the whole time—"

"I'll do my job."

"You don't like me very much, do you?"

"Not really."

"Why not?"

"I don't know. It's hard to put a finger on it. There's just something about you that turns me off."

"What?"

"I don't know. I knew someone like you once. He was a jerk."

"In what way was he like me?"

"He was sexist, and something of a racist, too."

"I'm not a racist! In fact, *I'm* black, too!"

"Say what?"

"My great-great-great-grandmother was a slave . . . or was she an Indian . . . ?"

"The other guy said the same thing. I believed him at first."

"His great-great-great-grandmother was a slave?"

"No, smart-ass. Everything else."

"So from your experience with him you conclude that I, too, must be a jerk."

"I didn't say that. It's just that you have all the attributes."

"Is there anything I can do to—"

"Look, we're just wasting time here. I'm going to do my damndest on this case, and you have a reputation for working hard. Let's get on with it."

"Okay, fine."

"Just leave any personal matters out of it."

"I said okay."

"Look, I'm engaged. Pregnant as hell, too."

"Oh. I didn't know that."

"I didn't either until a couple of weeks ago."

"Who's the lucky guy?"

"You don't know him."

"Is it the guy you told me about?"

"No comment."

"I have to ask you: Will the pregnancy interfere with your work on this case?"

"That's a sexist comment, jerk!"

"All right! Let's just get on with this thing, shall we?"

"That's what *I* said."

"Good. As you know, my dad and I have put in a lot of time on the case already. It's all in these folders. We had just filed the Complaint when he got sick. In fact, he missed the press conference."

"How'd that go?"

"About as usual. You know—'Do you really think you have a chance of winning this case?' 'Are you attempting to take on the whole medical establishment here?' That sort of thing. Anyway, look this stuff over, will you, and let me know if you have any questions or suggestions."

"Fine."

"And here's our list of experts and the reports they've submitted. Please look that over, too. We haven't gotten Mercer's Answer to our Summons and Complaint. But you might as well get into the pharmaceutical research. I'll take care of the legal stuff for now."

"Sounds reasonable."

"Shall we meet again on, say, Friday?"

"I'll try to get a handle on the basics by then, at least."

"Good girl."

"Bad boy. You never learn, do you?"

*

"Hi, Dad. How're you doing?"

"The pain's not as bad as before, I guess."

"Good. Great. The chemo must be doing something already."

"I doubt it. It's probably the painkillers."

"Whatever it is, I'm really glad to hear you're feeling better. No side effects?"

"Not yet. They say my hair, what I have left, will probably fall out."

"Hair today, gone tomorrow."

"Brilliant. Point is, they don't even guarantee that. The whole thing's just a crapshoot."

"Maybe you'll roll a seven."

"So what? The game's rigged. Even if I get out of here alive, I'll die of old age in a few more years, anyway."

"C'mon, Dad. You're not that old."

"Might as well be."

"A lot of people live to be a hundred these days. No reason you shouldn't, too."

"Not sure I want to."

"They treating you all right otherwise?"

"They're okay. Enough about me. I'm bored to death. What have you been up to?"

"The usual."

"Anything interesting?"

"Well, I think I told you I'm taking on a new partner in the Mercer case, didn't I? Just temporarily, of course. Until you get out of here."

"Don't hold your breath. Who's helping you on the case?"

"I told you about her already, didn't I?"

"Not me. Must have been some other old fart. Or else my memory is going, along with everything else."

"*My* memory, more likely. I've been covered up lately. You know how it is."

"I used to."

"Well, anyway, she was a brilliant student, and seems to know something about medicine and drugs. She even worked for a drug company for a while."

"Just what the doctor ordered."

"Only she has some personal problems."

"Like what?"

"She's pregnant."

"So?"

"So she'll probably be taking a couple of months off at some crucial time."

"Probably not that long. When your mother had you, it didn't slow her down much."

"But she stayed at home the whole time."

"You're beginning to sound like a sexist pig."

"That's what *she* said."

"Can't help you with that. How's the lawsuit going, anyway? You have the drug analyzed for impurities yet?"

"We're still working on that. Those labs seem to take forever. But we finally got the file on the doctor."

"Any professional problems?"

"Not that we could raise in court."

"Find out who's defending, yet?"

"Osterfield and Nay. Eddie St. Clair and company."

"Eddie? Uh-oh."

"Yeah, I know."

"Say hello to old Ed for me, will you, son? We go back a long time."

"I'll do that."

"Well, whatever happens, it'll be a learning experience. This is your biggest case so far, isn't it?"

"Yep."

"I just have four words of advice for you."

"What are they?"

"Don't screw it up."

"Jesus, Dad—"

"Now don't be so sensitive. A good lawyer doesn't let a thing like that get to him. That's why I said it. Of course you can't help it—you got it from your mother. How is she, by the way?"

"She's fine. Didn't she come in to see you?"

"Once or twice. What I meant was, this is the kind of case that can make or break you. Don't shirk on this one, even if you think you can't win it. Give it everything you've got."

"I wasn't going to shirk, Dad!"

"Okay, okay. Want one final piece of advice?"

"Is that a promise?"

"No. An old lawyer can't stop giving advice. Unless he's dead. Anyway, here it is: If Eddie makes any kind of reasonable offer, I'd advise you to take it."

"What would you consider a reasonable offer in a case like this?"

"Anything over half a million would be worth considering, don't you think?"

"Maybe. But remember, the public's going to be on our side."

"I wouldn't be too sure about that. Anyway, what counts is whose side the jury's on."

"Thanks for the advice. Quick game of checkers before I go?"

"No, thanks. I'm a little tired today. All this legal work . . ."

"I appreciate it, too."

"Enough to come and see me before another month goes by?"

"It hasn't been a month, Dad. Only a little over a week. Been pretty busy. You picked a very inopportune time to get sick."

"Is there ever an opportune time? Say hello to your mother when you see her."

"I will, Dad. When are they letting you out of here?"

"They say tomorrow or the next day."

"Call me when you know. In the meantime, take care of yourself."

"What else can I do in a place like this?"

*

"Could you spare a quarter so's I could get somethin' to eat?"

[HONK!]

"Huh? Oh, hello, 'Seinfeld.' Sorry, no change today."

"For a quarter I won't tell you the one about the lawyer and the Pearly Gates...."

"That's worth a buck."

*

"Tony? Hi, this is Marcus Allen. How are you? . . . Good. And Elmira? . . . Sorry to hear that . . . . I'm fine, thank you. The reason I called is that we've had a response from the defense lawyers to our 'Summons and Complaint' and they've asked for a couple of things we don't have yet . . . . Well, one thing is an accounting of the number of pills that were left in the vial . . . . Oh. Okay . . . . No, that's fine. The other thing they want is an authorization to look into Angela's health records. Would you sign the document if I send it over to you? . . . Sorry, I'll be in court tomorrow, but you could leave it in the office . . . Okay, very good. Great. Then I'll expect . . . Well, when we get everything together, we'll file what's called a 'Response to Bill of Particulars.' After that, defense may want to take a deposition from you and Elmira—remember, we talked about that earlier? . . . Yes, I know it's been three months since we talked about it, but that's how these things proceed. Anyway, we'll certainly want to depose the drug company as well, but once that all takes place we'll be ready to go on the docket . . . . The court calendar . . . . A few more months, at least . . . . Yes, it does . . . . We all have to be patient, Tony. It takes time to get defendant's responses, there are motions for postponements, all that is out of our hands . . . . We're working on it, believe me . . . . Thanks, Tony—I appreciate that. Hope Elmira feels better soon . . . . You, too."

"Whew."

*

"Hi, Candy. Sorry—Candace. How's the pregnancy coming along?"

"We've established the fact that that's none of your business, haven't we, counselor?"

"Yes and no."

"What's that supposed to mean?"

"It means you're right—it has nothing to do with me. On the other hand, people are supposed to be concerned about the problems facing their friends and neighbors, aren't they?"

"You're not a friend and you're not a neighbor."

"All right! I'm sorry I asked, okay?"

"Look. I'm no longer pregnant. And no longer engaged. Happy?"

"Yes and no."

"Listen. I've got a client coming in half an hour. May we please proceed?"

"Fine. Let's get this over with as soon as possible. Let me bring you right up to date: the Calvecchis have complied with all the defense's requests. They agreed to turn over the girl's health records, and they had kept back the two capsules that were missing from the vial."

"Just in case someone tried something funny."

"Exactly."

"Not so stupid, really."

"Maybe. Point is, they didn't overdose the girl."

"According to the autopsy report, the girl died because of a heart arrythmia. Do we know if that's what happened in the case of the others who died?"

"Sorry. I meant to send you over copies of those. Same thing—probable arrythmia."

"Why 'probable'?"

"You can't diagnose an arrythmia on autopsy. You can only rule out everything else. You should know that, shouldn't you?"

"I did. I wanted to see if *you* knew it."

"Uh-huh."

"So what's our strategy?"

"Well, I have some thoughts on that. But I'd like to hear your ideas first."

"At the moment I don't have any. Not until we have all the information from Mercer."

"Such as?"

"Such as: What procedures were used by the company, and did they comply with all the FDA requirements? How effective was the drug in reversing the disease in animals? Which animals were used in the toxicity tests and how many of each? Anything with human tissues? What about phases one and two of the clinical trial—any problems there, especially vis-à-vis heart arrhythmias? Stuff like that."

"Now I see why Lew brought you into this. Why don't you write all this up in the form of a motion and we'll go from there."

"Are you asking me to write the Discovery & Inspection?"

"Why not? The medical parts, anyway. You're the expert here, aren't you?"

"Fine. But it's going to take me a while to do all the research on this. The FDA rules and regulations are a rabbit warren."

"We have sixty days to file."

"Then I'd better get started."

"Later on, we'll talk about courtroom tactics, okay?"

"You're the boss."

"Why don't we meet for dinner some night to go over our courtroom strategy? There are some things about Eddie St. Clair and company we ought to discuss."

"Fine. But not over dinner."

"You're a hard nut to crack, aren't you?"

"You don't even begin to have the hammer for it."

*

" . . . Any other business? Marc, how are you and Candace coming along on that liability case?"

"Well, Lew, it's turned out to be a bit more complicated than we thought."

"Aren't they all?"

"I suppose, but this one's hard to nail down. We're not going to get anywhere going after the doctor. So we're going to focus on Mercer Pharmaceuticals. Our only chance is to show that there was something wrong with their safety standards or the procedures themselves."

"What's the basis for these standards?"

"I'll let our medical expert answer that. Candace?"

"Well, it's kind of vague. The FDA requires toxicity testing in animals for all new drugs, but doesn't specify which animals or how many, except that one species has to be a rodent. Doesn't specify which rodent. Rats, mice, guinea pigs, whatever. Usually it's rats or mice. Which are notoriously poor indicators of what a chemical is going to do once it gets inside a human being. But they're cheap and have been used in these kinds of tests for decades. Basically, the FDA leaves it up to the company to determine the safety of its products. Same for a drug's carcinogenicity and teratology. The fact is, there's no way to be sure whether a compound is safe and effective even if it's tested in chimps, which are virtually the same as us, biologically speaking."

"Matter of fact, there are two or three sitting on the bench in this district even as we speak."

"I'd say our best bet—maybe our only bet—is to show that the company cut corners on one or more of the safety tests."

"The judge, whoever he is, isn't going to buy that without some strong evidence."

"Anyway, that would involve suing the FDA itself, wouldn't it? What happened to the donuts?"

"Marc, Candace, have you learned anything along these lines from the D and I?"

"The company is perfectly happy to provide us with all the test results we want. Pretty standard stuff. No indication of toxicity problems in rats or rabbits, even at fairly high doses. Assuming their results are legit and so on."

"What about the deposition?"

"Scheduled for next month."

"Any brilliant ideas on what you should be looking for?"

"We've sent all the stuff to our experts. We're waiting for *their* brilliant ideas."

"What about the media? Anything happening there?"

"Well, you all know about the McBain series in the *Post*. The first couple of articles have been pretty sympathetic to our side."

"And why not? Angela was a very bright kid. A prodigy, apparently. Not only a straight-A student, but a pretty good violinist, too. Even wrote some music. She had a brilliant future, no doubt about it, except for the diabetes, which might have caused her some problems down the road. Wanted to be a doctor, though, not a musician. Wanted to do research, find a cure for her own affliction. When I read the McBain articles I wanted to go after the drug company myself."

"Let's hope the prospective jury reads the *Post*."

*

"Hi, Mom. Where's Tim?"

"Said he was going to ride his bike over to the park."

"How's he doing?"

"Well, his grades aren't getting any better, if that's what you mean. He spends too much time on his computer."

"Twelve was a hard age for me, too. I wouldn't want to go through it again."

"But you did, and so will he."

"Yes, but it wasn't easy. Have you been to see Dad lately?"

"Are you kidding? Last time I was there he wouldn't talk to me."

"Maybe he wasn't feeling well."

"If that's the case, he hasn't been feeling well most of his life."

"Well, I don't want to get into that again. I just thought you might have—"

"Not until he apologizes."

"Mom, he might be at death's door. Can't you bend a little just this—"

"Oh, he's nowhere near 'death's door.' He'll probably outlive all of us."

"All right, all right—I'm sorry I asked."

"When was the last time *you* saw him?"

"Last week. He seemed to be doing pretty well."

"That's what I figured. He was always a terrible hypochondriac, you know."

"I don't think he's imagining this one, Mom."

"Okay, I'll try, try again. But if he won't talk to me, it'll be the last time."

"He asked about you when I saw him."

"He did? Maybe he *is* at death's door."

"C'mon, Mom, can't we let bygones be bygones until we find out whether the drugs are going to work? If he gets well, you can always go back to the way it was."

"You think the divorce is all my fault, don't you?"

"No! I don't blame you. I know how he is. He can be pretty hard to live with. But I don't think it's all his fault, either. Anyway, people change, especially when they've gone through what he has."

"He's always been the way he is, Marc, and he always will be. I just couldn't put up with it any longer. I'm sorry he got sick, but it doesn't change anything. If he came back here, it would be just like it was before."

"Maybe not. Maybe he's learned something from what he's been through."

"Not him. He'll always be the center of the universe, his own universe."

"He's done a lot of good things for people, Mom."

"Yes, he has done that. He's the most generous man in the world. Except to his own family."

"He's only human, Mom, believe me. Maybe more human than ever. Give him one more chance. Please?"

"I said I would go see him. But tell me one thing first: Why are men so afraid of death? Does it have something to do with their libido?"

"How would *I* know? I've got to go, Mom. I just stopped in to see how you and Timmy are doing with all this. Tell him I was here. I haven't seen him for a while. Maybe we could go to a ball game or something, will you ask him about that?"

"You know he worships you, don't you, Marc?"

"I can't imagine why."

"I think it's because you're so much older than he is. You're kind of like a second father to him. Or used to be. I wish you'd call him once in a while...."

"I will, Mom. Tell him I'll give him a call sometime soon."

"At the rate you're going, he'll be the only son you ever have."

"Now, Mom, don't start."

*

"Dr. Small? How are you, sir? . . . Good. This is Marcus Allen, the lead attorney in Calvecchi vs. Mercer Pharmaceuticals. You got Ms. White's letter and the information packet? . . . Good. What do you think? . . . Yes . . . . Yes . . . . Uh— . . . No, we're not sure at all. That's why we need your help . . . . Probably May or June, but we'd like to have your report as soon as possible, say in 30 days? . . . Okay, I think we can work with that . . . . Sorry? . . . Sure, that would be perfect . . . . Okay, good. Is there anything else you need that we can provide you with? . . . Great. Fine. I'll send that right out and we'll look for your report in four or five weeks . . . . Good. Right. Ms. White or I will be in touch as soon as we get the information, okay? . . . Hello?"

"Any problem?"

"He hung up."

"Yeah. He did that to me, too."

"We may have to put some clamps on him—he seems a teensy bit weird to me."

"I told you about that. But he's brilliant, nonetheless, and we're going to need someone like him to convince the jury that a respected company like Mercer isn't a creation of the gods."

"Our friend St. Clair is certainly going to try to make them think it is."

"So would you, if you were on their side."

"Point is, is this guy the best we can do?"

"He's the only one I could find who knows all the FDA rules and regulations forward and backward and is willing to testify. Look: He worked there for almost twenty years before he was let go. He knows it like the back of his hand, how it functions, the whys and wherefores, how a drug is approved for clinical trial, everything."

"He wasn't exactly 'let go.' He was fired."

"That might not be a problem if we handle it right."

"Maybe. But we'd better let the jury in on that right away. So Eddie St. Clair doesn't have a chance to spring it on them."

"Have you made any inquiries? Talked to any of the lawyers he's worked with before?"

"One or two. They say he's fine on the stand, but you've got to let him know what to expect from the defense. He can be unpredictable, but he can also be contained."

"I think we can do better."

"Do you know how difficult it is to find someone who knows the FDA from the inside and is willing to testify?"

"All right, all right. But you examine him. Can you handle that?"

"I'm willing to try."

"Good. Just make sure he doesn't take the stand with his fly open. Anything else?"

"You want to hear what I've dug up on the defense witnesses?"

"Sure."

"Okay. They have five: Angela's doctor; one of the vice-presidents, no less, of the Mercer Corporation; Szybalski, the research director; the head of the CRO, the organization that administered the clinical trial; and last, but not least, their own FDA man. The last one is a johnny-come-lately. They brought him in to counter Small's testimony, I suppose. Anyway, he goes by the book and he swears that the company's testing procedures were not only adequate, but 'superlative.' None of these people are going to be easy to trip up."

"Who's our best bet?"

"I'd say Szybalski. I think the buck stops with him. I'm going to dig into his background a little more, see if there are any skeletons rattling around in his closet."

"Everyone has skeletons. It's just a matter of getting into the closet. What else have you got?"

"Not much. I'm still reading everything I can get my hands on about the procedures used for toxicity testing. Something obviously went wrong in the case of Angela Calvecchi, and I'm determined to find out what."

"Well, let me know what you come up with. Maybe we could discuss it over lunch or something."

"Maybe. But I doubt it."

*

"Marc, Jr.! How the hell are you? Haven't seen you in a coon's age!"

"Hello, Eddie. How've you been?"

"Fine as froghair! You know my associate, Bob Baxstresser, don't you?"

"Sure. How are you, Bob?"

"Couldn't be better!"

"And these old boys are Mr. Kron, Mr. Steuben, and Mr. Carafolio."

"Hello, hi, how are you? And this is *my* partner in crime, Candace White. Candace, Eddie St. Clair *et al.*"

"A pleasure, young lady. A genuine pleasure."

"I've heard a lot about you."

"Lies, I'm afraid, all lies. What they say about you, on the other hand, is obviously true."

"Thank you, I think."

"That was definitely a compliment. Meet Bob Baxstresser."

"Hi, kid."

"Coffee? Tea? Bourbon?"

"No, thanks."

"Well, let's all sit down at this here little table. Nice facilities, eh?"

"If you call this a 'little table,' I'd hate to see your office."

"I'd show it to you, little lady, but there's a football game going on in there right now. By the bye, Junior, how's your pappy?"

"Holding his own, I guess."

"Good. We go back a long time, your daddy and me."

"I know. He asked me to say hello, Eddie."

"Did you know we were in the first grade together?"

"Sure did."

"We had some great times, your old daddy and me. Tell him I'll try to get up and see him one of these days, will you do that, son?"

"Absolutely. He'd be very glad to see you, Eddie."

"You're paw did me a big favor once . . . . And you, you little whippersnapper—when the hell did you grow up? I can't believe you're a gen-you-wine lawyer already. Why, I can remember when you were barely bigger than a grasshopper."

"I remember you, too, Eddie. You seemed like a giant to me then."

"Time rolls along, don't it, son? Well, folks, 'scuse the reminiscin'. Let's get on down to business, shall we?"

"That's why we're here."

"I thought it was for the strudel and croissants."

"That, too."

"You know, you remind me a lot of your daddy. Chafin' at the bit, rarin' to go."

"I'll take that as a compliment."

"All righty, then! Let's get this goddamn show on the road! Pardon my French, young lady."

"That's all right. I speak French."

*

" . . . Did you ever see more luxurious quarters?"

"Hm? Well, I've seen it before, but now that you mention it—no."

"Maybe that's why St. Clair has such a red face—chronic embarrassment."

"What? Oh. Could be. But he's always looked like that."

"Partner, what are you thinking about?"

"Well, if you must know, I was wondering how Eddie and his cohorts knew about the Calvecchis' own medical history."

"How do you know they did?"

"A couple of little things. You remember Baxstresser asked Elmira about her 'nervous condition'? And whether she knew who made the medication she was taking for it?"

"Yes. But she did seem pretty nervous."

"Sure. Most people are, in that situation. But a 'nervous condition' requiring medication? Hell, *we* didn't even know about that."

"Well . . ."

"And St. Clair asked the coroner about Angela's eye problem? That wasn't in her medical records. Her doctor—Mangan—it was new to him, too."

"So she went in to get her glasses and the optometrist noticed some minor thing. So what?"

"Maybe nothing. Or maybe someone's leaking information to the defense team."

"You mean someone in the firm?"

"It's possible."

"Who?"

"I don't know."

"Maybe there's a simpler explanation."

"Who else would have this kind of information?"

"Well, the grandparents, maybe."

"I asked them only yesterday whether anyone from Osterfield Nay had talked to anyone else in the family. Or to any close friends of theirs. They said 'no'."

"I think you're making a mountain out of a molehill."

"In this business molehills sometimes have a way of growing into mountains, Ms. White. But that issue aside, how do you think our people did?"

"I think the coroner is going to be a strong witness. Very self-confident, well within himself, and he knows what he's doing. Best of all, he seems to be on our side."

"Maybe he's had a run-in with a drug company before. We'd better defuse that so they don't charge him with being biased against them. What about the Calvecchis?"

"Tony's okay. Elmira is a different story."

"Don't be too sure. Juries hate the kind of bullying tactics St. Clair and Baxstresser used. If she goes to pieces on the stand, it could be a positive."

"Still, you might have asked for a couple more recesses."

"You finished eating? I never knew a skinny woman could eat so much."

"One more thing. Didn't St. Clair grow up with your father?"

"That's right."

"Then why does he talk with a southern accent?"

"I don't really know. That's just what he does. I'll have to ask Dad about it."

"He must be pretty impressive in a courtroom. Was he a football player, by any chance?"

"Matter of fact, he was. Tackle. All-American."

"And that big, deep voice is going to command a lot of attention, too. Not to mention that snow-white head of hair. Everybody's nightmare grandfather. Does he have any weak points?"

"None that I know of. Did you know he's written half-a-dozen crime novels?"

"No way!"

"It's the truth. You can look him up on the web. His pen name is Tom Drake."

"Tell me: Why doesn't a big corporation like Mercer have their own lawyers?"

"They do."

"Then why—"

"Because no one can remember when Eddie St. Clair lost a big case like this one. Now if you're finally finished, we'd better get back up there. We've still got Mangan and the guy from Mercer—what's his name—Szybalski."

"Thanks for the lunch, partner."

"Damn it to hell, Candace, I wish you'd call me Marc."

"Is that an order?"

"Not at all. But it would make things so much easier."

"What sorts of things did you have in mind?"

"Ah, forget it. Let's go back up."

*

"What are you looking for in a man, anyway?"

"Who says I'm looking for a man?"

*

"According to this report, Dr. Szybalski, Mercer and company tested the effectiveness of the drug you call Mercipine on mice. Is that true?"

"Yes, it's all right there in the report."

"And are those animals susceptible to Type I diabetes, Doctor?"

"Yes, of course."

"So you're saying that if a drug fixes some problem or other in mice it's guaranteed to do the same in human beings?"

"No animal can predict the effectiveness of a new drug with 100% certainty. Animals are only models for us humans. But the results with mice were strong enough to suggest we move on to a clinical trial."

"How strong?"

"Ninety-one percent of the diabetic mice responded very well to the medication."

"Responded in what way?"

"Their blood sugar levels were significantly reduced compared to control levels."

"'Control' meaning mice who didn't have diabetes?"

"No. The controls were mice with diabetes who didn't get the Mercipine."

"What did they get?"

"Exactly the same food and water and exercise as the experimental mice, but no Mercipine."

"You said that 'ninety-one percent of the diabetic mice responded very well to the medication.' What about the other nine percent?"

"They responded, too, but not so well."

"But their blood sugar levels went down, too?"

"Yes, but not as much."

"Well, did some of them have health problems after taking the Mercipine?"

"Not really. One of them developed a little problem with walking—"

"What kind of problem?"

"It was staggering around in its cage for a few days."

"So you expected a number of the people who took the drug to stagger around for a few days before—?"

"Now, Marcus, Jr., let's not go off half-cocked here. The point is, the drug showed enough promise to get it a fair hearing."

"Sorry, Eddie. I didn't realize you'd finished your nap."

"Haw, haw, haw. You're Marcus's boy, all right. Please proceed, counselor."

"Dr. Szybalski, did the rats and rabbits you used also show any reduction in blood sugar levels after they were given the drug?"

"That parameter wasn't tested in those animals. They were used merely to ascertain the safety of the product."

"And was the product found to be safe in rats?"

"Very."

"And in rabbits?"

"Very safe."

"No side effects?"

"Only some hair loss."

"Does that mean that some diabetes patients treated with Mercipine could expect to lose their hair? Would Angela have been bald if she had survived the Mercipine treatment?"

"Not at all. You can't predict that sort of thing from animal studies."

"You can't predict whether a drug will make you bald, but you *can* predict it won't cause more serious effects? Is that what you're saying?"

"Animals have hearts, lungs, kidneys, livers—all the things people have. If a drug causes no damage to any of these organs in animals, the chances are it won't cause any such damage in humans."

"Dr. Szybalski, were there any heart problems in rats or rabbits as a result of Mercipine treatment?"

"Not at all."

"But you're aware, are you not, that several people's hearts have stopped as a result of taking this drug?"

"That's not true, Junior, and you goddamn well know it!"

"Thanks, Eddie. I'd prefer to hear the good doctor's answer to that."

"That is an allegation that has not been proven."

"But it's pretty suggestive, wouldn't you say, sir?"

"Not really. There are several hundred patients in the Mercipine study who haven't had any heart problems whatsoever."

"Well, are six deaths pretty standard results in the clinical testing of a new drug?"

"Yes, I would say that's fairly typical. We're dealing with some very sick people in Stage III clinical trials."

"And was Angela Calvecchi one of those 'very sick people'?"

"No, she was not. She was in the earliest stages of the disease."

"Thank you, sir. That's all I have at the moment. Candace, do you have any other questions for Dr. Szybalski?"

"Only one or two. Was the safety of Mercipine investigated using animals other than rats and rabbits, doctor?"

"No."

"Why not?"

"The FDA specifies no such requirement."

"Does the FDA specify that those animals in particular be used for this kind of study?"

"No."

"Sir, if you *had* used a different animal species and found that these animals died from a heart arrythmia or other cause, would you still have gone ahead with the clinical testing program?"

"Whoa, young lady. You know that kind of feeble speculation wouldn't be allowed by any judge in this here district."

"Yes, I know. But this isn't the trial. I'm just curious."

"Doctor Szybalski, sir, you don't have to answer that question."

"The answer is obvious, anyway."

"I think we would all agree with that answer, doctor. And just out of curiosity, did you in fact try any other animals in the safety studies?"

"Not *per se*. We used mice in the assessment of possible carcinogenicity."

"Why is that, sir?"

"Because the FDA requires the use of two rodent species in those studies."

"I see. And did the mice or rats come down with cancer in one form or another?"

"No."

"One last question: Who decided to put Mercipine into clinical testing?"

"A committee."

"And who heads up that committee?"

"It rotates. But everyone on the committee participates in the decision to go forward with any new drug."

"Who was head of the committee at the time of the Mercipine discussions, do you remember?"

"I think I was. But it doesn't really—"

"And what is the committee's decision based on, normally?"

"Everything. The animal studies, computer mockups, any preliminary testing on human tissues, the complexity and cost of production, it all figures in."

"And 'the animal studies' refers to the considerations of safety and effectiveness you've already mentioned—is that right?"

"That's correct."

"And this is the procedure that was followed in the case of Mercipine?"

"Yes, of course. As I said, it's followed with any new drug."

"And Mercipine passed all the tests with flying colors."

"That's right."

"Any studies with human tissues?"

"Yes. Several."

"Which ones?"

"Skin, liver, lung, kidney."

"Any negative results there?"

"None at all."

"Computer simulations?"

"No."

"Why not?"

"Computer simulations are normally done to test the interactions of various substances at the molecular level. In the case of Mercipine, the effect is at the cellular level."

"Finally, doctor, are there any tests you did with Mercipine that we don't know about?"

"No. It's all in the report you have."

"Nothing to suggest that Mercipine might not be safe and effective in humans?"

"No."

"Thank you, sir."

"Any other questions, Marcus, Jr.? I don't want your pappy to think we treated you unfairly at Osterfield and Nay."

"Not just now, Eddie. We're saving the best ones for the trial."

"I sure hope so, boy, for y'all's sake."

*

"Marc, you busy?"

"'Course I'm busy. C'mon in, Bill."

"I just heard that you got Norma Bates for Calvecchi v. Mercer."

"That's right. Is there anything I should know about her? I've never tried a case in her courtroom."

"She's a loose cannon."

"Yeah—that's what I've heard."

"Don't be too discouraged. That's exactly the kind of judge you need if you have any hope at all of winning a case like this."

"You mean she'll be unbiased."

"Scrupulously. The main thing is, she's not brain dead like some of the others. With her, I think you actually have a slim chance of winning this suit."

"You mean you expected us to lose it?"

"I never 'expect' anything, counselor. I just play the odds."

"The odds may have turned against us, Bill."

"What do you mean?"

"We may have a mole in the firm."

"A mole? You mean a spy? What the hell makes you think that?"

"Certain things the defense knew about the Calvecchis that they shouldn't have known."

"Really? And who do you think the 'mole' could be, Marcus, Jr.?"

"Everyone in the firm has been here for a long time. Except one. And she used to work for a drug company."

"Are you talking about your partner in the Mercer case?"

"She's the only one it could be."

"Are you sure they couldn't have gotten the information some other way?"

"No, I'm not. But—"

"You're not becoming paranoid about this case, are you Junior?"

"I hope not."

"Unless you have some damn good evidence . . ."

"None at all. At the moment."

"Marc, if this is going to interfere with—"

"Don't worry. I'll still give the case my best efforts."

"We expect nothing less around here. And speaking of giving your best—how's your dad doing?"

"Okay so far. Goes in for his chemo every week. Otherwise he's doing fine. Weak, of course, and bald as an egg. Even his arms and legs. You should see him."

"I'll try to do that. Right now, I've got to run. Just wanted you to know we're all behind you a hundred per cent. We were, anyway, until you started spouting off about 'moles' in the woodwork."

"Forget I ever said it."

"I'm going to do that. You know, you're more than a junior partner to Lew and me. You're more like a nephew . . . ."

"I know that, Bill."

"Anything you need . . ."

"Thanks. We'll try not to let you down."

*

"Hi, Dad. How are you today?"

"Marc, you ask me that every time I see you. It makes me feel like I should be doing worse than I am."

"I'm just pretending to be interested in your health."

"That's better. Tell you what. If you stop asking me how I am, I'll promise to tell you when I feel like shit, okay?"

"Deal. Anyway, you've been taking the chemotherapy for several weeks now, and you seem to be doing pretty well. That's a good sign, don't you think?"

"If you say so."

"Love your hat, by the way."

"Thanks. I've got three more of them, all different colors. Courtesy of your mother. Now tell me what's been going on at the office."

"Well, you'll be interested to know that the Mercer case has finally been put on the docket."

"Really? Who's presiding?"

"Judge Bates."

"Norma? She's a tough one. Unpredictable. But you could've done a lot worse."

"Bill says she's a loose cannon."

"Like I said, she's unpredictable. But fair. More integrity than Abe Lincoln."

"You'd know more about that than I would, Dad."

"Funny. I waited all week for that? Anyway, I'm not that much older than you are, my friend. What you're looking at is yourself in another forty years."

"If I could've had your life, I'd trade for it in a minute."

"What's *that* supposed to mean? Is there a problem at the office?"

"No, no, no, nothing like that. I guess I'm just getting tired of being a carefree bachelor."

"You mean your mother hasn't found you the 'perfect' girl yet? She's been trying for three decades."

"I know. You remember Sondra Castle?"

"No. Which one was she?"

"She was in my kindergarten class. I mentioned her to Mom one time and from then on she had Sondra and me engaged. She was very disappointed when we broke up."

"When was that?"

"First grade."

"So all right. If you're tired of being a bachelor, why not get married?"

"Because I haven't found the right girl. I know, I know—that sounds corny. But not one I'd want to spend the rest of my life with at the breakfast table, anyway."

"I thought there was that one—what was her name? Last year...."

"Oh, you mean Tasha. Good God, I'd almost forgotten about her."

"So what was wrong with Tasha?"

"Not too much, if you discount the teeth. But it just wasn't right, you know?"

"There have been a few others, haven't there?"

"Same story."

"Are you seeing anyone right now?"

"Not really. There's someone I might be interested in, but she barely gives me the time of day."

"Your assistant in the Mercer case."

"That's right. How did you know?"

"Little things you've said lately. Your voice gets softer when you mention her name. Stuff like that. Take my advice and marry her."

"Marry her? We haven't even gone out!"

"Then find some excuse to *get* her out. You're a lawyer aren't you? Lie to her if you have to. Why won't she give you the time of day?"

"I'm not sure. For some reason she can't stand me."

"What the hell did you do to her?"

"Nothing, Dad! She just doesn't like me. She was engaged when we started on the case. And pregnant. I guess both of those are over. Maybe she can't stand men in general any more."

"Maybe. Or maybe you're trying too hard."

"I've only tried to be friendly, Dad. She won't have any of it."

"How important is this girl to you? If she went off to Timbuktu, would you go after her?"

"Maybe. The longer I work with her, the more it hurts. Whenever she comes in, my pulse doubles. I can't breathe. It's terrible."

"Maybe you're allergic to her perfume."

"She's beautiful, too. But there's a small problem."

"There always is."

"She may be leaking information to Eddie St. Clair. I'm not sure I can trust her anymore."

"Marc, I probably shouldn't say this, but I think you've been working too hard. If Eddie's finding some things you didn't give him, he's probably getting it legitimately. He's very good at digging up obscure information. Anything he thinks might help him win."

"You're probably right. Bill thinks I'm paranoid."

"My advice is to forget about it. Above all, don't let it affect your work on the case. Even if it's true, which it isn't. Lew's pretty careful when it comes to bringing people into the firm."

"Either way, she's on my mind all the time."

"Have you tried my technique?"

"You mean ignore her?"

"It's a psychological thing. That's how I got your mother. Not that we had anything like a successful marriage. But she was wonderful then. Wouldn't even give me a second look. Have I ever told you about that?"

"Only about a million times."

"Doesn't always work, but in a case like yours—"

"Can't hurt to try it, I guess. By the way: are we part black, or part Indian?"

"Part native American, my politically incorrect friend. Why?"

"Nothing. Just curious."

"As I was saying, if it doesn't work, maybe you ought to ask her to withdraw from the case. Or withdraw from it yourself. You can't perform effectively as a lovesick teenager, never mind the paranoia."

"I can't withdraw from the goddamn case, Dad!"

"Then maybe you ought to see a shrink about the problem."

"I'll work it out somehow. You had any visitors lately?"

"Bill and Lew showed up once or twice. And, of course, your mother. She was here a few days ago."

"How was it?"

"Lasted about five minutes."

"What happened this time?"

"Same old same old."

"Can't you try, Dad?"

"I do try. It's hopeless. What else is happening in *your* life?"

"Not much. Game of checkers?"

"Okay. But let me win for once, will you?"

"You miss playing bridge, don't you, Dad?"

"Some of the best times of my life. Did you know I played with Goren once? We killed our opponents, too. And in a few tournaments against Omar Sharif. Great bridge player...."

"I wish I could've followed in those footsteps, Dad, but I was never in your class. I must have been a great disappointment to you, not to have carried on your bridge legacy."

"Just be a good attorney, son. That'll be legacy enough for me."

*

"Marc! How are you? Case coming up?"

"Hello, Mario. Meeting with the judge this week."

"I figured. That's usually when I see you."

"Got to look your best for the court."

"Sure . . . Managing to keep warm?"

"Just barely. It's colder than a witch's tit out there."

"I know. Couldn't even get my car started this morning. The regular?"

"No, let's make it a mohawk this time."

"Very funny, Marc. Your dad always had a great sense of humor, too."

"Still does, Mario."

"I didn't mean—"

"That's okay."

"How's he doing?"

"He's slowed down a lot since you saw him last. But he's doing okay."

"Who's cutting his hair?"

"He doesn't have any."

"Oh . . . . I remember the last time he was here. He didn't look too well then. Said it was his back again."

"He was still in his denial stage at that point."

"I told him he should take it a little easier, but he just kinda snorted like he always did when I'd tell him that."

"He's taking it pretty easy now. Except for the chemo. He has another scan coming up. That should tell us something about how he's doing."

"I hope it's a good one. He's too fine a man to lose."

"I'll tell him you said that."

"I remember one time a homeless man came into the shop. I told him to move on, but your dad reached into his pocket and gave him a five. Not many people would've done that."

"He's always been generous to people."

"Maybe I shouldn't say this, but did you know he lent me ten thousand dollars one time?"

"No, I didn't!"

"I was having a tough time because of—Well, I won't bother you with the gory details. And I didn't even ask him for it. He asked *me*! I don't even know how he knew I was having financial problems."

"Dad's a very perceptive guy. That's why he's such a good lawyer."

"Wait a minute . . . . Here."

"What's this?"

"A picture of my grandson. You show this to your dad, will you? He'll understand."

"Sure, Mario. Be glad to . . ."

"Okay, Marc, Jr. How's it look?"

"Good. As always."

"No charge today."

"C'mon, Mario. I insist."

"Nope."

"Here, damn it!"

"Nope."

"I'll leave it over here. So long, Mario."

"Marc, you're just like your goddamn father!"

*

"Marc!"

"Yeah, Lew?"

"Come on in here a minute."

"What's up?"

"Junior, what the hell are you accusing Candace of?"

"Huh? Nothing, Lew."

"I just talked to Bill and he says you think she's leaking shit to the enemy."

"I didn't say that, Lew. It's just that somebody around here—"

"I don't know what your personal relationship with her is, but I don't want to hear anything like that from you ever again. Do I make myself clear?"

"Very."

"Good. We don't operate that way around here. Now go out there and kick some ass. But not anybody's in the firm. Understand?"

"Perfectly."

*

"Mr. Allen, your mother's on the phone. Says it's urgent."

"All right. I'll take it in my office.... Hello?... Mom! I've been meaning to call you! But it's been one thing after anoth—... On oxygen? What happened?... Uh-huh.... When was this?... So he's okay?... He's what?... Oh—resting comfortably. Okay. Well, I can't get over there this afternoon—we've got a meeting with the judge in the Mercer case—tell him I'll see him after that. Or tonight sometime.... No, the case isn't more important than Dad, but—... No, Mom, I'll get over to the hospital as soon as I can... I will. 'Bye, Mom.... Yes, I understand that.... 'Bye, Mom. I'll talk to you later.... What?.... No, I haven't had a chance to call Tim yet.... Yes, I know that.... 'Bye, Mom.... Yes, I will.... Talk to you later. 'Bye."

*

"You're Marcus Allen's son, aren't you?"

"That's right."

"Your father is a fine attorney. I'm sorry about his medical problem. Give him my best, will you, Mr. Allen?"

"I will, judge. Thank you."

"And Eddie, how are you?"

"Fine and dandy, ma'am."

"Good for you. Gentlemen, shall we proceed? I've been looking over my notes on this case, and it looks to me as if a settlement is quite possible. Do either of you disagree with that assessment?"

"Not at all, judge."

"It's possible, of course."

"Good. Now where do we have differences? Mr. St. Clair, do you think plaintiffs have a legitimate case against your client?"

"Not really, your honor. My client asserts that all required procedures were followed, and some others that weren't required. The drug was approved for clinical trial by the FDA. It's a safe drug. But even if it weren't, it was FDA approved, which lets the Mercer Corporation off the hook. Moreover, all new drugs carry certain risks, and the parents signed a waiver stating they were aware of these risks. My client is not liable for damages in this case, plain and simple."

"Are you contending it's not possible that the girl's death was caused by this drug?"

"No, ma'am, we're just saying it's highly unlikely. Mercipine was found to be safe in animals and also in humans in preliminary studies. She could have died for other reasons unrelated to the treatment. But even if the drug was involved in some unforeseen way, plaintiffs knew the risks involved."

"What about the other six deaths?"

"Again, your honor, any connection is pure speculation."

"Mr. St. Clair, is it your position that we're wasting our time here attempting to reach a settlement?"

"No, Judge Bates. I'm only saying that my client has a very strong defense against the complaint."

"But you'd consider a fair settlement. To put this thing behind us, if nothing else. Avoid any bad publicity, etcetera."

"A fair settlement? Of course, your honor."

"Good. And what would you consider to be a fair settlement, counselor?"

"I think five hundred thousand would be a fair settlement in this instance but, confidentially, we're willing to go to seven fifty if this would end the matter once and for all."

"Mr. Allen, what say you?"

"Your honor, the girl who died after taking the drug they call Mercipine was a brilliant student with a very bright future. She wanted to be a doctor. She wanted to find a cure for diabetes. Given her intelligence and motivation, who can say she wouldn't have done just that? Her loss, not only to her parents, but to society in general, comes into the category of 'priceless.'"

"Pure speculation, your honor."

"Agreed. Let's stay out of the realm of future medical discoveries for the moment, shall we, Mr. Allen?"

"It's possible she wouldn't have found a cure for diabetes, your honor. Maybe only for cancer and heart disease. All we know for sure is that she would certainly have enjoyed a very productive life and a distinguished career in medicine."

"Maybe, judge. Or maybe she would have gone on to be a clerk at K-Mart."

"Mr. St. Clair, I know someone who works at K-Mart, and she is a very special person."

"No offense meant, your honor. But the issue here is the potential financial worth of plaintiff's daughter, not some pipe dream of Nobel prizes and the like."

"Mr. Allen?"

"Your honor, we'd prefer a jury's opinion on what the 'worth' of this girl might have been."

"What's the bottom line, Marcus, Jr.?"

"In our opinion, judge, all the tea in China wouldn't be a fair settlement in this case. But to expedite the matter and save time for the court and everyone else concerned, we're willing to settle for seven point five million."

"Mr. St. Clair?"

"Not possible, your honor."

"All right. On one side we have seven hundred and fifty thousand, and on the other we have seven point five million. It seems to me these figures aren't so far apart that something can't be worked out. A workable compromise would be something like three to four million. Mr. Allen, would you entertain that amount if I can get defense to go there?"

"Your honor, there's another factor to put into the equation. As you pointed out, there are six other people, two of them adolescents, who have died after taking the drug Mercipine. If defense gets off the hook with a slap on the wrist—and for a megacorp like Mercer, three or four million, or even seven point five, is petty cash—there may be others who will follow them to the grave."

"Mr. St. Clair?"

"It's just the other way 'round, judge. If my client gives in to plaintiff's demands, everybody who ever had a bad reaction to a painkiller would be after Mercer & Co. Something like that could have a chilling effect on medical research everywhere."

"Are you asking for an admission of guilt, Marcus, Jr.?"

"Only a tacit admission, your honor."

"Eddie?"

"No can do, Judge."

"Where would you draw the line?"

"We might be willing to come up a little, Judge Bates, but anything over a million would be an admission of guilt, even with a nondisclosure clause, and Mercer isn't guilty of anything. There are risks in any medical procedure and plaintiff was aware of those risks. The girl's death was a tragedy, but in this particular case plaintiff's request is unreasonable, in our opinion."

"How far down are you willing to come, Mr. Allen?"

"Five million, your honor. That's our floor."

"And the non-disclosure clause?"

"As far as we're concerned, your honor, defense can have the non-disclosure. But the clinical trial would have to be halted."

"Mr. St. Clair?"

"One million would be an extremely fair settlement, judge. And the Mercer Corporation isn't about to cave in to plaintiffs' other demands."

"It's going to cost you more than that to proceed with this case, Eddie."

"It's a matter of principle, Norma. A figure like Marc, Jr. is asking would be out of the question, even if the clinical trial goes forward."

"Well, gentlemen, it looks like we go to trial. But keep in mind that somebody here is going to lose his shirt. Maybe both of you. If either of you changes his mind about a compromise, my chambers are open."

"Thanks, judge."

"Thank you, your honor."

*

"My, God, Marc—it was a close call."

"What happened?"

"They're not sure. They think it might have been a small embolism."

"You're sweating, Dad. Do you have anything to mop that with?"

"There's a towel in the bathroom."

"I'll get it . . . Here. Are you hot?"

"No. Freezing. Marc, I'm scared shitless. I've never come this close to dying before."

"C'mon, Dad. How do you know how close you came?"

"Stop talking like a lawyer! They told me, goddamn it! If the nurse hadn't been in the room I'd probably be dead by now!"

"Then you're a very lucky man."

"Why—'cause I almost croaked?"

"No. Because the nurse was here. And because it happened when you were in here for your chemo in the first place."

"Right. I'm the luckiest SOB on the face of the Earth."

"I can tell by the sarcasm that you're feeling better, Dad."

"It's better than being dead, but not much."

"But you're okay, now. They fixed you right up. Somebody just told me you're in no immediate danger. In fact, they said your chemotherapy is looking very promising."

"Nobody's in any 'immediate' danger an hour before they croak!"

"Dad, you're not going to 'croak' in an hour. If you were, you wouldn't be here, you'd still be in intensive care or whatever. I'd be visiting someone else in this room right now."

"Is that what you call gallows humor? Marc, it's going to happen again. I can feel it."

"What do you mean, you can 'feel' it?"

"I can't explain it. I just feel funny. Like I'm on the outside looking in. Did you ever wake up and you couldn't breathe? I'm afraid to wake up any more! God damn it, Marc. I'm *scared*!"

"Okay, Dad. Okay. Try to take it easy. If you want to know the truth, you look fine. But I'll see if I can find the doctor and get some information. Try to relax for a minute. I'll be right back, okay?"

"Easy for you to say. You're not dying."

"Dammit, Dad, you're not dying, either. Just hang on for a minute till I see the doctor...."

*

"Don't tell me, Mr. Allen. A dozen long-stemmed red roses."

"That's right. And knock off that stupid grin, will you? I haven't found your theory to be worth a damn."

"You mean sending the flowers *before* the crisis? Is this pre- or post-?"

"Pre- or post-what? Oh, I don't know. Pre-, I guess."

"Maybe you're trying too hard. How about some nice yellow roses for a change?"

"What's the difference?"

"Less pushy."

"Okay, sure. Why not?"

"I'll put them on your bill...."

*

"Hi."

"All right—what were the roses for?"

"You're welcome. They were for all your help on the case so far. I read Small's report again. Maybe getting him on board wasn't such a bad idea after all."

"Thank you. But—"

"Yeah, I know. This doesn't change anything. Did you notice they were yellow roses? A gesture of friendship, not an expression of some silly romantic notion."

"I did notice. And thanks again, Marc."

"Thank *you*."

"For what?"

"That's the first time you've called me 'Marc.'"

"Doesn't mean we're pals."

"No, but maybe it's a start."

"And that's as far as it goes. By the way, I heard about your dad. Is he doing all right?"

"He's okay. I spoke with the doctor. His blood had thickened for some reason. Probably had nothing to do with the drugs he's taking. They gave him some thinners. But now he's convinced he's at death's door."

"I suppose you can't know what it's like until you're in his shoes."

"Sometimes I feel like I *am* in his shoes. Anyway, to answer your question, he's fine at the moment. In fact, he's home again already."

"I'm glad to hear that. The longer I work here, the more I appreciate the kind of attorney he was."

"Thank you, Candace. I'll tell him you said—Yes, Mrs. Felana?"

"Your eleven o'clock is here."

"Thanks. Please send them in . . . . Hi, Tony. Elmira. How have you been?"

"Fine, thank you."

"Fine. And you?"

"Not too bad. Please sit down."

"Thank you."

"Okay, I'm sure you're both busy. I know *we* are. So I'll get right to the point. The trial starts on Monday. We asked you to come in one last time to go over what to expect. Nothing we didn't discuss before your depositions. We just want to make sure we're on the same page about the testimony and so on."

"We understand."

"Okay. You read over the transcripts of those depositions?"

"Yes."

"Several times."

"Good. And have you decided whether both of you will be testifying?"

"Yes, we have. Like we said before, I'll be testifying and Elmira won't."

"We're sorry you feel that way. You know we think it would be advisable for both of you to take the stand."

"Oh, I just couldn't. I would go all to pieces up there."

"Well, it's not as terrifying as it sounds. It won't be much different from your depositions, except that a jury will be present. And the judge, of course. Candace or I, and one of the lawyers for the defense will be asking you a few questions about what happened the morning Angela—the morning you found her. We'll take some breaks if necessary and I promise you we'll hold our questions to a minimum."

"Yes, we know all that, but—"

"Elmira, would it be better if I asked the questions instead of Marc?"

"I don't think so."

"Candace—and Marc—my wife doesn't want to live through that experience again. Especially not in public. She's nervous enough without all that."

"All right, we can't force Elmira to testify. Just think about it a few more days and let us know for certain by Friday."

"We're certain."

"Okay, if that's your final decision we'll do the best we can without your testimony. But if you change your mind . . . ."

"We'll let you know."

"Fair enough. Now the other reason we asked you to come in was to lay out the procedures for you so you'll know what to expect. Basically we, and the opposing lawyers, will select a jury that we hope will be at least fair and impartial, if not sympathetic to our case. In other words, we wouldn't want to accept someone who is a nurse or a laboratory technician, for example, because they would probably be biased in favor of any and all standard medical and laboratory procedures. If we could seat an ideal jury, it would be composed of people much like yourselves, people who can identify with your situation. The opposing attorneys, of course, won't want anyone sympathetic to your plight. So the jury we finally arrive at will be a compromise, people somewhere between our ideal jury and theirs.

"Once that's finished, I'll present opening arguments. Which means I'll be telling the jury what happened to Angela, and why we think Mercer Pharmaceuticals should be held responsible. Then Mr. St. Clair or one of his associates will tell the jury why they think Mercer should not be held liable. After that, we'll present witnesses to support our case. The first witness we call would most likely be you, Tony."

"I'll be first?"

"That's right. But then you won't have to worry about it anymore. When you get on the witness stand you'll be asked to swear you're telling the truth, and then Candace or myself, probably me, will ask you some questions pertaining to Angela's tragic death—how she came to be taking the drug she was taking, were you given ample warning about possible side effects, who found her that morning, and so on. Keep in mind this isn't a test. You won't be asked any questions you won't know the answer to. It's just that the jury doesn't—shouldn't, anyway—know anything about the case, so we have to present it to them in a clear, straightforward, logical manner so they will understand the situation as nearly as possible from your perspective."

"I understand."

"Good. Now when I ask you a question, try to answer it simply and directly, without bringing in a lot of extraneous material, do you see what I mean?"

"I think so."

"Don't ramble. Think about the question I've asked you and answer it as truthfully and as directly as you can."

"I'll try."

"Fine. My questions and your answers constitute what's called the 'direct examination.' After that, the opposing attorneys will have additional questions for you. This is called the 'cross examination.' These will be a little different. They will ask you some questions that you might find a little more difficult to answer. For example, they might ask you whether you signed a release form allowing Angela to take an experimental drug, and that you understood there was a risk of death if she took part in the trial. We've gone over this many times, but they might try to phrase it in a different way to shake you up. Some of their questions may seem a little belligerent. Now this is very important: I want you to keep your cool during all of this. Their lawyers are working for the other side and they will try to confuse you and trip you up if they can. They'll just be doing their job, do you understand?"

"Yes. Sure."

"I can't emphasize this too much: don't get flustered by their questions, just answer them to the best of your ability. And don't get angry, or start yelling, or anything like that. Okay? I mean, it's all right to be annoyed if they ask you the same questions over and over again, or try to twist your words around. But it's very important that you stay calm, answer their questions, and let us do the lawyering."

"All right. I'll do the best I can."

"Good. We don't think you'll have any problem at all with their questions, but we wanted you to know that Eddie St. Clair can be very tough and the whole thing could get out of hand if we let it. Remember: answer all his questions as directly and as calmly as you can. But that doesn't mean you should be an ice cube. Just try to relax and be yourself. If they get out of line, it's our job to get them back on track. Okay?"

"Okay."

"Fine. After they cross-examine you, your job will probably be over. You could be recalled to the stand later in the trial, but that doesn't happen very often. If it does, it will just be to clear up some point or other and will be very brief. The judge will see to that. So after you've testified you can just sit with Elmira and us, cross your fingers, and listen to the rest of the trial."

"How long will it take?"

"Your testimony?"

"No. The whole thing."

"We estimate a couple of weeks."

"I guess we can wait that much longer."

"Now about the settlement offer I told you about: you never know what's going to happen in a trial like this, but in case we find ourselves in another negotiation over terms, I'd better ask you one last time how much your insistence on taking Mercipine out of the clinical trial is worth to you."

"We're not going to change our mind about that, Marc. Even if they offer a trillion dollars, they would still have to get that drug out of circulation, or we wouldn't take the money."

"Well, for a trillion dollars, you could *buy* Mercer and company, Elmira. But let's be realistic. We might be able to get them to go as high as two or three million at some point—"

"Not interested. We owe it to Angela to see that this doesn't happen to anyone else."

"Okay, if that's the way you want it. Candace, did you want to add anything?"

"Just to say that we'll be there to answer any questions you might have during the trial. And Tony, if you feel uncomfortable while you're on the witness stand, just let Marc know and he'll ask the judge for a recess so that you can compose yourself."

"I understand. I'll be okay."

"We think so, too. Now, do you or Elmira have any questions about the hearing?"

"What should I wear?"

"Good point, Tony. Do you have a suit?"

"Yes."

"It's not polkadotted or anything, is it?"

"It's dark blue."

"Fine. Wear that. No jewelry except for your wedding band. Anything else?"

"Will we win?"

"Good question, Elmira. We think you have a strong case. But in the final analysis it's all up to the jury, and no one can predict what a jury will do. Anything else? Good. Okay, are you ready? I'm going to pretend to be Mr. St. Clair and I'm going to ask you some of the questions we think he might come up with . . . ."

*

"Say 'Ah.'"

"Ahhhhhhh."

"Good . . . heart sounds fine . . . now breathe deeply. Through your mouth. That's it . . . nice deep breaths . . . good . . . good . . . lungs are clear. Now lie back—I'm just going to palpate your abdomen . . . good—nothing going on down there."

"Mike, I want to ask you something."

"Shoot."

"Is Dad going to make it?"

"I don't know, Marc. It could go either way."

"But he could beat this thing?"

"Based on his response so far to the therapy, there's a fair chance, yes. Okay, you can get up."

"That it?"

"Not quite—just pull down your shorts for a minute . . . okay, now turn your head and cough. Good . . . again . . . good. Any problem getting an erection, anything like that?"

"Not so far."

"Good. Now back up on the table and assume the fetal position. That's fine."

"The only thing I like about this is that it's the 'end' of the exam."

"Ha ha. Never heard that one before."

"I'll bet. Umm."

"Prostate is nice and small, just like it should be. Okay, fella, you can get dressed. C'mon on out when you're finished and we'll get Cathy to take some blood and urine and send you on your way."

"How was the physical part?"

"You take care of yourself, you'll live to be a hundred and ten."

"Great. Always wanted to be a hundred and ten."

"You'll make it. But take some time off work once in a while. Get a little exercise."

"Easier said than done. By the way, I'm curious: what do you think of the Mercer case?"

"What 'Mercer case'?"

"Haven't you heard that we're taking the Mercer Corporation to court in a wrongful death suit?"

"Mercer? Are you kidding? Do you know the drug that's pulled your dad from the brink of death was produced by Mercer Pharmaceuticals?"

"Uh—no, I didn't."

"Without the Mercer Corporation I'd be out of business."

*

"Hey, Mr. Allen! I read about your case! It was in the *Post* yesterday! It's about to start, ain't it?"

"That's right, Goose. Starts Monday."

"Looks like a big one!"

"Big enough for us."

"You can do it, Mr. Allen!"

"I hope so."

"Say, wasn't it too bad about that girl! What a shame! She was only thirteen, wasn't she?"

"That's right. Gimme a bagel, will you, Goose?"

"Sure, Mr. Allen! The usual?"

"Yeah."

"You got it! Poppyseed with cream cheese and chives . . . ! Here you go, Mr. Allen!"

"Thanks, Goose."

"Give that company that killed that little girl what for, Mr. Allen! Tell them I told you that!"

"Sure will, Goose. Here. Keep the change."

"Thanks, Mr. Allen! Good luck on that case!"

"Thanks."

"I'll be rootin' for you!"

"Thanks, Goose, I appreciate that."

"Good luck, buddy!"

"Thanks, Goose. See you later."

"Okay, Mr. Allen! Take care, now!"

"I'll try . . ."

*

"Good morning, Candace."

"Morning, partner."

"Morning, *Marc*."

"All right. Morning, *Marc*."

"Thank you. I thought we'd go over some jury strategy today. You got into the case a little late and we haven't had much time to talk about that. I'll be doing most of the interviewing, but I'd like to have your input. Besides, if I get food poisoning or something, you may have to take over. Keep that in mind."

"It's already in there."

"Good. Okay—tell me what you think we want in a juror. And don't want."

"Well, first of all, we should try to get men and women—"

"Perfect! You get an A+!"

"As I was saying, *Marc*, we should try to get men and women, especially women, I think, who have a family, especially a teenage girl, if possible."

"Those may be difficult to come by."

"Or as close as possible to that situation."

"Good. What else?"

"Well, I think we would want people who are, for want of a better term, open-minded. I mean, people who don't automatically accept things the way they are. People who aren't immediately intimidated by doctors in white coats, or necessarily awed by companies that have a reputation for doing wonderful things for humanity, that sort of thing."

"What kind of person did you have in mind?"

"Professional people. Educated people. Maybe people who have a position of authority themselves."

"Very good. Anything else?"

"People who are healthy."

"Why is that?"

"If they're taking medications they're dependent on, they would probably be more likely to go along with whatever a powerful drug company tells them. To let the scientists do what they want as long as they come up with the drugs they need. Especially if they have a life-threatening condition."

"And how do we know if they have a life-threatening condition or not?"

"In law school I was taught that the best way to interrogate a juror is to make your questions open-ended and let them talk. They'll usually tell you what you want to know."

"So who else would be an ideal juror for the Calvecchis?"

"Anyone with a broader vision—artists, writers, and so on—parents, grandparents, poor people, giving types."

"And who do we not want on our jury?"

"Stockbrokers, shopkeepers, dinks, yuppies—anybody with his or her own agenda to think about instead of the case at hand."

"Okay, we've got the jury and the trial is underway. What about terminology?"

"You mean *our* terminology."

"That's right."

"Well, whenever possible, we should refer to a medication or a pharmaceutical compound as a 'drug.'"

"And why is that?"

"Because the word 'drug' has a negative connotation for a lot of people. Pot, cocaine, that sort of thing. 'Medication' or 'pharmaceutical' good, 'drug' bad."

"What else?"

"It might be a good idea *not* to refer to the defense witnesses as 'doctor' all the time."

"What would you use instead?"

"Sir. Or nothing at all."

"Because . . . ?"

"Because there's a certain magic in the word 'doctor.' People tend to respect doctors."

"Given a choice, would you refer to a defense witness as 'Doctor,' or as 'Doctor so-and-so'?"

"I'd probably call him 'Doctor so-and-so.'"

"Why?"

"Like I said, the word 'doctor' has a magic ring to it. More than 'Doctor so-and-so,' which dilutes the effect. With our own witnesses, of course, we would use 'doctor.'"

"What about the drug company? Do we refer to them as 'Mercer Pharmaceuticals'? Or 'The Mercer Corporation'? Or what?"

"I would refer to them as 'Mercer' or 'Mercer and company' whenever we can."

"Why is that?"

"Because 'Mercer' or 'Mercer and company' could be anything. A company that produces nuts and bolts. 'The Mercer Corporation' sounds more impressive, so we should steer clear of that. 'Mercer Pharmaceuticals' sounds downright omnipotent, and we should avoid it at all times."

"Okay, what about Angela Calvecchi?"

"We should refer to her as 'little Angela' or 'young Angela Calvecchi' whenever we can. And we should personalize her connection to Mercer. She was taking 'her medicine' rather than 'the medicine,' for example."

"Very good. I'm impressed. Anything else? How do we get the jury over to our side?"

"Well, for one thing, we don't want to snow the jury with a lot of charts and tables."

"But I like charts and tables."

"A few are fine. But not too many."

"Okay, what else?"

"At the same time, we don't want to oversimplify. We want to make them feel that they understand our position. That they're brought into the discussions. As Bill always says, 'Never underestimate the intelligence of a jury.' It annoys them when you talk down to them."

"You know something, Ms. White? I think you have the makings of a fine attorney."

"Thanks."

"You want to have lunch? Finish the strategy session over a beer and pizza? God knows you've earned it."

"No."

*

"Hello, Marc."

"McBain! Long time no smell!"

"What the hell is *that* supposed to mean?"

"Not a thing. It's just that some skunk might be leaking information about the Mercer case to the defense lawyers."

"What kind of information?"

"I read your story about the Calvecchis. There were some things in there *I* didn't even know, at least not until their depositions."

"Like what?"

"Will you put away that stupid pencil for a change? Like the fact that Elmira's brother is a pediatrician."

"You probably never asked them about that."

"No, I didn't. Did you?"

"Of course."

"Why?"

"Because it's another angle. An interesting—"

"It's always 'angles' with you, isn't it? You don't give a rat's ass who wins this case. Just so you get your fucking story. That's your only motive—"

"And what's *your* motive, Marcus?"

"What?"

"What's *your* motive in taking the case?"

"To do my best to win it for my clients, of course."

"Bullshit."

"What the hell do you mean, 'bullshit'?"

"You took the case for the same reason you take any case. To win for Marcus Allen, Jr. To make money. To keep your job. To move up the ladder, if at all possible."

"So? Is there something wrong with that if the result is the same?"

"You tell me."

"We're getting off the subject here, McBain. Point is, maybe it's you who's 'leaking shit to the enemy,' as one of our senior partners put it."

"You haven't told me anything yet that's worth leaking, my friend."

"And I'm not telling you anything else, either. Stop looking at me that way. All right. Maybe I'm paranoid. But in the legal profession it pays to trust no one."

"Probably true in any profession."

"Yeah. Maybe you're right. Buy you a beer?"

"Sure."

"SARGE! TWO MORE OVER HERE!"

"The piece on Marcus Allen, Jr. is article number four in the series. Here's the copy."

"Oh, God."

"What?"

"I don't want to read a piece about me."

"Why not? The other articles have been fair, haven't they?"

"Up to a point."

"Any case, the folks at Mercer have finally decided to let me talk to a few of their people as well."

"They did? Why?"

"I think they're worried about the publicity. They're afraid I'm making you guys look too good."

"I wouldn't go that far."

"One thing, though . . ."

(Urrrrp) "Yeah?"

"I'm not going to show you their copy in advance."

"SARGE! CANCEL ONE OF THOSE BEERS!"

"That's all right. I don't have time for a beer anyway. I'm meeting my wife for dinner at Cal's."

"You have a nice wife?"

"She's wonderful."

"She have a sister?"

"No, but she has a couple of ugly cousins."

"You have their phone numbers?"

The Case For The Plaintiffs

"All rise. Come and you shall be heard . . . . Honorable Judge William Binns presiding . . . . Be seated."

("My God—how old is he?")

("Close to ninety. But he's semi-retired.")

"Good morning. The court apologizes for the heat and the noise. We're trying to get the air conditioners repaired as soon as possible."

("He's also semi-dead.")

"Ladies and gentlemen, I will not be presiding in this case. My duty here is to aid in the selection of a jury. The case you'll be hearing, if you are elected to serve, is Calvecchi v. Mercer Pharmaceuticals Corporation. This is a civil case. The plaintiffs are suing for damages incurred by the Calvecchi family as a result of the death of their daughter, Angela. After all the testimony is presented, you will be asked to decide whether or not to award damages to plaintiffs and, if you find in plaintiffs' favor, to determine the amount of such damage. On the other hand, you may decide that plaintiffs' claim is without merit, in which case you will find for the defense and no damages will be awarded."

("How can anyone speak so slowly?")

("Ask me again when I'm ninety.")

"Each of you has been selected at random from the jury pool to appear in this courtroom. This morning some or all of you will be interviewed by the attorneys in this case to determine whether, in their opinion, you can be fair and impartial jurors. This process is known as 'voir dire,' from early French meaning "to speak the truth." And that's exactly what we're here for. Nothing more, and nothing less."

("I think he's talking in his sleep.")

("Wouldn't be surprised. He's probably recited that speech ten thousand times.")

"I would estimate that the case will last two to three weeks. If any of you has a problem with this time frame, please approach the bench at this time . . . ."

"You're—"

"Sarah Wong."

"Do you have a problem with the three weeks this trial might take?"

"Yes, your honor. I have a two-month-old baby—"

"Dismissed."

"Thank you, your honor."

"And your name is—"

"Bob Dellinger, judge."

"What's your problem with the time frame, Mr. Dellinger?"

"I can't take that much time off work."

"What work do you do?"

"I'm a real estate broker."

"Do you work alone or with a firm?"

"With Druckmiller and Shaw."

"Please return to your seat, sir. If we excused everyone who has a job, we wouldn't have a jury system."

"But—"

"Are plaintiffs ready for jury selection?"

"Yes, your honor."

"Defense?"

"Ready, your honor."

"The clerk will draw the names of six prospective jurors. When your name is called, please take a seat in the jury box, from right to left over there, in the order you're called. Mr. Allen for the plaintiffs and Mr. Baxstresser for the defense will ask you certain questions to determine whether or not you can be a fair and impartial juror in the case of Calvecchi v. Mercer Pharmaceuticals. If there is anyone present who feels he or she cannot hear this case in a fair and impartial manner, please so indicate and you may approach the bench at this time . . . ."

"You're—"

"Olivia Stone."

"Ms. Stone, you don't think you can be fair and impartial in this case?"

"It's that I can't judge another person, sir. Only God can do that. Jesus said—"

"You're dismissed with the thanks of the court."

"Thank you."

"Very well. The clerk will draw the first six names."

"John Zedick."

"Mr. Zedick, please take seat number one in the jury box."

"Orville Steiner."

"Mr. Steiner, please take the second seat."

"Rebecca Elwell . . . ."

"Ladies and gentlemen, in courtrooms under state jurisdiction, the judge does not participate in jury interviews. At this time I shall excuse myself until the attorneys have completed their interrogations."

"All rise . . . ."

"Do you swear or affirm to . . . ."

"I do—I do—I do—Yes, I do—I do."

"Please be seated."

"Ladies and gentlemen, I'm Marcus Allen, Jr., attorney for plaintiffs. As Judge Binns indicated, I'm going to ask you some questions about your background and previous experience with the courts. We need to do this in order to determine whether there are any factors that might preclude your being an unbiased juror in this case. I'll start with juror number one. Sir, do you pronounce your name ZEDick?"

"That's right."

"Mr. Zedick, please speak up. With the windows open, the noise from outside makes it difficult to hear you."

"THAT'S RIGHT."

"Thank you. Much better. Mr. Zedick, what sort of work do you do?"

"I'm a stockbroker."

"And do you own any stocks yourself?"

"Yes, of course."

"Any stocks in a pharmaceutical company? Anything of that nature?"

"Well, I'm not sure, now that you mention it. It's possible, though."

"Any stocks in the Mercer Corporation?"

"No, I don't think so."

"Ever been to a stockholders meeting of any medical or pharmaceutical companies?"

"Not that I can recall."

"Any of the rest of you own stocks in the Mercer Corporation?"

"No—No—No—No—No."

"Mr. Zedick, do you think that scientists can make mistakes?"

"Yes, I guess so. Sure."

"And if you were asked to find that the scientists at Mercer and company had rushed to judgement and had produced an unsafe drug for treatment of their daughter's affliction, would you hesitate to find for the plaintiffs in this case?"

"Well, if I thought they produced a bad drug and should have known they did that—no, I don't think so."

"You would be able to find for the plaintiffs if that were the case?"

"Yes."

"Would any of the rest of you hesitate to reach that conclusion if plaintiffs were to show that Mercer and company produced a drug that was instrumental in the death of a young girl if there was a question about the safety of that drug?"

"No—no—I don't think so—no—no."

"Mr. Zedick, do you know anyone who works in a hospital or a pharmacy or drug company?"

"Well, let me see . . . . No, except my own doctor. And our pharmacist, of course."

"Well, do you know any doctors or pharmacists intimately? Anyone you'd have lunch with, for instance?"

"No, not really."

"Have you read anything about this case? Heard anything about it on radio or television, anything like that?"

"I've read a few articles. In the *Post*, I think."

"And would this prevent you from being a fair and open-minded juror in this case?"

"No, I don't think so."

"What sort of organizations do you belong to?"

"The golf club. Chamber of commerce . . . ."

"Anything political?"

"No, nothing you would call 'political.'"

Thanks you, sir. Jury number two—Mr. 'STEINer'? As in a stein of beer?"

"That's right."

"Again, Mr. Steiner, please speak louder."

"THAT'S RIGHT."

"What sort of work do you do, Mr. Steiner?"

"I work in a camera store . . . ."

"Uh—Ms. Washington, is it? Good morning."

"It's *Mrs.* Washington."

"I'm sorry—*Mrs.* Washington. Now, Mrs. Washington, as I did with the other five jurors, I'm going to ask you some specific questions pertaining to the case of Calvecchi vs. Mercer. As I've said before, these questions are to help us determine whether you can be an impartial juror in this case."

"I understand that."

"Good. Mrs. Wash—"

"Hmmm-ffffff-ha-CHEW!"

"Bless you, sir."

"Hmmffff. Thank you."

"Now, Mrs. Washington, have you ever served on a jury before?"

"Yes, several times."

"Civil or criminal?"

"Both."

"Okay. And were the juries you served on able to render a verdict in all cases?"

"All but one."

"Was that one a criminal or civil case?"

"Criminal."

"All right. Now—do you know anyone who works for a pharmaceutical company?"

"No, not that I know of."

"Or any other laboratory or research institution?"

"I have a niece who used to work in a place where they develop film."

"Anyone else?"

"No."

"Besides your own physician, do you know anyone who practices medicine, or is a nurse, or works in a hospital—anything like that?"

"I have a second cousin that works in the laundry room at St. Luke's."

"Does he or she know any of the medical staff well enough to—say—have lunch with them?"

"I don't imagine so."

"When was the last time you spoke with her?"

"At her mother's funeral."

"When was that?"

"'Bout ten years ago."

"All right. Now, Mrs. Washington, do you take any prescription medications? Or have you ever done so? You don't have to tell us which ones, just whether you have ever been given a prescription for any kind of drug by a doctor."

"Yes, I have."

"Any of these drugs made by the Mercer Corporation?"

"I wouldn't have any idea."

"Well, if the evidence in this case indicates that Mercer did not comply with all the safety regulations imposed on it by the federal government, or if they cut corners to get the drug known as Mercipine on the market faster, or did anything else that might have increased young Angela Calvecchi's risk in taking this drug, would you have any hesitation in finding for the plaintiffs, Mr. and Mrs. Calvecchi, and against Mercer and company?"

"No, I don't think so."

"One final question, Mrs. Washington: Are there any personal reasons—your health, a demanding job, anything of that nature—that would not allow you to serve on the jury in this case for a period of several weeks, if necessary?"

"No—none."

"Thank you."

"And I'll ask all the rest of you the same question: Are there any personal problems that would make it difficult for you to serve on this jury for a period of several weeks?"

"No—No—No—No—No."

"And are there any of you who would not be able to render a fair and impartial verdict in this case?"

"No—No—No—No—No."

"Thank you all. Mr. Baxstresser?"

"Thank you, Mr. Allen. Mr. Zedick, have you ever taken a prescription drug?"

"Yes."

"Was this medication produced by the Mercer Pharmaceuticals Corporation?"

"Well, I don't know . . . ."

"Can you remember whether it was produced by an American pharmaceutical company?"

"I can't say. Probably, I suppose."

"And did you have any doubt about the safety of the drug when you took it?"

"No, I don't think so. I never thought much about it."

"Sir, are you aware that all such drugs produced by American pharmaceutical companies are regulated by an agency of the federal government known as the United States Food and Drug Administration?"

"Yes, I've heard that, I think."

"Are all the rest of you aware of that fact?"

"Yes—I suppose so—maybe—uh—"

"And, Mr. Zedick, did you know that questions of drug safety are the sole responsibility of this governmental agency?"

"Yes. Sure."

"Thank you, Mr. Zedick. Now, Mrs. Washington: Mr. Allen asked you whether you were taking any prescription medications."

"Yes."

"And you said you were taking such a medication at this time?"

"No, I said I've had medications prescribed to me by a doctor."

"Then let me just ask you: Have you ever been involved with the clinical trial of a new medication?"

"No, I don't believe so."

"As far as you know, you've not been involved in a study involving any kind of drug or medication."

"That's right."

"Do you know of anyone who has ever been harmed in any way by taking an experimental drug?"

"No."

"Mrs. Washington, have you ever worked for a government agency?"

"No."

"Or do you know anyone who has worked for the government?"

"No, not that I know of."

"Do you have any pets at home?"

"Yes, we have a dog."

"Mrs. Washington, do you belong to any animal rights organizations?"

"Any what?"

"Any organizations whose goal it is to give certain basic rights to animals. Such as not using them in laboratory experiments, for instance."

"No."

"And you've never contributed money to one of these groups?"

"No."

"What do you do for a living, Mrs. Washington?"

"I work in a department store."

"Which department?"

"Women's apparel."

"In your job do you handle any apparel that comes from animals? Such as fur or leather."

"Not usually. We sell skirts and blouses and dresses. Mostly cotton and synthetics."

"If your buyer brought in a skirt or blouse containing leather or fur trim, would you refuse to sell it?"

"I don't think so."

"Mrs. Washington, do you know of any reason you could not be a fair and impartial juror in this case?"

"No."

"Do you have any conflicts or personal problems that might prevent you from serving on this jury?"

"None that I know of."

"Thank you. I'm finished with this group, counselor."

"Fine. Ladies and gentlemen, just relax for a few minutes while we go talk to the judge. And please don't discuss the case among yourselves . . . ."

*

"Okay, Mr. Baxstresser, is there anyone you want to challenge for cause?"
"Only one, your honor."
"Mr. Allen?"
"Two, your honor."
"Who's the first one?"
"Ms. Skrowaczeski."
"What cause?"
"Her brother is a pharmacist."
"Granted. Who's the other one?"
"Mr. Davis."
"What cause?"
"I don't think he understands what's going on, your honor."
"That is a peremptory challenge, son. You want to take one of your peremptory challenges for this juror?"
"Yes, your honor."
"Very well. Mr. Baxstresser?"
"Only one. Ms. Elwell."
"What grounds?"
"She belongs to a lot of animal rights organizations."
"What's the relevance of that?"
"Your honor, the Mercer Corporation uses animals to test the safety and effectiveness of all their products. She would undoubtedly be prejudiced in favor of plaintiffs."
"That sounds peremptory to me. Do you want to take that?"
"Your honor—"
"Yes or no, Mr. Baxstresser?"
"Yes."
"Very well, we have the first three jurors. Let's proceed with the next group."

*

"Okay, partner. Let's talk about the jury for a minute. Do you see any problem jurors?"
"Not really. I think it shapes up as a fairly impartial group. Nobody stands out as a particular leader, except for one person, maybe."
"Who's that?"
"Mrs. Washington."
"Why do you think she's our 'strongman'?"
"She has a direct, almost steely look. Like she ought to be a warden or something. But there's a heart in there, and I get the feeling that nothing would surprise her. The rest of the jury will listen to her, I think."

"You think she's strong enough to convince the others that a giant corporation like Mercer Pharmaceuticals might be the bad guys in this affair?"

"If anyone on the jury can do that, it would be her."

"I agree. Now how do you propose to convince her?"

"Well, she has grandchildren about Angela's age when she died. Of course we'll focus on the terrible loss the Calvecchis have sustained."

"Is 'focus' the right word here?"

"How about 'pound'? 'Reiterate'? 'Belabor'?"

"Better."

"But I don't think we want to overdo it. To make it sound like we're pandering to this lady. She has a lot of pride and I think she's very perceptive."

"We'll just have to play it by ear. Learn to read her signals."

"But we don't want to make the other jurors think they're being ignored, especially Mr. Olivera and Ms. Chin. I think they would give us a fair hearing even without Mrs. W's influence."

"Very good, partner. And what else would you belabor?"

"Well, since most of the jurors are middle-class workers, and Mrs. W's African-American, we ought to emphasize the size and power of Mercer and company. Make them seem cold and uncaring—establishment, for want of a better word. Make them and their witnesses seem like cogs in a giant machine."

"All of this is fine, Ms. White, but how do we convince Messrs. Steiner and Zedick? If we're wrong about Mrs. W, how do we get them over to our side?"

"Well, for one thing, they also have teenage grandchildren. And they're both taking prescription medications. We've got to convince them that anything could go wrong in the production of a new drug. That they or their grandkids could be the next victims."

"Good. Anything else?"

"One of the jurors is never going to come our way."

"Who's that?"

"Mr. Corrigan."

"Why is he a problem?"

"He's very conservative. Couldn't you strike him?"

"I tried. But we can't strike everybody who's old and crotchety. Remember, we only need four votes to win. If we present a good case, we have a fair chance. Now let's go over our legal strategy again . . . ."

*

"A quarter for a joke so's I can get somethin' to eat?"

"Is this your permanent location now?"

"One of 'em."

"All right, here's a couple of bucks. Don't bother me again for a while."

"What am I supposed to do——wait for you to come to *me*?"

*

"Do you ever get nervous before opening arguments?"

"No."

"Why not?"

"Because I grew up with it. I learned everything I know from my dad. When I was a kid I used to come in and watch him work. I love being in a courtroom. Any courtroom . . ."

"All rise . . . . Honorable Judge Norma Bates presiding."

"Good morning. Please be seated. Ladies and gentlemen of the jury, the case you'll be hearing is a wrongful death lawsuit. A civil, as opposed to a criminal, matter. You will be asked to decide whether a new medication produced by the Mercer Pharmaceutical Corporation caused the death of Angela Calvecchi, the daughter of the plaintiffs in this trial. And, if so, whether the Mercer Corporation should be held liable for her death. Counsel for plaintiffs, are you prepared to make your opening statement?"

"We are, your honor.

"Proceed, Mr. Allen."

"Thank you, your honor. Members of the jury, As Judge Bates indicated, in the case before you we'll be dealing with a civil lawsuit, not a criminal case. You will not be asked to send anyone to jail here, but to determine whether there are reasonable grounds to find that certain actions and procedures carried out by the defendants, the Mercer Corporation, were instrumental in the death of plaintiffs' daughter, thirteen-year-old Angela Calvecchi. And, if so, what damages Mr. and Mrs. Calvecchi are entitled to receive.

"Over the next several days we will show that young Angela's untimely death was a direct result of her participation in the clinical trial of a new, experimental medication called Mercipine, which is produced by that corporation. More importantly, we will show that Mercer and company should have known that this new drug might have been unsafe, and the principals involved should have conducted additional tests to determine whether this was indeed the case. And that the risk to little Angela Calvecchi was far too great to subject her, at the tender age of thirteen, to all the unknowns associated with this new experimental drug.

"The preponderance of the evidence will show that Mercipine did, in fact, cause the death of this little girl. We will show further that this budding teenager would almost certainly have gone on to become a successful and respected doctor in her own right, had she not been cut down in the flower of youth by an experimental drug given to her by a physician she trusted, and produced by one of the best-known drug companies in the world.

"But aren't there risks associated with the testing of any new drug in human beings regardless of the care with which it is manufactured? Of course. And aren't there procedures and regulations in place to assure that the risk to people who agree to participate in the experimental testing of a brand-new drug is minimized? Absolutely.

"But what if these required safeguards weren't properly carried out in the case of Mercipine? What if the governmental regulations weren't followed to the letter? Or even in spirit? And what if, by costcutting and the rush to get a new drug on the market, corners were cut? Ladies and gentlemen of the jury, plaintiffs will show that defendant acted in precisely this fashion, cutting costs, using the barest minimum safety testing procedures, hurrying these procedures in order to get this new drug on the market, pursuing profit above safety, and allowing young Angela Calvecchi, a girl with virtually unlimited potential, and at least six others to die as a result of their own greed and negligence in this matter!

"What I am suggesting to you is not merely speculation or wishful thinking on the part of Angela's parents or her attorneys. We will present evidence that will *prove* negligence on the part of Mercer and company. We will bring forth expert witnesses who will attest that this giant corporation should have done much more to determine whether this new drug, Mercipine, was safe for use in human beings, especially in children, before pushing it into a clinical trial to test it on Angela Calvecchi and a thousand other people, including forty-one adolescents.

"Ladies and gentlemen, you can be sure that attorneys for the defense will attempt to convince you that young Angela's death was merely an unfortunate data point in Mercer and company's records. That her tragic experience is part and parcel of any drug testing program, that risks must be taken in the interest of science and medical progress. But consider this: thirteen-year-old Angela Calvecchi was not some ninety-five-year-old man attached to tubes and machines, someone who was bound to die naturally in a very short time regardless of what was done to her. She was a young girl at the very beginning of her adolescence. A brand-new teenager with an enormously promising future. A girl who was bright, popular, brave, and dedicated to becoming a doctor. Her ambition was to work with diabetes patients such as herself, to help find a cure for this terrible disease, which she knew might be debilitating and even fatal at some future time in her life.

"Ladies and gentlemen, Angela Calvecchi was robbed of that promising future by a megacorp that cut corners in order to place an experimental drug on the market sooner than it should have been there, before all the safety questions had been answered . . . .

"What price do we put on a life like little Angela's? The answer to that question, of course, is a matter for you, the jury, to decide. Here is a girl who loved to play the violin. Who had countless friends and admirers. Who was bright and lively and courageous. Who was beloved by her parents, her grandparents, and everyone else who knew her. Who would've enjoyed almost limitless earning potential for decades. And beyond that, what price do we put on the suffering that Angela's parents have been forced to endure as a result of this unforgivable negligence? This, too, is for you to decide. I'm confident that, after you've heard all the evidence in this case, you will find that the Mercer Corporation was clearly negligent in this matter and that the Calvecchi family well deserves to be fairly compensated for such a terrible, such an enormous—and such a *preventable*—loss. Thank you."

"Mr. St. Clair?"

"Thank you, your honor. Good morning, ladies and gentlemen, good morning. You've just endured a very touching speech by one of the attorneys for the plaintiffs in the case of Calvecchi v. the Mercer Pharmaceuticals Corporation. Pretty convincing, wasn't it? I'd vote for him myself if the trial ended with that speech. But the trial doesn't end with that speech. It doesn't even begin with that speech. Why? Because counsel for the plaintiffs left out several important facts in his impassioned address to you. He left out the *fact* that Angela Calvecchi's parents were notified of all the possible risks associated with the medication known as Mercipine and, indeed, they signed an acknowledgment of their acceptance of these risks. He left out the *fact* that the pharmaceutical compound called Mercipine was approved for clinical testing by the United States Food and Drug Administration, the agency of the federal government responsible for the safety of all new medications. He left out the *fact* that all of Mercer's procedures were found to be completely satisfactory by this governmental agency and that, in *fact*, the Mercer Corporation could never have put Mercipine, or any other pharmaceutical, on the market *without* FDA approval. And, most importantly, he left out the fact that without courageous patients like Angela Calvecchi, and their parents, *no* new medications would ever appear on your pharmacy's shelves . . . ."

("What happened to his Southern accent?")

("He drops that in the courtroom.")

("Pffft.")

"As counsel for plaintiffs pointed out, it's an unfortunate fact that there are risks associated with the clinical testing of any new pharmaceutical product. On rare occasions, the medicine itself can cause illness or even death. That is why it is usually tested in the elderly or on volunteers who have something to gain. But there are exceptions to this rule. One of the best examples is the polio vaccine of the 1950's, which was tested on children because it was children who ordinarily came down with this terrible affliction. And aren't we all glad that this testing was done! As a result of this brave experiment we now have the Salk and Sabin vaccines, and poliomyelitis is a thing of the past. And can you imagine a world without the polio vaccine? Can you imagine the FDA telling Dr. Salk, 'Sorry, there is some risk associated with these tests'?

"Ladies and gentlemen of the jury, that is still the case today. There are always risks in this kind of testing, especially in the case of diseases like Type I diabetes, which usually originate in children. And other terrible diseases whose causes are still unknown. It's unfortunate that some sick patients become even sicker when they try a brand-new medication, and in the worst possible scenario, some will even die. And no one is more saddened by the death of young Angela Calvecchi, or any other patient, than every single employee of Mercer Pharmaceuticals. But we will show you that it is a necessary risk, a risk worth taking, a risk that *must* be taken if we are going to have any sort of medical progress in this country and around the world . . . ."

("God, it's hot in here.")

"Members of the jury, I could give you a long list of all the medications you would find in your own neighborhood pharmacy that have been discovered, developed, and produced by Mercer Pharmaceuticals. Plaintiffs' attorney has made much of the fact that Mercer is a large corporation. But there is a reason for that. The best companies in any enterprise expand and grow because of the excellence of what they do. The Mercer Corporation has a well-deserved reputation, both in the industry and among the general population, as one of the finest, most trustworthy pharmaceutical companies on this planet. Plaintiffs' attorneys would ask you to stifle the production of new medications by this or any other company and send all of them, along with the rest of us, back to the Dark Ages. As Mercer's representative in this courtroom, I ask you to reject that proposal out of hand, to reject plaintiffs' attempts to stifle medical progress, to reject the claim that any one individual or corporation is responsible for all the setbacks, large or small, that must accompany the production of new pharmaceutical compounds in this or any other country.

"And finally, ladies and gentlemen, and most importantly of all, I ask you to remember that the outcome of this case rests on a simple matter of law. Throughout these proceedings I ask you to keep in mind this question: 'What law has been broken here?' And to remember that your job in this trial is not to determine whether or how much Angela's Calvecchi's family suffered as a result of the girl's death, tragic as that may be, or even whether this incident was the natural result of proper clinical testing of a promising new drug, but whether, *in fact*, Mercer Pharmaceuticals fulfilled every single one of the regulations *required by law* in the production of their highly promising new diabetes medication known as Mercipine.

"I'm quite certain that when you have heard all the evidence presented by both sides in this case, you will find that the Mercer Corporation acted in accordance with industry standards and with the complete and willing approval of the U.S. Food and Drug Administration. And I am equally certain that you will not be swayed by the extraneous matters that counsel for plaintiffs will try to distract you with. Keep that all-important question in your mind: *What law has been broken here?* If you will do just that, and I'm confident that you will, I'm sure you will come up with a just and reasonable verdict in this case. Thank you, ladies and gentlemen."

"Thank you, Mr. St. Clair. Ladies and gentlemen of the jury, several workmen will be coming early this afternoon to see if they can get some temporary air conditioning set up in the courtroom. I apologize for the delay. Court is adjourned until ten o'clock tomorrow morning."

*

"Hello! Anybody home . . . ?"
"Hi, Marc."
"Hi, kid, where's Mom?"
"I think she went out shopping."
"Did she say when she'd be back?"
"Not really."
"Oh. So—what are you up to?"
"Nothing. Want some ice cream or anything?"
"Sure."
"Let's see . . . we've got Chunky Monkey and Cherry Garcia."
"Maybe a little of both."
"Me, too."
"How are things in school?"
"Okay."
"What are you taking now?"
"Oh, English, math, science, ceramics, gym, and—uh—did Mom tell you what happened to Sally?"
"No, she didn't. What happened?"
"She died."
"She *died*? What happened to her?"
"I don't know—it was like a heart attack or something."
"Well, I suppose it was her time to go. She must've been seven or eight."
"Mom said she was almost eleven."

"That's pretty old for a parakeet!"
"I buried her."
"Really? Where?"
"Over in the corner by the woods. So she can hear all the other birds."
"That's a good place. Sally would have liked that."
"Marc?"
"Hm?"
"What's it like to die?"
"Oh, c'mon, Tim, you're too young to worry about dying."
"I'm older than Sally was."
"Sally was a bird. You'll probably live to be a hundred and ten."
"But what's it *like*?"
"You got me, kid. I've never done it."
"Maybe Dad's going to do it."
"I don't know, Timmy. I really don't."
"Mom said the cancer came back."
"I know, but they're trying another drug combination . . ."
"Do you just stop living? Is it like going to sleep only you—like—don't wake up?"
"I suppose so. Eat your ice cream."
"But what does it *feel* like?"
"It's probably not so wonderful, but the good news is: it doesn't take long."
"How long does it take?"
"Tim, I doubt that when you die you even know it. So it doesn't matter much how long it takes."
"Does it hurt?"
"I don't know, Tim. I don't think so."
"I tried to hold my breath yesterday for as long as I could. It felt awful."
"But you didn't die."
"Maybe it would be even worse."
"It's probably a lot better. I've heard stories about people who became very calm and peaceful right before they stopped breathing or whatever. Sometimes they even smile. Maybe it's a very pleasant experience."
"Do you believe in heaven and hell?"
"I really don't know what to believe, Timmy. Are you worried that Sally is going to go to hell or something?"
"Not exactly. I was thinking about Dad."
"Have you been talking to him about this?"
"We were there on Sunday."
"I hope nobody is going to hell, Tim. But for God's sake, that's not something you need to worry about for a long time."

"It doesn't seem fair."

"Life isn't very fair sometimes, kiddo. You just have to learn that. I guess it's a part of growing up."

"Marc?"

"What?"

"I think I'm going to be a minister when I get out of school."

"Really? Where did this come from?"

"I don't know. I've just been thinking about it."

"You want to be a minister because you think life's unfair?"

"I guess so."

"That's the reason I wanted to be a lawyer!"

"I don't want to be a lawyer, though."

"Why not?"

"Dad said there aren't any lawyers in heaven."

"Might not be many ministers, either, Timmy, from what I've heard."

"Who's there, then?"

"I don't know. Maybe nobody."

"Because nobody's good enough?"

"Timmy, the best of us are bad sometimes and the worst of us are sometimes good."

"Then maybe everybody's there!"

"That's as good a guess as any. Gotta go, kid. Thanks for the Ben & Jerry's. Tell Mom I'll call her later."

"Can't you stay a little longer, Marc? You haven't heard any of my new CDs . . . ."

"I'm pretty busy right now. Big case in court. But when that's over—"

"Sure."

*

"Hi, Dad. How are you today?"

"I could go any minute."

"C'mon, Dad. You're not going 'any minute.' And I wish you'd stop telling Tim stuff like that. He's becoming preoccupied with death. Yours, primarily."

"Your point is well taken, counselor. I'll pretend I'm not dying when he comes over, which isn't very often."

"Thank you."

"What does it all mean, Marc?"

"What does what mean?"

"What does it mean that we live and die?"

". . . ."

"Don't look at me like that. I've been giving this a lot of thought for the last few weeks and you know what I think? I think it doesn't mean anything."

"Uh—"

"Let me finish. You're born, you grow up, get married, have children, work, grow old, and die. What's the point? I mean, after you're dead, what does it matter that you were ever alive?"

"Well, your life obviously means a lot to me. If it weren't for that, I wouldn't be here."

"Is that so? What if you were never born: would my life be worthless? If I had twenty-five children would my life be worth twenty-five times as much?"

"You're joking, aren't you?"

"I've never been more serious in my life. Give me the answer: once you're gone, what does it matter that you ever lived?"

"Damn it, Dad. I can't answer that. Maybe nobody can."

"Try."

"Well, surely if you do good, or make a contribution to the world, your life was meaningful."

"What about Hitler? Was his life meaningful?"

"I suppose so, but in a different way."

"So what?"

"What do you mean, 'So what'?"

"I mean, what's the difference whether you do good or evil? Your life has just as much meaning, or lack of it, either way."

"Are you suggesting it's okay to go out and murder people?"

"Not okay. It just doesn't matter. Unless—"

"Unless what?"

"Unless the theologians are right: There is a God, and he appreciates what you've done while you've been on Earth."

"Are you getting religion, Dad?"

"I didn't say that. I said 'unless.' If there's no God, then yes—it doesn't matter whether you kill people or not. When you're dead, you're dead, and *nothing* matters!"

"And if there is?"

"Then maybe it matters."

"Are you saying this proves there's a God?"

"For a lawyer, you miss a lot, son. It doesn't prove a damn thing. Just because you might like there to be a God doesn't mean there is one."

"So we're back to square one."

"No, we're on square two. If there's no God, life is certainly meaningless. But even if there is a God, it could *still* be meaningless."

"Now you're saying that good and evil don't enter into this?"

"Pay attention. I'm saying that God may not care whether we're good or not. Maybe He isn't paying any attention. Or maybe He cares and *is* paying attention, but doesn't reward or punish anyone, regardless. If any of those things are true, life is still meaningless."

"Not necessarily. But for the sake of argument, where does that leave us?"

"The only way life would have any meaning at all is if there is a God, and He cares whether we're good or not, is paying attention to everything we do, and rewards the good things we do and punishes the bad ones."

"Not true."

"Ah. You're learning. Why isn't it true?"

"There could be no God, and even if there is a God who isn't paying any attention and doesn't hand out rewards, life could have meaning anyway."

"Very good. And what meaning do you suppose it would have?"

"I can't quantify it, but I think you'd have to say that life at least has meaning while you're living it. If so, then it also has meaning after you're gone, regardless of whether you know it or not."

"Exactly. Now what is the evidence that it has meaning while you're alive?"

"Well, my life has meaning for me. And since you've played a big part in creating my life, then your life has to have meaning, too."

"You mean sex gives life its meaning?"

"No, dad. I'm talking about all the things you did to help form my life *after* I was born."

"In other words the only thing that gives life any meaning is the effect you have on other people."

"I would say that's true."

"Wrong."

"What's wrong with it?"

"All you've said is that life *might* have meaning because of the effect you have on others. Even if you have some effect on others, good or bad, it still might not mean anything."

"Well, for that matter, maybe you're a figment of my imagination, or life is but a dream."

"Sounds like a catchy tune, but if that's the best answer you can come up with, I pity your clients."

"Dammit, Dad, you've done a lot of good things for a lot of people!"

"Irrelevant, incompetent, and immaterial."

"All right, what can I say? Life may have meaning and it may not."

"And?"

"And while you're living it, you've got to assume that it does have some meaning. Because if you don't, then your life will not be a good life, whether you're right or wrong."

"So what?"

"Look, Dad. Here's what I think: Everyone has to decide this question for himself. We can never really know whether our answer is right or wrong. You just have to live the best you can, based on your own answer."

"A very feeble summation, for a lawyer."

"It's the best I can do."

"It's the best I can do, too. Sickening, isn't it?"

"I hadn't really thought about it that way."

"And if you had, would it make any difference?"

"No."

"Exactly. Tell me something, Marc: Did you hate it when I argued with you when you were a kid?"

"I loved every minute of it. That's why I wanted to follow your footsteps. You made it so much fun."

"That sounds like a load of crap, but I'm glad you said it."

"I should do what they do in all the movies now, Dad, and say, 'I love you.' I imagine you'd find that sappy, but the fact is, I *do* love you!"

"Maybe this is what gives life some meaning."

"If that doesn't, what would?"

"I love you, too, you little shit, and Timmy, too. Hell, I even love your mother. If she hadn't been such a harpie . . . But enough of this. Why aren't you in court this afternoon?"

"They had to fix the air conditioning system."

"They ought to tear the whole damn building down and start over. How did opening arguments go?"

"Okay, I guess. Anyway, the members of the jury know they're in for a battle."

"Good. That's the way they *should* feel at this point. What did you think of Eddie's opening remarks?"

"He's going to be a formidable opponent."

"The most formidable you're likely to encounter for a while. But he can be beaten. If he starts to stutter, or starts to speak southernese, you've got him on the ropes."

"Stutter?"

"I've known Eddie since we were kids, remember? Do you know why he speaks with a southern accent outside the courtroom?"

"No. Why? I always thought it was just some sort of affectation."

"Nope. He has a stuttering problem. Outside the courtroom he's always had a problem with that. For some reason he's fine when he's in front of a jury, or if he speaks with some kind of dialect. But if you get him on the defensive—no pun intended—shake his confidence, he'll begin to stutter. That's when you know you're on to something. Whatever it is that made him stutter, hammer away at it."

"Dad?"

"Yes?"

"You're interested in this case, aren't you?"

"Sure."

"Why?"

"Why? I don't know. Because I want my son to do a good job, I suppose."

"Why?"

"I don't know."

"I think the fact that you care what happens to me, or with this case, or with anything else, shows that your life has some meaning, at least for you."

"As long as I'm still alive."

"And it has meaning for me, too. Even after you're gone."

"We'll soon see."

*

"Ladies and gentlemen, I'm sure you've noticed the difference in noise and temperature this morning. Perhaps it was worth a brief delay in the trial. Mr. Allen?"

"We agree, your honor, and we call Mr. Anthony Calvecchi to the stand."

"Anthony Calvecchi . . . ."

"Raise your right hand. Do you swear to tell the truth, the whole truth, and nothing but the truth?"

"I do."

"State your full name."

"Anthony Mariano Calvecchi."

" . . . Good morning, Mr. Calvecchi."

"Good morning."

"How are you this morning?"

"A little nervous."

"Of course. Who wouldn't be? We'll try get through this as quickly as possible."

"I would appreciate that."

"Mr. Calvecchi, I'm going to have to ask you some questions pertaining to your daughter's death. Some of these may be difficult for you, but they must be addressed. Please take your time, and if you need to stop for a minute or two, just let me or the judge know."

"All right."

"Mr. Calvecchi, please tell us in your own words what happened to your daughter Angela a little over a year ago."

"Well, she was suffering from diabetes. There wasn't much the doctor could do for her except prescribe insulin, and we knew that wasn't really a cure, that she would probably have problems down the road . . . ."

"Take your time."

"Angela was very bright. Very smart. She told us when she was—oh, four or five—that she was going to be a doctor. She was always going to be a doctor. She told us she was going to find a cure for diabetes some day. She *knew* that, even before she could pronounce it right. She read everything she could find about it. By the time she was ten, she probably knew as much about it as her doctor."

"And who was her doctor?"

"Doctor Mangan."

"Richard Mangan?"

"Yes, that's right."

"Okay. Now tell us, if you will, how she happened to be taking Mercipine when she died."

"Objection!"

"Sustained."

"Please tell us how Angela became involved with the experimental drug Mercipine."

"Doctor Mangan called us."

"*He* called *you*?"

"Well, he called my wife. And then I called him."

"What did he tell you and your wife when you spoke to him?"

"He said there was a new drug on the market which might be able to help Angela."

"Did he tell you the name of the drug?"

"Not right then. We found out later it was called Mercipine."

"How did you find out?"

"He told us."

"Okay. And did he tell you at that time that there might be some risk involved in taking this drug?"

"Yes. He said there might be some side effects, and that the drug might not work. In fact, he told us that she might not get the drug at all, but a placebo."

"And do you know whether she got the drug or a placebo?"

"We found out after she died that she was taking the real thing."

"All right. Now, did Dr. Mangan tell you what kind of side effects you might expect if Angela began the treatment?"

"He said headaches, muscle aches or stiffness, nausea and diarrhea, that sort of thing. He called them 'flu-like' symptoms."

"He didn't tell you that there could be a fatal reaction to Angela's taking the drug?"

"Not in the beginning."

"Did he *ever* tell you about this possibility?"

"He said there was always the possibility of a serious reaction to any new untested drug. But that the chance of a fatal reaction was usually very, very small."

"Did he tell you what his confidence was based on?"

"No."

"Did he tell you anything about the chance of a fatal reaction to Mercipine specifically?"

"No, except that it was very, very small."

"So based on that assurance you decided that it was safe for Angela to—"

"Objection, your honor."

"Sustained. Please refrain from making this kind of leading statement, counselor."

"Very well, your honor. Mr. Calvecchi, after speaking with Doctor Mangan, you and your wife decided to go ahead with the experimental treatment, is that right?"

"Yes . . . ."

"Your honor, may we have a short break in order for Mr. Calvecchi to compose himself?"

"No, I'm all right."

"Are your sure?"

"Yes."

"Mr. Calvecchi, can you tell us how you obtained the drug recommended by Dr. Mangan?"

"He gave it to us."

"He didn't give you a prescription?"

"No."

"Did he tell you why he didn't give you a prescription?"

"He said there was only a limited amount available for the tests and it wasn't in the drug stores yet."

"So he gave the drug to you directly."

"Yes."

"Could you describe the form of the drug he gave you?"

"Yellow capsules."

"In some kind of container?"

"Yes. A little plastic bottle."

"Did he give you instructions on the dosage to give Angela?"

"Yes. And the instructions were also on the bottle."

"And what were those instructions?"

"To take one capsule twice a day."

"Did he say what time of day?"

"He said breakfast and dinner. They should be taken with a meal."

"Did he mention any particular danger of taking the capsules without food?"

"Just that they might upset her stomach more. And also that the drug might be absorbed into her system better with food."

"And when did you start giving Angela the drug?"

"That evening at dinnertime."

"One capsule."

"That's right."

"Was there any kind of immediate reaction?"

"Not right away."

"Was there any evidence for a reaction later on?"

"Yes."

"Would you describe these symptoms for us?"

"The next morning she felt achy and tired. Like she had the flu or something."

"Did you tell the doctor about this?"

"We spoke to his nurse."

"And what did she tell you?"

"That this was normal and we should continue the treatment."

"So you gave her another capsule at breakfast?"

"Yes."

"What day was this?"

"Satur—mmmmm—Saturday."

"Would you like a Kleenex or a glass of water, Mr. Calvecchi?"

"Thank you . . . I'm all right."

"So you were home that day?"

"Yes. My wife did some shopping and I stayed home with Angela."

"Did her symptoms get any better?"

"She seemed to be better that morning. In the afternoon she felt worse again. I asked her where it hurt. She said she hurt all over."

"What did you do?"

"As soon as my wife got home I called the doctor. It was Saturday, so he wasn't there, but his answering service gave him the message."

"What time was this?"

"About three o'clock."

"In the afternoon?"

"Yes."

"And did Dr. Mangan call back that afternoon?"

"He called us back about seven o'clock that evening."

"What did he tell you when he finally returned your call?"

"Objection."

"Sustained."

"What did Dr. Mangan tell you when he called back?"

"I told him how Angela was feeling, and he said it was nothing to worry about, and that we should go ahead and give her another capsule at dinnertime and two the next day and call him on Monday if she wasn't feeling any better."

"And that's what you did?"

"Well, we had already finished dinner, but yes, we gave her the capsule then."

"How long before that had you finished dinner?"

"About an hour."

"And the next day?"

"She was dead . . . . Mmmmm . . . ."

"We'd like a brief recess, your honor."

"You may have ten minutes, counselor."

*

"Here, Tony, take this glass of water. There's some Kleenex over there."

"Thank you . . . thank you."

"Go on back and sit with Elmira for a minute . . . ."

"What was the jury's reaction to the questioning?"

"I'd say they're paying attention."

"How about Mrs. Washington?"

"Completely inscrutable. One good thing, though: some of the others peek at her from time to time to see how she's reacting."

"That's a good sign."

"Unless she goes the other way. Meant to ask you: how's your dad?"

"He's doing okay. Claims he's dying, but he's not. Not right away, anyhow. But he's got my little brother obsessed about it."

"How old is he?"

"Twelve."

"I was twelve once. A very impressionable age."

"I bet you were very cute at that age."

"I was ugly, ungainly, and smart-assed."

"Well, you've changed a lot since then. Anyway, two out of three ain't bad."

*

"Mr. Calvecchi, I just have a few more questions for you. Are you all right?"

"Yes. I'm sorry about the delay."

"That's all right. I know this is very difficult for you, sir. But, when you're ready, could you please tell the jury what happened after you gave Angela her third capsule after dinner that Saturday evening?"

"I think she felt worse. Anyway, she went right to bed."

"Did Angela say anything before she went to bed?"

"Yes . . . . She said, 'I'm glad this is—I'm glad this is happening to me. I need to know how my patients would feel when—when—if they take this drug.'"

"Do you need another minute?"

"No—I'm all right. I'm sorry."

"We all know how you must feel, sir. Now you've testified that you told Dr. Mangan that Angela felt 'very tired and ached all over'—is that right?"

"Yes, I did."

"And he wasn't at all concerned about that?"

"Not as far as I could tell."

"Well, did Angela seem all right except for the aching and fatigue?"

"She seemed to be. We didn't take her temperature or anything like that. But she didn't feel hot."

"And did Dr. Mangan suggest that you take her temperature?"

"No."

"Did he suggest you do *anything* to relieve her distress?"

"He suggested a children's Tylenol capsule."

"And you gave her one?"

"Yes."

"And did Angela complain of any other symptoms? Stomach cramps, anything like that?"

"She didn't eat much dinner. But she didn't say she felt sick to her stomach. She just didn't feel like eating."

"But she did eat something?"

"A little, yes."

"That was an hour or so before she took the yellow capsule?"

"Yes."

"Did Dr. Mangan say an hour after eating was okay?"

"Yes, he did."

"And then what happened—after she went to bed?"

"We watched television for a while and went to bed ourselves."

"And as far as you know Angela was all right when you went to bed."

"As far as we knew."

"What time was that?"

"About twenty after nine."

"And Angela was sleeping?"

"Yes."

"Did you check on her?"

"My wife went in to look at her. I watched from the doorway. She sat on Angela's bed and felt her cheek. Then she pulled the covers up around her and kissed her on the forehead. Angela turned over, so we thought she was okay."

"And then?"

"We went to bed."

"And the next morning?"

"She was gone."

"How did you know she was gone?"

"She was very cold. Like ice. And she didn't respond when her mother screamed at her."

"No further questions, your honor."

"Mr. St. Clair?"

"Thank you, your honor. Mr. Calvecchi, I'm Edward St. Clair, attorney for the defense. Are you all right, sir?"

"Better, thank you."

"I'm glad to hear that. First let me say that we are all very sorry about Angela's death. It must have been very difficult for you and your wife."

"Yes, it was. It is."

"Of course. Now, Mr. Calvecchi, I need to ask you a few more questions. I'm sure you understand. I'll be as brief as possible."

"I'll try to answer them."

"Thank you. You stated earlier that Dr. Mangan explained to you that there could be serious risks involved in taking an experimental drug. *Any* experimental drug. Isn't that right?"

"Well, yes and no."

"Could you elaborate on that answer?"

"He told us there might be some side effects. But we got the impression that they wouldn't be very serious."

"But he did tell you that they *could* be serious, did he not?"

"Not really."

"Mr. Calvecchi, I remind you that you are under oath. Didn't you sign a waiver stating that you understood the risks involved and that there might be a fatal reaction to using this medication? And if there were such a reaction you would not hold the doctor or the clinic responsible?"

"Yes."

"Is this a copy of that waiver with your signature at the bottom?"

"Yes."

"If it please the court, defense would like to enter this into the record as Defense Exhibit A."

"So ordered."

"I'm going to read a portion of that waiver to you, sir, if I may. Uh . . . 'The patient or guardian understands that there may be significant risks involved with the taking of this medication, and that these risks may include possible serious and, in some cases even fatal, side effects.' Do you remember reading that warning?"

"Yes. We read it."

"So you *were* warned about the possible dangers involved in taking the drug and you signed the waiver anyway."

"Well, actually we didn't read the whole thing. It was very long and the print was very small. But Dr. Mangan had led us to believe that there wasn't much danger in Angela taking the drug."

"You signed the waiver without reading it?"

"No, we read some of it. It sounded like a lot of complicated legal stuff."

"Weren't you given enough time to read it?"

"Well, the nurse told us to take our time, but we knew the doctor was in a hurry. He's always in a hurry."

"So you were given plenty of time to read the waiver but you only read part of it."

"Yes."

"And did you understand the part you read?"

"Not all of it."

"Did you ask your lawyer to look it over?"

"We didn't have a lawyer then."

"So you signed it anyway."

"Yes, we signed it."

"Without any pressure or coercion on anyone's part."

"Well, no, not exactly."

"Mr. Calvecchi, did your daughter show any signs of a heart problem—difficulty in breathing, perspiring, that sort of thing—when she went to bed on the night of March the twenty-second?"

"Not as far as we could tell."

"So she seemed perfectly all right."

"No. She wasn't feeling well at all."

"When did she start feeling unwell?"

"She hadn't been feeling good all day."

"But she wasn't feeling much worse that night than, say, at noon?"

"I'm not sure. Angela didn't like to complain. But I think she felt a lot worse that night than she did that morning."

"Mr. Calvecchi, wouldn't you know if Angela were suffering from a heart irregularity after she took the medication that evening?"

"Objection. Mr. Calvecchi isn't a doctor and hasn't been trained—"

"That's true, counselor, but he was in a position to closely observe any symptoms she might have experienced. Overruled."

"Thank you, your honor. Mr. Calvecchi, did your daughter show any symptoms of great distress on the evening of May twenty-second of last year?"

"Not as far as I know. I mean, I wouldn't call it 'great distress,' exactly."

"Well, if Angela had shown signs of distress during the night, wouldn't you have known about it?"

"Of course I would have known about it."

"Sir, are you a sound sleeper?"

"I sleep all right."

"And your wife?"

"No, she usually hears any noises, anything like that."

"Sir, do you snore at all?"

"Objection, your honor."

"Overruled."

"Please answer the question, sir."

"Sometimes."

"Now if you were snoring, would your wife be able to hear Angela if she were having serious difficulty in her room, twenty or thirty feet away?"

"Objection, your honor. Defense is calling for speculation on the part of the witness."

"Sustained."

"No further questions, your honor."

"Mr. Allen, any re-direct?"

"Mr. Calvecchi, did Dr. Mangan tell you personally that there was a significant chance of death if—"

"Objection."

"Sustained."

"Did Dr. Mangan tell you that there was a significant risk of Angela's having a serious reaction to Mercipine?"

"He said the risk was very, very small. We figured he meant like getting hit by lightning, something like that."

"Thank you. No further questions."

"Mr. St. Clair?"

"No further questions, your honor."

"Court stands adjourned until two o'clock this afternoon."

*

"I'm glad that's over."
"You did fine, Tony. As well as anyone could have done."
"What happens next?"
"We go on to our expert witnesses."
"How long will that take?"
"Oh, maybe the rest of the week or a little longer. Now folks, you go out and have a nice lunch. We'll see you back here a little before two, okay?"
"All right. We'll be back by 1:45."
"See you later . . . . Some lunch, Ms. White?"
"No, thanks. Going to the library. Besides, I'm not hungry."
"You're not pregnant again, are you?"
"That's hilarious, counselor. You really should go on the road with that routine."
"I'm sorry. I was just trying to lighten things up a bit."
"Well, try something else."
"Do you need any help at the library?"
"That's much better."
"No—I'm serious. Can I help you find something?"
"Thanks, but you wouldn't know what to look for."
"What *are* you looking for?"
"Some little chink we might have overlooked in toxicity testing for new drugs. It's such a complicated mess."
"I can be a 'gopher.'"
"It's mostly computer searching."
"I know how to use a computer."
"Like I said. You wouldn't know what to look for."
"I can—"
"Go have some lunch, Marc. I'll see you at two."
"Can I bring you anything? Something to drink, maybe?"
"Marcus—go to lunch!"

*

("You're late.")
("I found something!")
("What?")
("Tell you later.")
"State your name, please."
"Felicity Brown."
"Do you swear . . . ?"
"I do."

"Miss Brown, good afternoon."

"Afternoon, Mr. Allen."

"Miss Brown, how long have you been a teacher at Governor's middle school?"

"For about ten years."

"And what do you teach?"

"Science and math."

"Do you find the job rewarding?"

"Very."

"In what way . . . ?"

"Your honor, in the interest of brevity, defense stipulates that teaching middle school can be very rewarding."

"Mr. Allen, what are you getting at here?"

"Your honor, Miss Brown's relationship with Angela will reveal what kind of person she was. This pertains to the value of the loss of Angela Calvecchi to her parents."

"Are you suggesting that not all thirteen-year-olds are of value to their parents?"

"In terms of emotional value, of course they are. But plaintiffs contend that Angela was a very gifted child, one whose future worth, in monetary terms, was at the highest level."

"Very well. Proceed."

"Thank you, your honor. Miss Brown, would you please tell the court why you find teaching middle school to be particularly rewarding?"

"I think it's because these are young minds that can soak up knowledge like a sponge when they are stimulated. They are young people right at the dividing line between childhood and adulthood. It's really very exciting and gratifying to be able to determine what interests and motivates an adolescent and to nourish and encourage those interests and watch him or her grow and blossom into an outstanding young man or woman."

"And how would you describe Angela Calvecchi as a student?"

"She was a perfect student, one of the best I ever had. Her mind was wide open and she learned very quickly. Not just one or two of her subjects, but all of them. And she was one of the most popular students in school. If I had a child, I'd want her to be exactly like Angela."

"Would you elaborate just a bit on her interests?"

"That's my point. She was interested in everything—in science, math, English, music—everything. She was a straight-A student. Despite her affliction, she played in the school orchestra and took part in other extracurricular activities. She was especially interested in science. So much so that she asked me for extra assignments so that she could learn more. It was as if she couldn't wait to grow up.

She was already talking about the colleges she might want to go to. She wanted to be a doctor, but she could have been anything, done anything."

"Do you think she would have become a doctor if she had had the chance?"

"Objection. Witness doesn't have a crystal ball."

"Sustained."

"Miss Brown, what made you think at the time that Angela would have become a physician?"

"It wasn't just because of her aptitude or her interest in the sciences. She sometimes acted as if she were *already* a doctor. When someone in her class got a cut or twisted an ankle, something like that, it was Angela who administered first aid. In fact, and I laugh every time I think of this, one time our principal had a splinter in his finger and the nurse was sick, so he came to Angela to get the splinter out. It was funny to see him sitting in one of those little chairs with Angela holding his hand, so serious but at the same time smiling and joking, trying to put him at ease. No, I have no doubt that she would've become a wonderful physician. In a way, she already was one . . . ."

"Do you think that might have been because of the diabetes?"

"You know, I never thought about that. Angela was one of those kids who are just what they are. But maybe that *was* what focused her mind on a career in medicine. I don't know. All I know is, she would've been a great doctor. I have no doubts about that whatsoever."

"Miss Brown, how smart was Angela, exactly? Were there IQ tests, anything like that?"

"Yes, we give those to all eighth-graders."

"And what did they show in Angela's case?"

"Angela's scores were in the 140's."

"Pretty smart girl."

"Very smart."

"And you testified that this level of thinking ability was reflected in her grades."

"It certainly was. She got A's in everything."

"Miss Brown, what percentage of your students have gone on to college?"

"Roughly forty per cent."

"And how would you compare Angela's interests and abilities and ambitions with that forty per cent who went on to college and later careers?"

"As I said earlier: Angela was one of the best students I ever had. Maybe the smartest one of all. There is no question she would have succeeded in college and later on in life."

"As a medical doctor."

"Yes."

"Miss Brown, did Angela know a lot of medical terminology?"

"Yes, she did. She even read some of the journals."

"Do you know which journals she read?"

"Oh, *The Journal of the American Medical Association*. Uh, *Diabetes Reports*. Things like that."

"Do you think she understood what she was reading in those professional publications?"

"Absolutely. For English assignments, she would almost always write about a case she had found in one of those journals."

"Anything else to suggest she would've become a doctor?"

"Yes. She had already picked out a medical school to apply to."

"At thirteen?"

"Yes."

"Which one was that, do you know?"

"Yes. The University of Minnesota."

"Why that school? That's pretty far away, isn't it?"

"Because her doctor came from there."

"Dr. Mangan."

"Yes, that's right."

"Thank you, Miss Brown. No further questions at this time."

"Mr. St. Clair?"

"Thank you, your honor. Good afternoon, Ms. Brown."

"Good afternoon to you, too."

"Ms. Brown, if I could have ten lives, one of them would be as a teacher. In fact, I almost became one once. And if I had met you way back when, I might have taken that road. You obviously enjoy your profession."

"Thank you, Mr. St. Clair."

"Now, Miss Brown, have you ever had any other students go on to become doctors?"

"Two or three."

"Ms. Brown, you testified that you've been teaching middle school for ten years, is that right?"

"That's right."

"Then the oldest of your graduates would be—what—twenty-three or—four?"

"I suppose so."

"Then they'd still be in medical school, wouldn't they?"

"Well, yes. But I meant that those graduates are *in* medical school. Obviously they're going to become doctors."

"Perhaps. And when these students were Angela Calvecchi's age, were they as focused on medicine as she seemed to be?"

"No, not at all. Not as much as she was, anyway."

"Well, what were they focused on?"

"Different things."

"At the time, would you have predicted they would go on to careers in medicine?"

"Probably not."

"In fact, isn't it virtually impossible to say where one of your middle school students is going to end up when they get to be adults?"

"For most students I suppose that's true. But in Angela's case—"

"Miss Brown, you testified earlier that Angela Calvecchi was interested in 'everything.' Do you recall that statement?"

"Yes."

"And wouldn't you agree that interests change as we grown older?"

"Yes, of course, but—"

"Then how can you be so certain that she wouldn't have become a musician? She played the violin, didn't she? Or, for that matter, a teacher? Or even a lawyer?"

"She didn't read journals about music or the law."

"Miss Brown, do you recall a student you taught several years ago named Patrick Chervil?"

"Yes."

"Was he a good student?"

"Yes, he was."

"What kind of grades?"

"All A's."

"Did he show any particular interests?"

"He was brilliant in math."

"And did he express any desire to go to college?"

"Yes, he did. He wanted to become an electrical engineer."

"Miss Brown, what happened to Patrick Chervil?"

"I think he's in prison at the moment."

("Oh, shit. She never mentioned this guy to us.")

"And before that?"

"He was arrested for selling drugs."

"What kind of drugs?"

"I don't know."

"Your honor, defense would like to enter into evidence the official police record for one Patrick Marion Chervil, dated January 25, 2004. This would be Defense Exhibit B."

"Your honor, may we see that?"

"Clerk will pass the records on to Mr. Allen . . . ."

" . . . Your honor, we fail to see the relevance of this document."

"It's relevant to your own suggestion that the girl would have become a physician, Mr. Allen. Clerk will enter it as Defense Exhibit B."

"Thank you, your honor. Now, Miss Brown, I'd like to read a paragraph from Mr. Chervil's police record. Um—'Mr. Chervil was apprehended in his apartment without a struggle. No weapons were found in the apartment. Four point six kilograms of marijuana, two kilos of cocaine, and 1/2 kilo of heroin were found under a bed and seized . . . .' Miss Brown, is that the promising student you knew in grades seven through nine, the one who wanted to be an electrical engineer?"

"Yes."

"Thank you. No further questions, your honor."

("Any quick thoughts, Candace?")

("Ask her what Patrick was like as a person.")

"Mr. Allen?"

"Miss Brown, were there any noticeable differences between Angela Calvecchi and this—uh—Patrick Chervil when they were in the eighth grade?"

"Yes. Pat had some problems with his parents and he had trouble fitting in with the rest of the class."

"In what way did he have trouble?"

"He was what you would call a 'loner.'"

"Well, did he have any friends?"

"Very few, if any."

"And was Angela Calvecchi a loner?"

"Just the opposite. She was very popular. Very sensitive to the problems and needs of others. Everyone loved her."

"Did everyone 'love' Patrick Chervil?"

"As I said, he was a loner. He never gave anyone a chance to get close to him. They were two entirely different kinds of kids. Pat got into trouble even before he got out of high school."

"And Angela—was she ever in any kind of trouble, as far as you know?"

"None whatsoever."

"So the two children were as different as apples and oranges, wouldn't you say?"

"Yes, I would."

"Thank you. No further questions."

"Mr. St. Clair?"

"Miss Brown, do all apples go to college and all oranges to prison?"

"I don't know what you mean."

"No further questions, your honor."

"Mr. Allen, is your next witness in the courtroom?"

"No, your honor. We scheduled him for tomorrow morning."

"Very well. Court stands adjourned until ten o'clock tomorrow morning."

*

"Okay—what did you find out?"

"I found something interesting. There are at least three cases where a company was forced to recall one of their drugs when somebody found they were toxic in animal species different from the ones they used in their safety tests! Even though they were approved by the FDA!"

"And how does that help us?"

"It gets our foot in the door! It opens up the possibility that if they *had* used other animals, the safety results might have been different!"

"Maybe and maybe not. I'd take you out to dinner and discuss this further with you, but I've some work to do on another case. Unless you—"

"Thanks. I've got a date."

"You're dating again?"

"I thought I should get out more."

"Sure. Good idea. But stay away from lawyers!"

"Too late for that!"

"You mean you're going out with another lawyer?"

"Not all lawyers are jerks, Marc."

*

"Marcus! What the hell you doing here so late?"

"Hello, Sammy. Oh, the goddamn Mercer case. Anyway, I could ask you the same thing."

"Just came in to pick up a few things. Back from a dinner date."

"Yeah? Who with?"

"Your partner in crime. Candace White. Didn't she tell you?"

"Candace? But—But—"

"How come you never asked her out? She's terrific."

"But—"

"See you later, alligator."

". . . ."

*

"Your honor, plaintiffs call Dr. Solomon Epstein . . . ."

"Do you swear . . ."

"I do."

"Doctor Epstein, you're the medical examiner for Hamilton County, is that correct?"

"Yes, I am. For the past twenty-six years."

"So you're responsible for determining the cause of any unusual or suspicious death occurring in this county, isn't tha—"

"Your honor, I object! There has been no evidence presented that Mercipine—"

"Sustained. Counselor, I remind you once again to refrain from unwarranted speculation."

"Very well, your honor. Dr. Epstein, would you briefly describe the nature of your responsibilities as County Coroner?"

"I'd be happy to. It's my job to determine the cause of death when this information is requested by the attending physician, in consultation with the family of the deceased, or in some cases upon request of the family themselves. And then, of course, there are times when an autopsy is required by law."

"In what sorts of cases would an autopsy be required?"

"Oh, homicides, suicides, cases when an unidentified body is found, things like that."

"What about the case of Angela Calvecchi?"

"Yes, in clinical drug trials the state requires an autopsy to determine the cause of death."

"Why is that, Doctor Epstein?"

"Well, it's part of the protocol. The public, as well as the pharmaceutical company involved, needs to know whether the medication is responsible for the death, or whether, in fact, the patient died of natural causes unrelated to the administration of the drug in question, or perhaps despite the treatment. Without this information the study would be useless."

"And is an autopsy the best way to determine the cause of death?"

"It's often the only way."

"And based on the results of the autopsy you performed, doctor, and all your years of experience, were you able to make a determination as to the cause of death in the case of Angela Calvecchi?"

"Yes, I was. Miss Calvecchi died of heart failure brought about by an arrythmia—an irregular heartbeat."

"Heart failure? At the age of thirteen?"

"That's right."

"Objection, your honor."

"What grounds?"

"An irregular heartbeat cannot be diagnosed on autopsy."

"Dr. Mangan, would you agree with that statement?"

"Yes, your honor. But when all other causes are ruled out, a heart arrythmia is virtually always the reason for the heart's suddenly failing to contract. This is a well-established medical fact."

"Objection overruled."

"Thank you, judge. Doctor, were you able to form an opinion on the cause of her heart irregularity?"

"Yes. Her heart was structurally normal, and there was no evidence of a prior history of irregular heartbeats or any other heart problems. That suggests an environmental factor. And the only drugs or other chemicals found in her system were the pharmaceutical compound known as Mercipine, plus a trace of acetaminophen."

"Which is the active ingredient in Tylenol, isn't that right?"

"Yes."

"And there didn't appear to be any other contributing factors?"

"No. My report indicated that the cause of death was Mercipine toxicity."

"Your honor, plaintiffs would like to submit the autopsy report for Angela Calvecchi, and signed by Dr. Epstein, as Plaintiffs' Exhibit One."

"So ordered."

"Thank you. Now, doctor, are you saying it would be unlikely that Angela's heart failure would have occurred without the intervention of the Mercipine in her system?"

"That's correct. Fatal heart arrhythmias, especially in children, are extremely rare."

"Even for children with Type I diabetes?"

"Yes. Children with diabetes usually exhibit normal heart function."

"Can you give us scientific odds on the likelihood that Angela's death was caused by the drug in question?"

"Given the circumstances of the case, I'd say there is a 99.5 per cent certainty."

"Objection! Again, this is pure speculation on the part of the—"

"Overruled. We're in the area of scientific probability here, counselor. I'll allow the answer."

"Thank you, your honor. Doctor, can you describe for the court the condition known as 'Type I diabetes'?"

"Type I diabetes usually begins in children and adolescents. It's basically an autoimmune disease in which certain cells in the pancreas, called beta cells, are destroyed by the body's own defense mechanism and stop producing insulin. Insulin is necessary for sugars to get inside of cells, so the sugar level in the bloodstream begins to increase and the cells are starved for sugars and can't function. So the patient becomes tired easily. Insulin injections relieve this problem, but not perfectly, and diabetes patients can have serious health problems later in life, and usually do. At present there is no cure for this disease."

"And is there a Type II diabetes?"

"Yes, but that condition usually occurs in older people, and is much less severe than the first type."

"So Angela Calvecchi was in the early stages of the childhood form of the disease, or Type I."

"Yes."

"Doctor, would this condition preclude young Angela, or anyone else, from going on to become a doctor?"

"No, not at all. With proper treatment, exercise, and diet, a diabetic can lead a reasonably normal life well into middle age and beyond."

"Dr. Epstein, in your opinion, did this condition play a role in Angela's death?"

"None whatsoever."

"And you testified earlier that Miss Calvecchi's heart was normal on autopsy."

"That's correct."

"Dr. Epstein, is it conceivable that the cause of death might have been due to an interaction between Mercipine and Tylenol?"

"No. Extremely unlikely."

"Why is that, sir?"

"Mercipine is a member of the biphenylmercaptan family. These compounds do not react with acetaminophen."

"Nor would Tylenol itself have caused the heart arrythmia that led to her death."

"Not at all."

"Based on all the evidence at your disposal, then, doctor, you were able to state conclusively that the drug found in Angela Calvecchi's system, the drug known as Mercipine, was the cause of her death?"

"Yes, and I so stated in my autopsy report."

"Thank you, doctor. No further questions."

"The court understands that Dr. Epstein will be unable to return this afternoon. Mr. St. Clair, do you anticipate a lengthy cross-examination of this witness?"

"No, your honor."

"Please proceed."

"Thank you, your honor. Good morning, Dr. Epstein. How are you today, sir?"

"I'm fine. How are you?"

"Very well, thank you. And might I say that I'm happy to be meeting you under these circumstances, rather than as part of your regular duties."

["Ha, ha, ha."]

"So am I, Mr. St. Clair."

"Thank you, sir. Now Dr. Epstein, you stated earlier that, in your opinion, Angela Calvecchi died as the result of taking an overdose of Mercipine?"

"Objection, your honor! Witness never mentioned an 'overdose' of the drug."

"Sustained."

"My mistake, your honor. Let me rephrase that. Were you able to determine the level of the drug in her blood stream at the time of your examination?"

"Yes. The concentration was eight point five micrograms per cc serum."

"Doctor Epstein, have you done any other autopsies involving the drug Mercipine?"

"No."

"Well, do you know of any other studies done on the concentration of Mercipine in patients who died while being administered this drug?"

"Yes, there are six other cases that I know about."

"And what were the results?"

"The concentration of the drug ranged from ten to twenty-seven micrograms per cc serum."

"And were these adults or children?"

"Both."

"How old were the children?"

"One was fifteen, the other seventeen."

"No one the age of Angela Calvecchi?"

"No. She was the youngest patient in the study."

"And could you tell us with "99.5 percent certainty" what serum concentration of Mercipine is sufficient to cause death in a thirteen-year old child?"

"No."

"Why not?"

"We don't know enough about the drug to pin it down to a figure like that."

"So Miss Calvecchi's Mercipine level might not have been sufficient to cause death in her case, isn't that right, doctor?"

"Well, technically that's true. Without additional evidence, that is. But it must have been a contributing factor."

"A contributing factor? Then there were other factors as well?"

"Not that we could find. Nor were any found in the other cases, of which five of the six also died of heart failure resulting from an irregular heartbeat."

"But the concentration of Mercipine in these cases was considerably higher than in the case of Miss Calvecchi, was it not?"

"Yes, but she was the youngest patient in the trial."

"Dr. Epstein, can you say with "99.5 percent certainty," or *any* degree of certainty, that eight point five micrograms per cc in the blood is sufficient to kill a thirteen-year-old girl?"

"As I said earlier, there aren't yet enough data to support that precise a figure. But it appeared to be sufficient to cause the death of Angela Calvecchi, in any case."

"Sir, have you ever personally encountered another case of death resulting from the administration of the drug Mercipine?"

"No, I haven't."

"Thank you. Oh, one more thing. Did this medication cause heart failure or arrythmias in the laboratory animals in which it was tested?"

"Not to my knowledge."

"Well, did it kill laboratory animals in some other way?"

"Not even at massive doses."

"And in phases one and two, when it was tested in healthy human volunteers?"

"There were no heart problems reported, as far as I know."

"In other words this is a very safe drug, wouldn't you say, doctor?"

"It would appear to be, yes. But—"

"Thank you, sir. No further questions."

"Any re-direct, Mr. Allen?"

"Yes, your honor. Dr. Epstein, you testified that the experimental drug Mercipine had not been found to cause heart failure in any of the human volunteers it was tested on for safety reasons, is that right?"

"Not as far as I know."

"Then how could it cause several deaths among the diabetic patients it was given to?"

"That's a good question. It's possible that it causes heart arrythmias only in diabetic patients, but this possibility hasn't been studied. Except, of course, for the clinical trial itself."

"Well, could the cessation of insulin injections have caused the irregular heartbeats?"

"No. There's no evidence that that would be the case. It seems more likely that there is something about the diabetic condition that predisposes people to a negative reaction with this drug."

"But it didn't cause such a problem for any of the diabetic animals tested in the laboratory, isn't that right?"

"Yes, that's true."

"Very well. Now, counsel for the defense argues that this would rule out the possibility that Mercipine could have caused the death of Angela Calvecchi and the other diabetics who died while taking this drug. Do you agree with that conclusion?"

"Not necessarily."

"Why not?"

"Because sometimes a drug that's found to be safe in animal tests can, in fact, be quite dangerous to humans."

"In fact, that's one of the reasons for conducting phases one and two of a clinical trial, is it not—to assess the safety of a particular pharmaceutical compound in human beings?"

"Yes, of course."

"And have there ever been any other drugs, besides Mercipine, that have been found to be safe in animals, but unsafe for humans?"

"Objection, your honor! Mercipine has not been proven unsafe for humans!"

"Sustained. Mr. Allen, you're walking a very thin line here."

"I'll try to stay on it, your honor. I'll rephrase the question, doctor: Have there ever been drugs found to be safe in animal tests that have turned out to be toxic to human beings?"

"Many."

"Thank you, doctor. Now I ask you once again: In your opinion, did Mercipine cause the death of young Angela Calvecchi, animal experiments and tests on healthy humans notwithstanding?"

"In my opinion, yes, it did."

"Thank you. No further questions."

"Mr. St. Clair? Any re-cross?"

"Thank you, your honor. I'll ask the stenographer to read back a remark Dr. Epstein made a few minutes ago in response to the question of what serum concentration of Mercipine is sufficient to cause death in a thirteen-year-old child . . . ."

"Question: 'And could you tell us with "99.5 per cent certainty" what serum concentration of Mercipine is sufficient to cause death in a thirteen-year-old child?' Answer: 'No.'"

"Thank you. Did you say that, sir?"

"Yes, I did."

"Do you want to change that testimony now?"

"No."

"That's all I have for this witness. Thank you, your honor."

"Your honor—"

"I think we've gone around this circle enough, Mr. Allen. Owing to the lateness of the hour, court stands adjourned until 2:30 this afternoon."

*

"Nice job, Marcus, Jr. Your old daddy would have been proud."

"Thanks, Eddie. He still is."

"Of course. Of course . . . Courthouse pissoires have their own characteristic aroma—have you noticed that, son?"

"Not particularly."

"I'd know which courthouse this was if I came in here blindfolded. So would Marcus, Sr. It takes a good long time for that kind of information to seep into your itty-bitty nervous system. Just like it takes time to get to know what kinds of little things irritate a particular judge."

"Are you trying to give me some free advice, Mr. St. Clair, sir?"

"Not at all, Junior. I never try to help out the opposing attorney while a case is in progress."

"Thank you so much."

"Just ask your pa what gets to Judge Bates. He'll be able to clue you in some."

"I'll do that."

"In the meantime, have you tried to get your clients to lighten up on their unreasonable demands?"

"They aren't interested in that, counselor. And neither am I. Unless, of course, your client is willing to consider taking Mercipine out of its clinical trial . . . ."

"Hold on, junior, don't have a conniption. You know that's out of the question. I just thought I'd try to save us all a little time, and a few of them filthy greenbacks to boot . . . . God damn—this place could sure as hell use a little air conditioning, too."

"Tell it to the judge."

"Haw, haw, haw. You've got your old man's sense of humor, that's for shit-sure."

"See you later, Eddie. May the better man win."

"Why, son, you don't have a dog's chance."

*

"Dad? How are you? . . . Really? You must be doing all right, then! . . . Oh, that's great! So they're going to continue with the same combination for a while? . . . Oh. But even if it *is* making you sick, it's worth it, don't you think? . . . Come on, Dad . . . . We'll talk more about it later. I'll come over and see you as soon as I get a break from the trial . . . . From right outside the courtroom . . . . Maybe this weekend . . . . All right. See you soon. Oh, by the way, I just saw Eddie St. Clair in the john . . . . Very funny, Dad. Anyway, he told me that there were some things that irritate Judge Bates. Any idea what he was talking about? . . . I haven't tried to put anything over on her, Dad . . . . Yeah, she's come down on me a couple of times for that, but . . . . You mean he was just trying to get into my head? I thought it might be something like that. Thanks, Dad. Gotta run. I'll see you sometime this weekend . . . ."

"Oh, hello, McBain."

"Marc, your fl—"

"Later, McBain. Got to get back in there . . . ."

*

("Why is everyone laughing?")

("I don't know.")

"Mr. Allen, is your next witness present?"

"Yes, your honor."

"Please call him to the stand. And Mr. Allen?"

"Yes, judge?"

"I would consider it a personal favor if you would zip up your pants."

["Ha, ha, ha, ha, ha, ha, ha."]

"Uh"—ziiiiip—"my apologies, your honor. Plaintiffs call Dr. Lawrence McCall."

["Ha, ha, ha."]

" . . . It's *Doctor* McCall, isn't it, sir?"

"Yes, but don't come to me with your problems. I'm not a medical doctor."

"You're a Ph.D."

"That's right."

"Dr. McCall, what's your area of expertise?"

"I'm a professor of biochemistry at Morgan State University."

"And how long have you been a professor of biochemistry?"

"For sixteen years."

"And before that?"

"I was an associate professor."

"At Morgan State?"

"Yes."

"Doctor, would you please tell the jury what sort of duties being a professor of biochemistry entails?"

"Sure. Teaching various courses and laboratories, research, committee work, supervision of several undergraduate and graduate students. And I also happen to be the editor of *The Journal of American Medical Science*."

"Is that a professional journal?"

"It's for the scholar and the layman alike. Something like *Scientific American*, except it's restricted to the medical and related biological sciences."

"Now, Dr. McCall, what is your specific area of research and expertise?"

"The comparative biology and biochemistry of mammals."

"And human beings are classified as mammals, isn't that right?"

"Yes, it is. Any vertebrate species that suckles its young is classified as a mammal. That includes us."

"Dr. McCall, could you tell us what other kinds of animals fit into the category of 'mammal'?"

"Besides humans, almost all the animals we're familiar with—dogs, cats, mice, rats, deer, elephants, and so on. As I said, it's all those animals that suckle their young. Almost all bear their young live, as well."

"As opposed to laying eggs—is that what you mean?"

"That's pretty much it."

"So your specialty is comparing the basic chemical processes occurring in human beings with those of other mammals, right?"

"Exactly."

"Does that include the response of various mammals to drugs and other chemicals?"

"Yes, it does."

"Doctor, have you published any books in your area of expertise?"

"One or two."

"What was the most recent?"

"*Animal Research: Fact or Fiction?* was published in 2003."

"Your honor, plaintiffs request that Dr. McCall's book be entered into evidence as Plaintiff's Exhibit Two."

"Any objection, Mr. St. Clair?"

"We do object, your honor."

"On what grounds?"

"Counsel for plaintiffs is embarking on a matter that is irrelevant to these proceedings. No one questions that human beings are different from mice. This case is about meeting certain safety standards as required by law."

"Your honor, we agree with defense counsel that this case is about drug safety. We're attempting to show that Mercer Pharmaceuticals did not properly assess the safety of the drug Mercipine before it was manufactured for human use. In order to establish this fact, we need to know the standards on which the company based their conclusions about the safety of this drug."

"Mr. St. Clair, you raised the issue of animal testing in your cross of Dr. Epstein. I'll allow this line of questioning for the time being, Mr. Allen . . . ."

"Thank you, your honor. Dr. McCall, what is the premise of your book?"

"It concerns the use of non-human animals as predictors for the safety and efficacy of drugs in humans."

"In terms of negative reactions to various drug therapies, that sort of thing?"

"Exactly."

"But doctor, don't all animals behave the same way in response to treatment with various drugs or other chemicals?"

"No. It's much more subtle than that, despite the gross similarities in anatomy and physiology between different animals. Even compounds as highly toxic to humans as curare and strychnine don't affect some other animals at all."

"And this applies to medicinal pharmaceuticals as well?"

"Well, curare and strychnine are used in certain instances as medicinal compounds. Under very controlled conditions, of course. But the answer to your general question is: yes, it does."

"And so there are drugs that can be safe and effective in animals that are not only useless, but actually unsafe for the treatment of the same or similar conditions in humans."

"That's quite true."

"And the reverse is also true: a drug that might prove to be a miracle cure for human beings can be ineffective or even harmful in certain other animals."

"Also true."

"Can you give us an example of the latter case?"

"Well, probably the best example is aspirin, which is one of the safest drugs around and has been used as an analgesic for decades. But it causes serious birth defects in mice and rats."

"In other words, doctor, if aspirin had been tested on these animals a hundred years ago, we wouldn't have it as a painkiller and a fever-reducer and a preventer of heart attacks today."

"Objection—pure speculation on the part of counsel."

"Sustained. You're straying off that narrow path, Mr. Allen . . . ."

"Very well, your honor, I'll rephrase the question. Would it be safe to say, Doctor McCall, that animal testing is, at best, only an approximation of how safe a drug will be in humans?"

"Objection—irrelevant and immaterial."

"Mr. St. Clair, I've already ruled on that. Proceed, Mr. Allen."

"Thank you, your honor. Please answer the question, doctor."

"Barely that. It's hardly even an approximation. It works sometimes, not others. There's simply no way to predict."

"So a drug that doesn't cause heart failure in rats or rabbits, or even chimpanzees, might still do so in human beings."

"Yes, and sometimes does."

"And this applies to other side effects as well, does it not?"

"To any you could think of, probably."

"Now, doctor, could you give us the names of any commonly-used medications that were found to be safe in animal tests but not in human trials?"

"Sure. Several. Thalidomide is probably the best known. It was tested in several animals and found to be safe for human use. But only rabbits and certain primates show the kind of catastrophic birth defects humans do. Other disasters would include diethylstilbesterol, accolate, chloramphenicol, isoproterenol, Flovent, uh—methysergide, Suprofen, zomepirec, Propulsid, Fen-phen, the antiviral agent fialuridine—well, the list goes on and on."

"How many drugs would you say are on that list all together?"

"Oh, dozens. Perhaps hundreds. More every year."

"So that if a pharmaceutical company bases its safety considerations on animal testing, there can be a false sense of security with respect to the drug in question."

"In the absence of other criteria, yes. In fact, a drug found to be harmless in one animal species may prove to be toxic or even fatal in any number of other species."

"In fact, there is simply no way to ascertain which animals would be a good predictor of human reaction to a particular drug or chemical compound, isn't that true, sir?"

"For the most part, with a new and untried drug, there's no way in hell to predict what will happen in humans."

"In other words, doctor, the use of animals to test new drugs before they go into human clinical trials is essentially useless, and potentially very dangerous, isn't that true?"

"In my opinion, yes."

"Your honor!"

"Let's not get carried away, Mr. Allen, shall we?"

"Dr. McCall, if the use of animals is not a good measure of drug safety, why does the FDA require these tests?"

"Well, for a lot of reasons. The first is tradition. It's been the method of choice for so long that it's become ingrained into our way of thinking. And then there's politics. Animal testing is a multi-billion dollar industry—"

"Objection!"

"Sustained. Take a different tack, Mr. Allen."

"Yes, your honor. Doctor, is there any other reason for the FDA's insistence on animal safety tests before a drug can move on to human trials?"

"Well, it's a vicious circle, really. The FDA requires the tests, so the drug companies do them in order to win approval for the clinical trials. And since the drug companies are set up to do animal testing, the FDA continues to require it. And around it goes. And there's one final reason why the drug companies do animal testing...."

"What reason is that, sir?"

"Well, there's the matter of lawsuits such as this one. Companies conduct endless animal tests basically to cover their asses in case somebody takes them to—"

"Your honor!"

"Sustained! Counsel will advise the witness to respect the decorum of this court!"

"Very well, your honor."

"Mr. Allen how much longer will you be leading this witness?"

"Only one or two more questions, if I may."

"Proceed."

"Dr. McCall, are you familiar with the chemical and biological nature of the drug Mercipine?"

"Yes, I am."

"In your opinion, doctor, is Mercipine a safe drug?"

"Based on animal tests, there's no way to know that. But if people are dying after taking this or any drug, it would seem clear that it is not."

"Even though it was found to be safe in certain animals."

"Even though it was found to be safe in *those* animals, yes."

[Kuff. Ha-kuff, kuff, kuff.]

"Could you elaborate on that answer?"

"Certainly. As I've tried to suggest, it's entirely hit and miss. The chances are good that a drug found to be safe in certain animals will be toxic in other species, including humans. I know of no drug that isn't toxic in *some* species or other. If all drugs were tested for safety on susceptible animals, we wouldn't have a single drug on the market today. On the other hand, we're throwing away dozens of possible miracle cures every day."

"Because they were found to toxic in mice or whatever, even though they might be safe in humans."

"Exactly."

"Thank you, sir. Your honor, plaintiffs have no further questions at this time."

"I'll see both attorneys in chambers. Court stands in recess for twenty minutes."

"All rise . . . ."

*

"Mr. Allen, what exactly are you trying to pull here? Did you coach your witness to make those inflammatory remarks?"

"Your honor, this is a product liability case. We're simply trying to show that defendant did not put a safe product on the market."

"Horseshit, judge. Pardon my French."

"Based on animal tests, Marcus, Jr.?"

"No, your honor. Based on *faulty* animal tests."

"But it's your contention that *all* animal tests are faulty, isn't that so?"

"Your honor, Marcus, Jr. is obviously making a desperate play to win the sympathy of the jury, not only for his clients, but for all those poor little ratties and micies that every company uses to determine the toxicity of a new pharmaceutical compound."

"Thank you, Mr. St. Clair. For your information, I wasn't born yesterday."

"I certainly meant no offense, Norma."

"It looks to me as if this isn't going to be as simple a case as I had thought. It's one of those things with 'facets.' Mr. Allen, how long do you estimate you'll need to finish presenting your case?"

"Two or three days, maybe."

"Uh-huh. And you, Mr. St. Clair?"

"Four or five days, max."

"That 'max' always has a peculiar way of turning into 'min,' doesn't it, Eddie?"

"Not always, Judge."

"Gentlemen, we can go on until the snow falls if it will get a reasonable judgment for both sides. Or we can negotiate a settlement in the next five minutes and get the damn thing over with. What say you?"

"Your honor, we've offered plaintiff a million dollars to take care of their emotional loss. As you know, this is a more than reasonable offer in our opinion. However, in order to save time and expense for both sides, as well as that of the court, we're prepared to increase that offer to a million and a half, with a no-fault provision, of course."

"Mr. Allen?"

"Your honor, that doesn't begin to cover the emotional loss incurred by our clients, not to mention the loss of their daughter's future income. Moreover, plaintiffs are seeking not only compensatory damages for themselves, but also punitive damages so that the same fate won't befall the next Angela Calvecchi who is railroaded into taking an unsafe drug."

"You see what we're up against, Judge?"

"What do you think would be a fair settlement for all concerned, counselor?"

"No less than four point five million, your honor, plus the withdrawal of Mercipine from further clinical tests."

"Your honor, that's an outrageous proposition, and Junior knows it."

"Mr. Allen, exactly what ax are you grinding here?"

"Merely protecting the interest of my clients, your honor, like my daddy taught me."

"Mr. St. Clair, I don't suppose you'd be interested in a compromise? Say, three million and a no-fault clause and non-disclosure?"

"Your honor, if we were up against a wall here, we might consider that. But plaintiffs can't possibly win this case. In the interest of expediency, and that alone, we're prepared to go to a million and a half. That's a very generous offer, in my opinion. With the no-fault and non-disclosure clauses, of course. And that's our final offer, no further negotiation possible, ever."

"'Ever' is a long time, Eddie. Mr. Allen?"

"I'll speak to my clients, your honor. But I don't think they're going to find his offer acceptable. Unless, of course, Mercipine comes right off the market."

"No way, judge."

"Give it your best shot, will you, Marcus, Jr.?"

"I'll twist their arms, your honor. But they have very tough arms."

"All right. Failing an agreement, we'll take this up again in—tch, tch, tch—eight minutes."

"Thank you, your honor."

*

"Tony, Elmira, we've got them up to a million and a half, plus absolution of guilt."

"What does that mean—'absolution of guilt'?"

"It means they don't admit they did anything wrong. That they did everything possible to assure the safety of Mercipine, and Angela's death was basically an accident."

"So they go on as before."

"Not necessarily. They may have learned something from this case. A million and a half dollars isn't exactly peanuts, even to a giant corporation like Mercer and company."

"We'll take the money, but only if they admit the drug isn't safe and they take it off the market. We owe that much to Angela."

"I don't think they'll agree to do that, Elmira."

"How about if we don't take *any* money, but they take the drug off the market?"

"I can try, but I seriously doubt they'd go for that, either. It's the admission of guilt, not the money, that bothers them the most."

"Well, that's one thing we and Mercer can agree on."

"So you want to contin—"

"Let's go back in."

*

"Court apologizes for the delay. Mr. St. Clair?"

"Thank you, your honor. Dr. McCall, we won't waste much of the court's time here. Just a few more questions."

"No problem."

"Good. Now, you stated earlier that you are a professor of biochemistry at—what was it?—Morgan State University?"

"That's correct."

"Dr. McCall, where is Morgan State University?"

"Montana."

"Beautiful state, Montana. Been there many times. Great fishing."

"Yes, it is."

"Sir, does Morgan State University have a graduate program in biochemistry?"

"Yes, we do."

"And how many Ph.D.'s do you graduate annually? Just a rough average will be fine."

"Well—uh—we only have the master's program at present."

"At present? Was there a Ph.D. program in the past?"

"No."

"Are there any plans to develop one in the future?"

"We've talked about it."

"Dr. McCall, do you do any research at Morgan State?"

"Yes, of course."

"At the undergraduate and master's level."

"That's right."

"Any publications in respected academic journals? In the past ten years, say?"

"One or two."

"What journals were those?"

"*The State Newsletter. The Zoo Animal Quarterly.*"

"Any publications in any of the leading biochemistry periodicals? *The Journal of Biological Chemistry? Biochimica Biophysica Acta? Nature? Science?* Anything like that?"

"Objection, your honor. Counsel is badgering this witness."

"He's your witness, Mr. Allen. Defense has a right to question his credentials."

"Thank you, your honor. Shall I repeat the question, sir?"

"That won't be necessary. I've never published in any of those journals."

"Dr. McCall, you actually do very little research, isn't that true?"

"Mr.—St. whatever your name is—have you ever taught at the undergraduate level?"

"No, sir, I haven't. But I suspect your teaching load is pretty heavy, isn't it?"

"Yes, sir, it is."

"That probably leaves you very little time to become an expert in matters involving this court, doesn't it?"

"Your honor!"

"Cool it, Mr. St. Clair. And get to the point."

"Now this book you've written—*Animal Research: Fact or Fiction?*—who published that book?"

"I did."

("Jesus Christ—why didn't you tell me that?")

("I didn't know!")

"Did you try to get it accepted by a reputable publishing house?"

("How did *Eddie* know?")

("I don't know, partner. *I* didn't tell him.")

"Academica *is* a reputable publisher!"

("*Somebody* must have!")

"But yours was a subsidy publication, was it not?"

"Yes."

"So even this little-known firm wouldn't publish your book unless you paid them to do it?"

"That's right. American publishing companies—"

"Now, Dr. McCall, you—"

"Your honor, he's not allowing the witness to answer the question!"

"Let him finish, Mr. St. Clair."

"Sorry, your honor. Go right ahead, sir."

"American companies don't like to publish books containing new or radical ideas. They don't sell all that well."

"Well, how many copies did your radical book sell?"

"Objection."

"Sustained."

"How many copies did your self-published book sell, Dr. McCall?"

"A few thousand."

"Five thousand? Ten?"

"Two thousand six hundred."

"Looks like the publishers were right, doesn't it, sir? All right, let's get to the crux of your testimony. Do you have any knowledge of FDA rules and regulations?"

"Yes, I do."

"And in your *expert* opinion, did Mercer Pharmaceuticals violate any of those rules and regulations?"

"In the general sense, yes. They were required to produce a safe drug for use in a human clinical trial. They did not."

"You're saying the regulations are imperfect."

"They're not only imperfect, they're archaic."

"Dr. McCall, the Food and Drug Administration isn't on trial here. Whether the FDA regulations are perfect or imperfect is not the issue. What is at issue is whether Mercer violated any of those regulations. I ask you again: Did Mercer violate any specific FDA rule or regulation in the testing of its new and promising medicinal compound Mercipine?"

"No *specific* regulation, no. But—"

"Thank you, sir. No further questions at this time. Oh. Just one more thing: Do you happen to belong to any animal rights groups?"

"Objection!"

"What grounds?"

"Whether Dr. McCall belongs to any such groups has no relevance to his testimony before this court."

"I tend to agree with that. Sustained."

"No further questions."

"Any re-direct, Mr. Allen?"

"Not at this time, your honor."

"Well, do you plan to bring the witness back again tomorrow?"

"No, your honor."

"Very well. Court is adjourned until ten o'clock tomorrow morning."

*

"Well, we blew that one."

"Maybe. But I saw Mrs W's ears come up when he said the drug companies only test on animals to cover their asses in case of lawsuits like this one."

"Anyone else's ears come up?"

"Not that I noticed."

"Goddamn it, Candace, didn't you bother to check out the guy's publisher?"

"No—did you? I gave you the book, remember? Didn't you read it?"

"Just the table of contents. Where did you find the reference to it?"

"In one of Dr. Small's reports."

"Didn't you realize he had published the book himself?"

"No. The cover said it was published by the Academica Publishing Company. I didn't know he paid them to do it."

"Bill and Lew are going to have our hides for this."

"Maybe we should recheck the credentials for the rest of our witnesses."

"Let's discuss it over dinner."

"Sorry. Got a date."

"With Sammy?"

"That's none of your business, is it?"
"What's he got that I haven't got?"
"I like him, for one thing. Separation from the case, for another."
"You mean that after all this is over—"
"Did I say that?"
"Not really."

*

"Candace—what are you doing here so late? I thought you had a—"
"Marc! I think I found a smoking gun!"
"What 'smoking gun'?"
"Mercer used the wrong animals to test the thing for toxicity!"
"How do you know that?"
"I found a paper by someone named Dalrymple. He says that rats and rabbits don't show any ill effects with biphenylmercaptans, but cats and guinea pigs do! So do certain birds and reptiles."
"Cats? He used cats??"
"Yes."
"What are you telling me?"
"Don't you see? This invalidates their safety reports. They should have been using cats or guinea pigs to test the drug, not rats and rabbits!"
"Didn't McCall mention this in his report?"
"No."
"Why not?"
"Maybe he didn't know about it."
"What about your ex-FDA guy, Small?"
"Him either, but I'm sure as hell going to ask him about it!"
"Maybe I could convince the judge to let us subpoena this guy Dalrymple and bring him in on Monday, if we can get him that soon."
"She would never agree to that, Marcus. Not at this late date."
"Let's bring it up at the 8:30 meeting tomorrow. See if anyone has any ideas about that—excuse me . . . . Oh, hi, Mom . . . . Well, I'm working, of course. Why else would I be in my office at— . . . . Mom, I'm there sometimes . . . . Well, I sleep there for one thing. Most of the time, anyway . . . . No, Mom, I'm not sleeping around . . . . This weekend? God, Mom. I don't know . . . . All right, but not for dinner. I've got to go see Dad sometime this weekend, too. Hey—why don't you have *him* over for dinner on Sunday? . . . Yes, I think he can drive . . . . Yes, he can eat some things . . . . I don't know, mashed potatoes or something . . . . So will you call him? . . . Pretty soon. I was just leaving, in fact . . . . I will . . . . 'Bye, Mom . . . Yes, maybe I will bring someone. See you on Sunday."

"Candace . . . ?"

*

"Hi, kitty. What a *good* kitty. Want your supper, Fuzzer? Supper? Oh, you *did* want your supper! All right . . . ."

" . . . Get down now, old girl. Daddy has work to do . . . . Oh, all right. Five minutes. Okay? Five minutes is all you get tonight. Daddy has important work to do."

"Rrrrr."

"Oh, you wanted to know what work? Well, a little girl died after she took a new drug produced by—"

"Rrrrrrr."

"Yeah, I know, you've heard it before. But did you know people test drugs and other chemicals on *cats*? Ha! I thought that might get your attention!"

"Rrrrrrrr."

"Then there's this *other* girl, the one I work with. Oh, you've heard that before, too, eh? All right. All right, Fuzzer. Just one question: Do you think Daddy's a jerk?"

"Rrrrrrrrrr."

"You *don't*? Well, thank you, my old lady friend. But my partner does—would you believe that? Listen: Would it be all right if Daddy shuts his eyes for a just a few minutes, Fuzzer? Would that be all right with you? Daddy's very tired . . . ."

"Rrrrrrr. Rrrrrrrrrr. Rrrrrrrrrrrrrr . . . ."

*

"Where's the coffee?"

"It's coming! It's coming!"

"You'd make a good judge, Bill."

"Not in a million years. Wouldn't be able to fake staying awake that long."

"Can't that be learned?"

"They all learned it, Bill. You could, too."

"Could we get started, folks? Candace and I have to be in court in an hour."

"Absolutely right, Marc." [Bang, bang, bang.] "The meeting, or whatever it is, will come to order. Is there something in particular you wanted to go over, Junior?"

"Yes, there is. Candace found some information that we didn't have before, something that might make a difference in the Mercer case. Without rehashing the whole damn thing again, our question is: Can we subpoena the guy who produced this information, even though we're wrapping up our case today?"

"Sure, if you have good cause."

"Not sure we do. It's old information we probably should have obtained earlier, before we filed."

"Why didn't you have it then?"

"It's a very complex case, Sammy. Even the rabbit warren has rabbit warrens."

"It's Judge Bates, isn't it? I tried a case in her court last year. She's a stickler for rules. If you send her a petition she'll deny it. Guaranteed."

"On the other hand, they can't lose much by trying it."

"Unless she considers it a delaying tactic. She hates delays."

"Whether she allows your petition or not is irrelevant."

"Also incompetent and immaterial."

"You younger guys never saw the old *Perry Mason* shows, did you? That poor damn Hamilton Burger . . . ."

"So why is it irrelevant?"

"Because all you have to do is get your last couple of witnesses to bring it up. If they testify about the information, you can introduce it as evidence. Not as good as the real thing, but close enough."

"What's the new evidence?"

"Somebody found that biphenylmercaptans like Mercipine are toxic to guinea pigs and cats and a bunch of other things. Mercer and company used the wrong animals for their safety tests!"

"But the FDA approved their application, didn't it?"

"Yes, but Mercer should have known they were using the wrong animal species because the info was already out there. So they submitted false and misleading evidence to the FDA. There are at least three precedents for a drug recall based on findings like this."

"Too bad you didn't find this stuff earlier."

"Maybe the Mercer people honestly didn't know about the cats and guinea pigs."

"Point is, they *should have*."

"That's for the judge and jury to decide."

"I'm not clear on something. This whole animal thing seems pretty iffy to me. It looks like a company would have to test a drug on every animal there is in order to be sure it wouldn't be harmful to humans."

"That's what we're beginning to believe, too, Lew. But the FDA doesn't take that into account. So we're stuck with trying to prove a company like Mercer knowingly or unknowingly picked the wrong ones for their safety studies. Either way, that information was available, so their application was false and misleading."

"Maybe you should've sued the FDA for basing their approval on outdated protocols."

"Too late for that now. But a class-action suit might nudge them into the twenty-first century . . . ."

"I was joking, Marcus."

*

"Will you state your name for the record, please?"

"Dr. Megan Leonard."

"Is your doctorate an M.D. or a Ph.D.?"

"Both."

"Double Doctor Leonard."

"That's right. And a couple of Master's degrees thrown in there somewhere."

"And where did you get all those degrees, doctor?"

"Harvard and Yale."

"The best of both worlds, eh?"

"I suppose you could say that."

"Dr. Leonard, are you familiar with the way drug companies determine the safety of their products?"

"I ought to be. I run one of them."

"What company is that, doctor?"

"Wilson and Leonard Biotechnics."

"In case anyone on the jury hasn't heard of this company, could you please describe it for us?"

"Yes, certainly. We're still a fairly small outfit, but we're growing. In fact, *The Wall Street Journal* says we're the fastest-growing pharmaceutical/biotech company in the country right now. Sales last year approached a hundred million dollars."

"And you are the head of that company?"

"Chief Executive Officer."

"Thank you. Now can you tell us: does Wilson and Leonard specialize in any particular area of biotechnology?"

"Yes. We specialize in 'designer' drugs. In other words, we produce and test pharmaceutical compounds based on genetic requirements."

"Could you simplify that for us?"

"We look at a disease or affliction in terms of its molecular biology. For example, we're working on—well, that's classified. Suffice it to say that if a medical problem is caused by a defective gene, or perhaps an overactive gene, we look for a drug that will have some effect on the activity of that gene, whether positive or negative. That's about as simple as I can make it."

"Sounds as though you're right on the cutting edge of pharmaceutical science."

"We like to think so. And so does *The Wall Street Journal*."

"Now tell us, doctor, do you ever test your products on animals?"

"Yes, of course."

"And why is that?"

"Because the FDA requires us to."

"That's the only reason?"

"Pretty much."

"Objection, your honor."

"On what grounds?"

"Your honor, once again counsel for plaintiffs is trying to raise a non-issue. The motives of the FDA are not at question here."

"Mr. Allen, is this taking us anywhere?"

"It certainly is, your honor."

"I'll allow plaintiffs to proceed for the moment. But get right to the point, counselor."

"Thank you, judge. Now, doctor, aren't animal tests the principal basis for the assessment of drug safety?"

"Not in the slightest. If anything, they're counterproductive. And not just in the sense that a drug found to be safe in animal tests can be toxic in humans. We look at the other side of the question: Are any of the drugs that have been discarded because they were found to be toxic in rats or hamsters or guinea pigs or what-have-you—might they in fact be absolutely safe in humans and effective in the treatment of certain diseases as well?"

"And have you found any such drugs?"

"Several."

"I imagine a lot of people are grateful for this approach."

"I think you could safely say that, yes."

"Now, doctor, let's look again at the first side of the question: whether it's possible for an unsafe drug to be approved by the FDA based on animal testing."

"Objection! Irrelevant and immaterial!"

"It seems relevant and material to me, Mr. St. Clair. Please proceed, Mr. Allen."

"Thank you, your honor. Doctor Leonard, I was about to ask you whether it's possible for an unsafe drug to be approved by the FDA based on the results of safety tests carried out on animals."

"Yes, of course. And it happens."

"But how could this be true? The FDA is charged with seeing that it doesn't, isn't it?"

"Yes, but in order to do that, they'd have to require that a drug be tested on every known animal species. And even then they couldn't be sure."

"Can you explain that, doctor?"

"Sure. The simple fact is, you can never know that the animals you use are going to predict the safety of any product made for human consumption."

"So you're saying that if Mercer had used enough different animals for the safety tests, they might have found one where Mercipine caused some heart problems."

"That's not only true, but highly likely."

"And if *that's* true, why doesn't the FDA require pharmaceutical corporations to test on a wider variety of animals?"

"Objection! The FDA is not on trial here!"

"Sustained."

"Very well, your honor. Dr. Leonard, does your company conduct clinical trials of the new drugs you produce?"

"Of course."

"Because it's required by the FDA?"

"It's required, but we would do that anyway because we need to know how effective the drug is before it goes into full production. We need to know also the proper dosage and regimen for the particular medication in question."

"But you first determine the safety of the drug before it goes into human clinical trials."

"That's right."

"Well if animal tests are useless in this regard—"

"Objec—"

"If animal tests are unreliable in this regard, how do you determine whether a pharmaceutical is safe to use in humans?"

"Several ways. We test on a variety of human tissues, we do computer mockups, we use the Ames and other tests for mutagenicity, and we use human organ studies as well, in most cases. In short, we use all the state-of-the-art technology available to us."

"In other words, to determine whether a drug is safe for use in humans, you basically try to find out whether it's harmful to live human tissues, rather than animals, is that right, doctor?"

"That and the computer simulations."

"How does that work?"

"It's a way to form a three-dimensional image of the drug and it's mode of interaction with DNA, RNA, enzymes, intact cells, and so on."

"But you say you also use animals in accordance with the FDA regulations."

"That's right. Tests using a rodent and a non-rodent species are required for certification."

"What happens if results of the animal tests are contradictory to those using other methods?"

"We try other animals until we find two, one rodent, one non-rodent, that agree with what we know to be the better assessment of a product's safety and effectiveness."

"And has this ever happened?"

"Many times."

"Dr. Leonard, are you familiar with the work of Joseph Dalrymple and his colleagues at the Waring Institute in Philadelphia?"

"Not intimately. I believe they study the effects of certain chemicals in animal models. As I say, we don't rely much on animal studies."

"Your honor, plaintiffs would like to introduce a paper by Renner and Dalrymple entitled—"

"Objection!"

"What grounds?"

"Attorney for plaintiffs is trying to sneak in new evidence that has no bearing on this case, and hasn't been brought forth either in deposition or during this trial."

"Mr. Allen, was this paper submitted as part of plaintiffs' brief?"

"No, your honor, but—"

"The proper time for introduction of this evidence, if it *is* evidence, has long passed. Request denied. Please proceed, counselor."

"Very well, your honor. Doctor Leonard, have you ever had a drug taken off the market because of a harmful reaction in human trials or in subsequent use by the general public?"

"No. Not one."

"And how many drugs has Wilson and Leonard put on the market in, say, the past five years—one or two? Half-a-dozen?"

"More like thirty to thirty-five. I don't have the exact figure at my fingertips."

"One final question, doctor. To your knowledge, does every U.S. pharmaceutical company use 'state-of-the-art' methods to determine drug safety before it's placed on the market?"

"Some do, some don't. Many of the bigger companies still tend to rely on the older, less reliable methods."

"Would you say the Mercer Company is one of those companies?"

"Objection, your honor. There's been no testimony—"

"I withdraw the question. Thank you very much, Dr. Leonard. No further questions at this time."

"Mr. St. Clair?"

"Thank you, your honor. Dr. Leonard, doesn't the FDA require testing on human tissues before a new medication goes into a clinical trial?"

"Yes, but we carry the requirement much further. We test on a greater variety of human tissues, and with a greater range of parameters than is required by law."

"So the answer is that the FDA requires testing on animals *and* human tissues, and you obey both those requirements, isn't that so?"

"Yes."

"Thank you. Now, doctor, are you familiar with a pharmaceutical compound called 'Exopene'?"

"Yes."

"Wasn't that one of your drugs?"

"Yes, it was."

"And wasn't it taken off the market?"

"Yes, but not because of safety considerations."

"Didn't it cause some kidney problems in children who took this drug?"

"Not exactly. It sort of 'unmasked' certain problems that were already there."

"But it was brought up for review at the Food and Drug Administration, wasn't it?"

"Of course."

"And wasn't there a recommendation that it be removed from the market?"

"A recommendation, yes. Not an order to do so."

"Then why was it taken off?"

"Because it turned out not to be as effective as we hoped it would be."

"So all your so-called 'modern' testing methods failed you in this case?"

"Mr. St. Clair, no one can predict with absolute certainty the efficacy of a drug that's introduced into a clinical trial."

"Isn't that true of a drug's safety as well, regardless of the methods used to determine it?"

"Well, yes. But—"

"Thank you. No further questions."

"Mr. Allen?"

"Any other so-called 'failures,' Dr. Leonard? Of the thirty to thirty-five new medications you've put on the market?"

"No. And we don't consider Exopene to be a failure. In fact, it's being used now in lower doses to confirm certain suspected kidney problems in children."

"No further questions, your honor."

"Are you prepared to bring forth your next witness?"

"No, your honor. We scheduled him for this afternoon, and he's not present in the courtroom at this time."

"Very well. Court stands adjourned until two o'clock this afternoon."

*

"Where the hell is he? It's almost two o'clock."

"I don't know! When I called his wife last night, she said he was en route. She didn't know where he was staying. Oh—there he is, I think."

"You didn't tell me he was black! I mean African-Amer—"

"Is that relevant, counselor?"

"No, of course not. It's just that . . ."

"Does the term 'jive turkey' mean anything to you, partner?"

"All right, never mind! Are you ready for this guy?"

"As ready as I'll ever be."

"Did you check his credentials again?"

"Except for the fact that he was fired by the FDA, they're first class."

"That's a big 'except.'"

"True, but if St. C tries to knock him down it might backfire. I've talked to him several times, and he's no dummy."

"Well, if he gets flustered you can always ask for a brief recess."

"We covered that in Litigation 101. Now let me get over there and ask him about Dalrymple."

"Too late. The door's opening . . . ."

"Call your next witness, Mr. Allen."

"Your honor, our next witness will be examined by my colleague, Ms. White."

"Very well. Call your next witness, Ms. White."

"Thank you, your honor. Plaintiffs call Dr. Robert Small to the stand."

"Please state your name and profession."

"Robert L. Small. Physician, lecturer, writer."

"Do you swear to tell the truth . . . ?"

"I do."

"Dr. Small, good afternoon."

"Ms. White."

"Doctor, will you please tell the jury about your professional experience?"

"Well, I got my M.D. degree from Case Western Reserve University in 1966. I did an internship and residency at Metropolitan General Hospital in Cleveland, and I practiced medicine there, as a pediatric oncologist, until 1980, when I took a position with the Food and Drug Administration. I was there until 1998."

"'Oncology' means you worked with cancer patients, is that right?"

"Primarily, yes."

"And what do you do now?"

"I work part-time at the Anundale Clinic in Albuquerque, and the rest of my time is devoted to research and writing."

"When you say 'research,' do you mean laboratory research?"

"No, I mean research for the articles and books I write for publication."

"In the area of cancer therapy?"

"More general than that. I write about the history of medicine, current trends in research and practice, new and promising methodologies, that sort of thing."

"Have you published many books in this area?"

"About a dozen."

"You've published a dozen medical books since 1998?"

"No, some of them were written while I was still at the FDA."

"And how many since then?"

"Three."

"And did you publish any of these books yourself?"

"Myself?"

"I mean, did you pay someone to publish them for you?"

"No, I've been well paid for my work."

"And how many copies have your books sold, on the average?"

"Oh, thirty to forty thousand. Two have become *New York Times* best-sellers."

"Which two?"

"*The Promise of Gene Therapy* and *Modern Medicine for the Masses*."

"Thank you, doctor. And the articles you've written: Have any of these appeared in the standard medical journals?"

"Yes. And some in newspapers and popular magazines. I write for the general public as well as the medical community."

"How many of your papers have been published in *The Journal of the American Medical Association*, for example?"

"Eight or nine, maybe."

"*The New England Journal of Medicine*?"

"Another six or eight."

"*Lancet*?"

"Three or four."

"And how many popular medical articles do you have in print?"

"Oh, I don't know—maybe a hundred or so."

"And have any of these popular articles been published in newspapers and magazines we would know about?"

"Oh, sure. *The New York Times, The San Francisco Chronicle, Reader's Digest*—"

"In fact, Dr. Small, you're a pretty well-known and respected figure in the popular medical literature, as well as the scientific literature, wouldn't you say?"

"I suppose so, yes."

"So it's safe to say that many of the your colleagues consider you an expert in the field of medical research?"

"Yes, I think that's true."

"And have you received any awards for any of your work?"

"A few."

"Such as?"

"Such as the Goodman award, an Oxford fellowship, and—uh—one or two others."

"Thank you. Now, doctor, will you please tell the court about your experience with the Food and Drug Administration?"

"Well, I was hired in 1980 as an assistant program administrator in the area of new drug treatments for leukemia and other childhood cancers."

"And could you describe the nature of your work at that time, please?"

"My job was to read applications requesting approval of experimental drugs for the treatment of various malignant diseases in children. To make sure all the guidelines had been followed, and all the requirements had been met in the application."

"'Malignant diseases' means 'cancer,' is that right?"

"Yes."

"And if these guidelines and requirements were not met, what happened then?"

"I passed the information on to my supervisor."

"You met with him or her—"

"Him."

"And went over the applications and pointed out the shortcomings of each one?"

"Yes, and gave him written reports as well."

"And your reports had to do mostly with studies of childhood cancers of various types?"

"At first, yes. Then I was asked to branch out into other areas."

"Could you be more specific?"

"I was given applications involving drug treatments for all childhood diseases."

"Sounds like a very responsible position."

"I think you could say that."

"And were your reports and your job performance in all these areas judged to be satisfactory by your superiors at the FDA?"

"I believe so. I was given an annual raise and high marks in appraisal reports."

"And how long did you stay at this particular level?"

"For almost ten years."

"During this time were there ever any complaints about your performance?"

"Not one."

"What happened after the ten years?"

"I took over my supervisor's job."

"After he retired?"

"Yes."

"Did he recommend you for this promotion?"

"Yes. Highly. The request was approved in a few weeks. Which is pretty fast for a governmental agency."

"And did the job description change much with that promotion?"

"Sure. Instead of reading all those drug applications per se, I had several assistants who did this and who gave me their reports and recommendations."

"So you never read another application after your promotion?"

"Well, not as many. And not in the great detail I had in the past."

"And what did your higher-level position entail other than reading your assistants' reports and recommendations?"

"My job was to pass judgement on these recommendations. To send on up the ones which in my opinion were good candidates for approval, and to write letters to those applicants who had failed to meet FDA standards. And to suggest what they might do to improve their chances next time."

"By pointing out deficiencies in their applications, things like that?"

"Exactly."

"And you had superiors in this job who approved your work and your salary increases, et cetera?"

"That's right. The department is set up like any other government agency, like a pyramid. There is always somebody above you until you get to the top."

"The FDA director."

"Yes. The director."

"And were your approval ratings satisfactory? And did you get a salary increase every year?"

"Yes."

"Dr. Small, why did you leave the Food and Drug Administration?"

"I was fired."

"Did you say 'fired'?"

"Yes. Although they called it something else."

"What did they call it?"

"Irreversible termination for gross insubordination."

"Whatever they called your leaving the FDA, they didn't give you much notice, did they?"

"They gave me twenty-four hours to clean out my office."

"In your opinion, sir, what led to this abrupt ending of an obviously productive and successful career?"

"I learned that several of the clinical trials I had not recommended for approval went ahead anyway."

"And why was that?"

"Well, it had to do with politics. The government wanted drug applications to move through the system faster to get the drugs on the market sooner."

"And in your opinion, sir, things were moving *too* fast?"

"That's right. The emphasis had shifted toward speeding up the approval process and away from product safety."

"In your opinion, then, some of the drugs being tested with FDA approval were unsafe?"

"In my opinion, yes."

"And you made this opinion known to your supervisors?"

"Yes, I did."

"And for your concern for the public safety and for your candor about it, you were fired, is that right?"

"Yes, that's right."

"And did you seek restitution?"

"I appealed the decision all the way to the top."

"And that failed?"

"Yes."

"Did you consult an attorney about this matter?"

"Yes, I did."

"And what was his advice?"

"Her advice was to forget the whole thing."

"Because . . . ."

"Because I couldn't win."

"Why not?"

"'You can't fight city hall,' was the way she put it."

"Your honor, haven't we heard enough of this saga? It's totally irrelevant to this case."

"Mr. St. Clair, as you have so eloquently pointed out, this case rests on whether Mercer Pharmaceuticals violated any laws. If laws were violated and these violations were ignored by the FDA, the issue becomes clouded. I see some relevance here. Proceed, Ms. White."

"Thank you, your honor. Now doctor, since you were kicked out of the establishment, you decided to write books about the way you were treated by the FDA?"

"Not at all. I don't hold that kind of grudge. Sure, I write about the methods and requirements used in selecting drugs for clinical trials, some of which are outdated and useless, but I have never gone after the FDA in particular."

"Can you elaborate on that? Which requirements do you consider to be outdated and useless?"

"Well, animal testing for safety and effectiveness of new drugs is the most egregious."

"Because . . . ?"

"Because the results do not accurately predict drug safety in humans."

"Well, could you give us some examples of unsafe drugs that were put into clinical testing or on the market with FDA approval, say in the past ten years?"

"There are many. In fact, I've prepared a list of them."

"And how many drugs are on that list?"

"Fifty-seven. But I may have missed a few."

"Thank you, doctor. Your honor, in order to save the court's time, plaintiffs would like to introduce Dr. Small's list of recently-approved animal-tested drugs that have been found to experience safety problems subsequent to their approval for human testing. This would be Plaintiff's Exhibit Three."

"Objection, your honor."

"Overruled. Clerk will admit the list as Plaintiffs' Exhibit Three. Please proceed."

"Thank you, your honor. Dr. Small, are you familiar with a drug called Mercipine?"

"Yes, I've read all the reports on its history and the results of the clinical testing."

"In fact, it's on the list we just introduced, is it not?"

"Yes, it is."

"Dr. Small, this drug was approved by the FDA for testing on humans, was it not?"

"Yes, it certainly was. Otherwise the clinical trial would never have begun."

"And the drug was approved by the FDA for treatment of Type I diabetes, isn't that right?"

"That's right."

"Can you tell us whether, in your opinion, the drug was safe to use in humans based on animal tests?"

"In my opinion, it was not."

"Objection, your honor."

"On what grounds, Mr. St. Clair?"

"Your honor, Dr. Small wasn't *at* the FDA at the time Mercipine was approved for clinical testing. His opinion in this matter is irrelevant."

"Mr. St. Clair, the witness seems to be quite familiar with FDA procedures. I'll hear his answer."

"Thank you, your honor. Dr. Small?"

"I've studied the test records. It seems to me the procedures were hurried and not well thought-out. In a drug like this, which is produced especially for use with a long-term and potentially debilitating disease, more attention should have been given to possible safety problems. Had I *been* at the FDA when this drug came up for approval, I would have rejected it. And, as it turned out, there *were* safety problems. Even Mr. St. Clair can't deny that."

"Objection, your honor. Defense *does* deny that."

"So noted, counselor. Please proceed, Ms. White."

"Thank you. Doctor, you're referring to the seven or more patients who died after becoming human guinea pigs for this experimental drug, are you not?"

"Your honor!"

"Sustained. Jury will disregard the reference to 'human guinea pigs.'"

"Doctor, you were referring to the seven patients who died after taking Mercipine?"

"Yes."

"Dr. Small, are you familiar with the work of Dr. Lawrence McCall?"

"I've read his book."

"In your opinion, is that a scholarly work?"

"Very. It's a brilliant analysis of the relationship between different animal species vis-à-vis their sensitivities to various chemicals in general, and to prescription drugs in particular."

"Despite the fact that all the major publishers rejected it?"

"Maybe that's *why* they rejected it."

"And do you agree with what Dr. McCall said in that book? Particularly with regard to the testing of new and experimental drugs on animals?"

"Absolutely. The testing of experimental drugs on animals is a vast waste of time and money. Unless, of course, you're looking for a drug to be used in treating that particular animal species."

"So you agree with the testimony of earlier witnesses that the safety of a new drug for use in clinical trials cannot be predicted from animal tests?"

"Not in the slightest."

"And that applies to the experimental drug called Mercipine."

"*Particularly* in the case of Mercipine."

"Why is that, sir?"

"The Mercer Corporation used the wrong animals in their testing protocols."

("Whew!")

"And how can you be so sure of that conclusion?"

"Because Dalrymple *et al.* had already shown that rats and rabbits aren't negatively affected by biphenylmercaptans."

("Yes!")

"Which is the class of drugs that Mercipine belongs to."

"That's right."

"And which species would have been more appropriate for the testing of Mercipine and other such compounds than rats and rabbits?"

"They found cats and guinea pigs to be susceptible to the toxic effects of this chemical family. And also certain birds and amphibians, I believe."

"And what were the effects of biphenylmercaptans on these species?"

"They caused certain heart problems. And they also caused seizures and other neurological disorders in some of the test subjects."

"Based on that work, sir, is it your opinion that if these other animals—cats, guinea pigs, birds and amphibians—had been used in Mercer's safety tests, that their new experimental drug Mercipine would never have reached the clinical testing phase?"

"Objection!"

"Overruled."

"Well, if they had used those animals, and reported their findings to the FDA, the drug would never have been approved, I'm sure of that."

"And based on the Dalrymple work, doctor, can you say with certainty that Mercipine was responsible for the deaths of those seven or more patients who died while participating in the clinical study?"

"Objection, your honor. The witness had nothing to do with this study, nor the autopsies, nor—"

"The court would be interested in the witness's expert opinion, nevertheless. Overruled."

"Sir?"

"No, not on that work alone. Those studies show only that rats and rabbits were the worst possible choice for the toxicity studies. Even if you used the other animals, you still couldn't say that Mercipine would be unsafe for human use."

"And why is that?"

"Because *no* animal species is a good model for drug safety in humans, whether the results are positive or negative."

"Then how can you be sure that Mercipine was responsible for the deaths of those patients?"

"Because they all died from heart failure and they were all taking that particular drug."

"Objection!"

"Overruled!"

"Could you elaborate on that conclusion?"

"Sure. In most clinical studies there are likely to be a few deaths, mostly because the patients are elderly or their disease is quite far advanced. The data coming from the Mercipine study fits an entirely different pattern. Most of those deaths were unexpected and occurred in a younger set of patients. This strongly suggests a causal relationship."

"Is there any doubt about this in your mind?"

"No. And the coroners involved probably reached the same conclusion."

"As a matter of fact, sir, they did. Doctor, is it possible that Mercipine is a safe and effective drug at lower doses than those proposed for the clinical study?"

"It's possible, but not likely."

"Why not?"

"There weren't any heart failures with the control group or with adult patients receiving the lowest doses of the drug, but it appeared to be ineffective at those doses."

"So it's a loser on both counts."

"You could put it that way."

"Once again, sir, is it your opinion that the FDA should not have approved Mercipine for human trials?"

"Objection, your honor! The FDA is n-not on trial here!"

"Sustained."

"One final question, doctor. Has it ever been your experience that when animal tests have found to be faulty after a drug has already entered clinical trials, the drug has been retroactively disapproved?"

"That's rare, but it has happened, yes."

"Can you give the court an opinion as to why this has not happened in the case of Mercipine?"

"Objec—"

"Overruled."

"The FDA is a very conservative outfit. Very slow to make changes, very slow to act on new evidence of this sort unless it's overwhelming."

"Do you mean to suggest that seven deaths brought about by a heart irregularity isn't overwhelming enough evidence to remove a drug from a clinical trial?"

"Objection, your honor! Plaintiffs have yet to prove—"

"Sustained."

"Thank you, Dr. Small. No further questions at this time."

"Thank you, Ms. White. Mr. St. Clair, it's almost three o'clock, and the court has some previous business scheduled for four. Can you wrap up your cross-examination this afternoon so the witness won't have to come back on Monday?"

"We'll sure try, judge."

"Very well. Court stands in recess for exactly ten minutes."

*

"How did I do, partner?"

"Beautifully. Couldn't have done better myself."

"Thanks. Hi, Elmira. Hi, Tony. How are you holding out?"

"Okay. We didn't know it was going to be so complicated."

"Neither did we."

"Anthony and I want you to know that we think you're both doing a wonderful job."

"Thank you. It's not an easy case."

"Maybe you and Mr. Allen can come over for dinner some night after all this is over."

"We'll see."

"You make such a good-looking couple."

"We're not a couple."

"Oh. I thought—"

"We're just colleagues. Partners for this case."

"Oh. I see. Well, you make a nice-looking couple just the same."

"That's what I've been trying to tell her!"

*

"Proceed, Mr. St. Clair."

"Thank you, your honor. Dr. Small, good afternoon, sir."

"Afternoon."

"Counsel for plaintiffs has brought you here as an expert on safety requirements for new pharmaceutical compounds as established by the FDA, is that right?"

"I would assume that's so."

"Sir, you testified that in your opinion some of the drugs—no, you said *many*, didn't you?—of the drugs approved by the FDA for clinical testing are unsafe. Is that true?"

"In my opinion, yes. Potentially unsafe, at any rate."

"Meaning . . . ?"

"Meaning there's no way to tell until they go into clinical trials."

"And if they were tested according to *your* standards, there wouldn't be any unsafe drugs, or even *potentially* unsafe drugs, on the market, is that what you're saying?"

"No, I'm saying there would be fewer than there are now."

"So no matter what criteria are used, there would always be some unsafe drugs out there."

"Probably. There's always some uncertainty in any medical procedure."

"And why is that?"

"Because the human body is so complex and so individualistic. No one can predict every eventuality."

"In other words, it's a crap shoot, isn't that so?"

"Objection!"

"Mr. St. Clair, would you please rephrase the question?"

"Very well, judge. Sir, the whole question of drug safety is just a gamble, isn't it?"

"I've already said there is always an element of uncertainty—"

"So in the case of Mercipine, there really isn't any way to be sure that the Mercer Corporation's methods aren't as good as, or better than, yours or anyone else's, isn't that so?"

"Mr. St. Clair, if that were 'so,' then there wouldn't be any need for having government regulations at all."

"So in your opinion, a governmental agency like the FDA is necessary to ensure the maximum safety of experimental drugs, isn't that true?"

"Sure, but—"

"Dr. Small, you worked at the FDA for a number of years, didn't you?"

"That's correct."

"How long did you say that was?"

"Eighteen years."

"And during that time, did you ever recommend approval of a drug that had been tested in animals?"

"Yes, of course."

"Well, if you think animal testing is inappropriate, why did you approve these drugs?"

"When I first started at the FDA, I thought animal tests were necessary. In fact, I was taught that in medical school. Since then, I've learned otherwise."

"So, again, it's just a matter of opinion, is that what you're saying?"

"No, I'd say it's a matter of education."

"So now you're saying that medical schools don't educate their students in the way you would have it?"

"In this area, that's correct."

"Thank you, sir. Now during the time you were at the Food and Drug Administration, did you ever come across a situation in which the legal authority of the FDA was usurped by any other governmental agency?"

"I don't understand the question."

"Very well, I'll rephrase it for you. Is the FDA, or is it not, the final arbiter of what new medicinal compounds are approved for clinical testing and later marketing?"

"Well, yes, but—"

"In other words—"

"Objection, your honor. Attorney for defense isn't allowing the witness to give his testimony."

"Sustained. Don't chop him off at the knees, Mr. St. Clair."

"Very well, your honor. Sir, shall I have the stenographer read back the question?"

"No. The answer is: of course the FDA makes these determinations. But sometimes they make mistakes, like all of us."

"So you are capable of making mistakes, Dr. Small?"

"Yes, and so are you."

"Thank you, sir. I appreciate that. Now I ask you once more: given that everyone makes mistakes, who has the legal authority and the legal responsibility for approving a drug application—the company or the FDA?"

"I'm not a lawyer, Mr. St. Clair."

"So you don't have a worthwhile opinion about whether the Mercer Corporation followed the law or not, is that right?"

"Objection!"

"Sustained. Stick to the point, counselor."

"Very well, your honor. Dr. Small, when you *were* at the FDA, before you were fired, that is, you were completely familiar with its regulations and requirements?"

"You know the answer to that, Mr. St. Clair."

"I'd like you to confirm that, sir."

"Yes, of course I was. Still am. They haven't changed much since then. Or in the last few decades, for that matter."

"Could you tell the court the regulations pertaining to toxicity testing of new pharmaceutical compounds?"

"The FDA mandates testing in a rodent and at least one nonrodent species."

"And doctor, did Mercer Pharmaceuticals follow these procedures to the letter?"

"Yes, but—"

"And they dotted all their i's and crossed all their t's?"

"As far as I know, yes."

"Thank you again. Now let's move on to something else. You testified earlier that you were fired by the FDA in 1998. Do recall saying that, sir?"

"Yes. And so does everyone else in this room."

"Let's hope so. Dr. Small, do you recognize this termination report?"

"Uh . . . Yes, it's mine."

"Your honor, defense submits this report as Defense Exhibit C."

"Any objection, Ms. White?"

("Do we want to object to this?")

("What's the point? We brought it up.")

"No, your honor."

"So ordered."

"Now, doctor, according to this report, you were fired for 'gross insubordination,' isn't that right?"

"That's the way they referred to it in the report, yes."

"And was this because you were complaining to your boss that certain pharmaceutical companies weren't following proper procedures? Dotting their i's and all that?"

"Not exactly. It was for complaining to him that *he* wasn't following the standards mandated long ago by Congress when it established the Food and Drug Administration."

"Dr. Small, how many other FDA employees at your level were fired for gross insubordination?"

"I don't know."

"Well, I do, as it happens. The answer is, that in the last ten years, you were the only person fired for gross insubordination."

"I can assure you there are others there who felt the same way I did, but who didn't come forward."

"If it please the court, I'd like to read a portion of Dr. Small's termination report."

"Go ahead, Mr. St. Clair."

"'The employment of Robert C. Small, M.D., was terminated for his refusal to appear at required meetings, for disregarding the orders of his superiors, and for general disruption of the normal functions and procedures of the FDA during the period 1994-1998.' Dr. Small, is any of this true?"

"Well, yes, but it's not that simple."

"Dr. Small, were you given a copy of this report?"

"Yes, I was."

"And you took it to an attorney, isn't that right?"

"Yes."

"And she felt it was a perfectly legal document, did she not?"

"Well—"

"Sir, did you try to get another job, in a hospital or the like? Or another governmental agency?"

"Yes."

"Were you successful?"

"No."

"No one would hire you after eighteen years in a top position with the Food and Drug Administration?"

"No."

"Thank you. No further questions, your honor."

"Ms. White, any re-direct?"

"Absolutely, your honor."

"Proceed. But please be succinct."

"Your honor, we'd like to follow up on a few of the misrepresentations made by defense. We'll try to make it as brief as possible."

"Very well."

"Will the stenographer please read back something from Dr. Small's previous testimony, the line that begins, 'And doctor, did Mercer Pharmaceuticals follow these procedures . . .'"

"Uhhhhhh—Question: 'And doctor, did Mercer Pharmaceuticals follow these procedures to the letter'? Answer: 'Yes, but—'"

"Thank you. Dr. Small, counsel for the defense didn't allow you to finish that sentence. Would you please do so now?"

"I was going to say that Mercer Pharmaceuticals followed the letter of the animal requirements, but not the underlying principle."

"Which is?"

"Well, the paragraph in question goes something like this: "In order to ensure the safety of any new pharmaceutical compound for human use, it must be tested in one rodent species and at least one non-rodent species."

"But isn't that what Mercer did with Mercipine?"

"They tested their drug on rats and rabbits knowing full well that these species were not the appropriate animals to test biphenylmercaptans with. Or should have known. In other words, they did not *ensure the safety* of their new pharmaceutical compound, as required by the FDA."

"And why should Mercer and company have known about this research?"

"Because they're a huge corporation with unlimited resources. I'm sure the papers on the subject were available in their library."

"And was the FDA aware of this problem?"

"They should have been."

"Now, doctor: Mr. St. Clair asked you whether you'd ever approved a drug whose safety had been based on animal tests while you were with the FDA."

"I remember."

"And you replied that you had?"

"Yes. But I based my judgement on other evidence than just those tests, which I've long thought were faulty. Anyway, things are very different now. Safety tests are becoming much more sophisticated. And everyone knows that animal testing for safety purposes is obsolete. The FDA is way behind the times in this regard."

"Thank you, doctor. And finally, defense has made a big point that you weren't able to find a position at another agency or in a hospital environment after your severance from the FDA. May I ask: What did you do when your position was terminated? Besides appealing that decision, I mean."

"I sent a letter to the Director."

"Of the Food and Drug Administration?"

"Yes."

"And did he respond?"

"Yes. He ordered an investigation."

"Isn't that what you were asking for?"

"Yes."

"And what was the result of this investigation?"

"There wasn't any investigation. It was a total whitewash."

"How do you know that?"

"Nothing happened. No one looked at the data, called me in, no one did anything at all."

"And you continued to complain."

"I wrote a few more letters, yes."

"To whom?"

"To various government officials."

"Including the highest officials?"

"Yes."

"The President?"

"Yes."

"The Vice-President?"

"Yes."

"Leaders in Congress?"

"Yes."

"And what happened as a result of this campaign?"

"Nothing."

"Dr. Small, how long did it take you to find your present position with the Anundale Clinic in Albuquerque?"

"Two years."

"Why so long for a man of your broad experience?"

"In effect, I was blacklisted."

"What does that mean, sir?"

"It means that the word went out that I was a whistleblower."

"Isn't there a law against recriminations against whistleblowers?"

"Yes, but it doesn't always solve the problem. The damage is done subtly and behind the scenes."

"Dr. Small, what usually happens to whistleblowers?"

"Objection, your honor! This is *totally* irrelevant and *completely* immaterial!"

"You raised the issue, Mr. St. Clair. I'll allow it."

"Dr. Small, what usually happens when someone blows the whistle on dangerous or corrupt practices in a governmental agency?"

"Your honor!"

"Objection sustained. Don't get carried away, counselor."

"Very well, your honor. Doctor, what happens when someone blows the whistle in a governmental agency?"

"They're usually fired."

"And where do they go after that?"

"It's very hard for them to find employment elsewhere, whether in government or in the private sector."

"Because employers are afraid the whistle will blow again."

"Objection, your honor! Counsel is trying to—"

"I'll sustain this one. I think you've made your point, Ms. White."

"Thank you very much, Dr. Small. No further questions, your honor."

"Mr. St. Clair?"

"Just one final question, your honor. Dr. Small, I ask you one last time: Did Mercer comply with letter of the law in the case of Mercipine?"

"I would say with the letter, not the spirit."

"No further questions, your honor."

"Ms. White? Mr. Allen?"

"That concludes the case for the plaintiffs, your honor."

"In that event, are you prepared to present the case for the defense, Mr. St. Clair?"

"Your honor, defense is prepared to begin first thing Monday morning."

"Very well. Court is adjourned until ten o'clock on Monday. Jury is reminded not to discuss this case among yourselves or with anyone else until that time."

"All rise . . . ."

*

"Mrs. W. didn't like the way St. Clair treated our witness."

"What makes you think so, partner?"

"She watched St. Clair rather than Dr. Small. And there was a scowl on her face."

"That sounds encouraging. What about the others?"

"Hard to tell, but they liked Small's testimony. There were little smiles here and there. And Mr. Steiner nodded his head in agreement a couple of times."

"That sounds pretty good, too."

"But Corrigan looked bored."

"Still—"

"Don't forget, though, the jury usually comes down on the plaintiff's side until the defense begins its case. Then they can go the other way."

"Not if we do a good job in refuting their testimony."

"I don't know about you, but I'm exhausted. How about a drink? We can go over the—"

"No, thanks."

"Damn it, Candace, it's just a lousy drink. And I won't say a word!"

"Sorry. I'm having dinner over at Lew's tonight."

"Lew? But he's never even—"

"I'll be in my office tomorrow morning if you want to discuss anything. Have a nice evening."

"Sure. Great. Same to you."

*

"Hello, Marc. How are things?"

"Oh. McBain."

"Buy you a beer?"

"Why not?"

"SARGE! TWO MORE AMSTELS OVER HERE! Got a question for you."

"I'm aghast."

"Do you think your dad will give me an interview?"

"What for? Are you starting a new series on cancer patients?"

"Not exactly. It's kind of a counterpoint to the Mercer case."

"You mean—"

"You know. He's fighting cancer while you're fighting the people who make the drugs he's taking."

"SARGE! CANCEL ONE OF THOSE BEERS!"

"No. You don't understand. I won't even mention the fact that Mercer is producing those drugs."

"What, then?"

"The article will be entirely neutral. It's the irony I'm interested in. Mercer is producing drugs that cure people like your father from deadly diseases despite certain—ah—setbacks. You're looking beyond that simplistic view—trying to do something to increase drug safety despite the fact that your father is, himself, taking a combination of Mercer drugs."

"I get to read it before it goes to press?"

"If you like."

"MAKE THAT TWO MORE BEERS, SARGE!"

"And when do you get into Mercer's side of the story?"

"In a couple of weeks."

"The trial will be over by then."

"But the story won't be. One other thing. I was wondering if you could give me your feelings about the trial now that you've wrapped up your case."

"If this is for another *Post* article, we've got it made in the shade."

"St. Clair knocked you around on some of your witnesses, though, don't you think?"

"He tried. But he may have actually helped us make our case. What matters, of course, is what the jury thinks."

"And what the judge thinks."

"I'd be interested to hear what *you* think about how we're doing, Mr. McBain."

"From where I sit, you've wrapped up your case and Goliath is still standing."

"I disagree. The fact that Mercer used the wrong animals in their testing procedures knocks down all their defenses."

"Is that the rock of your case?"

"No, it's a damn boulder."

"So you think you can win this one?"

"No question in my mind at all."

"And *off* the record?"

"We haven't got a dog's chance."

*

"Hi, Marc. Come on in."

"Thanks."

"Tell me: Why does it always rain on Saturdays?"

"I don't know, Lew. Is that what you wanted to see me about?"

"No. Not exactly. Just trying to postpone discussing a little personal matter with you before you take off for the weekend."

"About Dad?"

"No. How's he doing, anyway?"

"He's doing okay. The cancer is still retreating, at least."

"Good. Good. No, the matter I wanted to discuss with you is your relationship with your partner in the Mercer case."

"Candace? We don't have a relationship."

"But you keep trying to develop one, don't you?"

"Now wait, Lew, if you think—"

"Calm down, Marc, Jr. I'm not accusing you of anything. But I think there's something you ought to know."

"Oh? And what's that?"

"Candace has a terminal illness."

"She—what??"

"So you shouldn't take anything she says personally, you understand what I'm getting at? She doesn't want to complicate her life any more than it is already."

"Jesus, Lew. I mean, I didn't know anything about this. She never mentioned—"

"She doesn't like to talk about it. I think she's afraid people will feel sorry for her."

"I do feel sorry for her."

"Yeah. So do I."

"Can you tell me what kind of problem—"

"Sorry, I'm sworn to secrecy on that."

"Well, can you at least tell me how long she's got?"

"I don't know, Marc. Could be months or years. Or tomorrow afternoon."

"My God."

"How's she doing, anyway? Been of any use to you?"

"She's great. She did a wonderful job with a difficult witness yesterday."

"I know."

"You know?"

"She told me."

"Oh. Right."

"Don't worry. She gave you high marks, too."

"Should I let her continue? Is she too sick to be trying this case?"

"Best thing that could happen to her. Give her all the work you can. It's the only thing she's got . . . ."

"All right, Lew. If you say so. But why didn't you tell me any of this before?"

"She asked me not to."

"Does this have anything to do with her abortion?"

"What abortion?"

"She—Never mind. I probably misunderstood something. Jeez, I can't get over Candy—I mean—"

"I know. Life is hell, and then you die. At least that's what your old man always says."

"Tell me about it!"

*

"Hi, Dad. How are you doing?"

"Don't start the funeral without me."

"Dad, for God's sake . . . !"

"All right! I'm doing okay for a man with cancer."

"But you're practically in remission!"

"All 'remission' means is the time between now and when the damn thing comes back."

"Who says it's coming back?"

"The doctor told me it could at some point. It's just a matter of time."

"Maybe it won't be for twenty or thirty years."

"Not likely. Anyway, I've been doing a lot of thinking lately. Whatever happens, I'd like to rewrite my will. Plan a funeral service. That sort of thing."

"You want to talk to Bill about it? He's the expert on—"

"Maybe. I wanted to talk to you first."

"Whatever you say."

"Here."

"What's this?"

"It's my new will. Read it over, will you? Tell me what you think."

"Right now? I've got a date in a little while."

"All right, all right. When you can. Just do it before it's too late, will you?"

"Sure. Soon as I can get to it."

"And then there's this."

"What's—"

"The funeral arrangements. I want you to take care of them."

"Dad, I'd be happy to. Only it won't be for a very long time."

"Or it could be next week."

"That's true for anyone, Dad. I just found out that—Well, never mind."

"Everyone should be prepared for death. It happens to all of us, you know."

"Good grief, you've even got the price of your coffin in here."

"Remember that discussion we had a while ago? The one about God and the meaning of life?"

"How could I forget it?"

"I shut my eyes and saw it."

"Saw what?"

"Heaven."

"Dad, I'm really beginning to worry about you."

"You know what it was like?"

"What?"

"It was exactly like southern Florida."

"If that's the case, I think I'd rather—"

"Yeah. Me, too."

*

"Who's 'Candy'?"

""Candy? Uh—that's a confection, isn't it . . . ?

"You called out her name last night."

"Last night?"

"While we were doing it."
"I meant *you*! All I—"
"And you talked about her in your sleep...."
"All right! She's a colleague in the law firm. I just heard that she's dying...."
"Oh, sure."
"Well, she is."
"When?"
"I don't know."
"What from?"
"I don't know that, either."
"Do you love her?"
"Well—uh—no! I mean, I don't know...."
"I mean, goodbye!"

*

"Hi, Mom."
"Do I know you?"
"I used to live here, remember?"
"Must've been a long time ago."
"Not so long. Anyway, this will always be home to me."
"Then why don't you come home once in a while?"
"Now, Mom. I know I haven't been around for a while. It's the Mercer case. You know how it is."
"Do I ever. I pity the girl you eventually marry, if you ever do."
"I'm sure you do, Mom. By the way, Dad told me you never called about dinner."
"What's the point? He wouldn't have come."
"I think he would if you asked him nice."
"*You* didn't show up. And you still haven't called Timmy."
"Mom, as soon as this case if finished—"
"Sure. And that's the only case you've got, right?"
"Well, no, not exactly...."
"Maybe you could work him in between some of your golf games."
"Mom, I haven't played golf in two years!"
"Uh-huh."
"Where is he, anyway?"
"He was in the garage a little while ago, working on his bike. I'm not sure he'd recognize you, though."
"Okay, Mom. You made your point. I'll be back in a minute. I don't want to miss him in case he runs off somewhere.... Tim? TIMMY?"

"Booo!"

"Jesus, Tim—where the hell were you?"

"In the garage. I heard you come up."

"So how you been?"

"Okay."

"Been to see Dad lately?"

"We're going this afternoon."

"Good. I saw him yesterday. He asked about you and Mom."

"Is he going to die this time?"

"You don't waste a minute, do you, kid? He isn't going to die for a long time, Timmy. Not before he's ready."

"How do you know if you're ready?"

"When you're so old that you can't see or hear or walk and nothing means much any more."

"What if you're *young* and you can't see or hear or walk and nothing means much? Or if you're old, but—"

"Dammit, Tim, you're too young to be worrying about death!"

"How old do you have to be?"

"Ninety-five."

"C'mon, Marc. Hardly anybody lives to be ninety-five."

"Well, *you* will. Have you been talking to Dad about this again? Has he been telling you stuff?"

"Dad says everyone has to die some time."

"That's true, kiddo, but most people live a long time, even if it's not ninety-five. Let's talk about something else, shall we? What have you been up to, lately?"

"Nothing. Mom got a new parakeet. Did you see him?"

"No. Want to go in and show him to me?"

"Okay. Then you have to go, right?"

"I can't stay too long."

"I figured."

"Sorry, pal. Got some work to do tonight. But after this case I'm on is over, let's go to a ball game or something, okay?"

"When will it be over?"

"In a week or two."

"That's what Dad always used to say."

The Case For The Defense

"Hey, Mr. Allen! How's it going?"

"Great, Goose. Couldn't be better."

"That's fine, Mr. Allen! I've been reading about your case—do you think you can beat those bastards?"

"We're trying, Goose. Can I have a—"

"The regular? Sure! I hope you get a bundle for that little girl's parents! What happened to her shouldn't happen to a dog! Here you go, Mr. Allen! And here's your hazelnut!"

"Thanks. Here. Keep the change."

"Thank *you*!"

"I'll see you later, Goose."

"Sure thing, Mr. Allen! And if any of them reporters come around here and ask me about the case, I'll tell them what for!"

"You do that, Goose."

"You take care, Mr. Allen!"

"I will. You be good."

"I'm always good! Give my best to your dad, Mr. Allen!"

"Sure will. So long, Goose."

"Tell him I've got some of the fat-free waiting for him!"

"I'll do that."

"Good luck, Mr. Allen!"

"Thanks—we're going to need it!"

*

"Mr. St. Clair, please call your first witness."

"Your honor, defense calls Dr. Richard Mangan . . . ."

"Raise your right arm, please. Do you . . ."

"I do."

"Dr. Mangan, from what institution did you receive your medical degree?"

"The University of Minnesota."

"In what year?"

"1978."

"Was there an internship or residency?"

"Stanford. Chief Resident my final year there."

"And how long have you been in your current practice?"

"Almost twenty-five years."

"And your practice is limited to pediatric medicine?"

"That's right."

"Thank you. Now, doctor, do you see Mr. and Mrs. Anthony Calvecchi in the courtroom?"

"I do."

"They are patients of yours?"

"No. I'm a pediatrician."

"Was Angela Calvecchi one of your patients?"

"She was."

"For how long?"

"Thirteen years."

"From the time she was a baby."

"That's right."

"So you saw her for routine checkups and minor illnesses and so on?"

"Yes."

"Was she a healthy young girl?"

"She was in excellent health except for a condition known as Type I diabetes."

"Can you describe the symptoms of this disease for the court?"

"It's a condition in which the body's cells are starved for sugar, which provides the fuel for cellular energy. So the patient tires very easily, and actually develops muscle pain on exertion, much like someone who's been exercising to exhaustion. The basic problem is that the body doesn't produce insulin, which is the agent that allows the sugar to get out of the bloodstream and into the cells."

"Dr. Mangan, is this a serious disease?"

"Very serious."

"Is it a fatal condition?"

"It can be, although sometimes people can live fairly long lives with the affliction."

"And until Mercipine came along, was there any treatment for this disease other than injections of insulin?"

"That plus a low-sugar diet and exercise."

"And wouldn't you say, sir, that a better treatment for this affliction would be quite a gift to mankind?"

"It would be a wonderful gift. Certainly for those suffering from this condition. Besides the health problems which are associated with the disease, there's an enormous amount of discomfort involved in regulating the amount of insulin required and in injecting it three to four times a day."

"Dr. Mangan, did you bring Angela into an ongoing clinical study involving the drug Mercipine?"

"I did."

"Sir, aren't clinical studies on experimental medications usually conducted on the elderly, or in patients in the final stages of a disease?"

"Yes, but not always."

"But Angela Calvecchi was in the early stages of the disease, wasn't she?"

"Yes, very early."

"Then why did you decide to offer Angela this new medication for her affliction?"

"Because she asked me to."

"She *asked* you to?"

"That's right."

"When did she ask you to allow her to try this new treatment?"

"Angela knew nothing about Mercipine. On several of her earlier visits she told me she wanted to become a doctor like me, and we usually talked a bit about that. On her last visit before the trial began she told me she would be willing to try anything if it would help her overcome her affliction."

"And did you tell her about Mercipine at that time?"

"Yes. It was only the week before that I had received information about this new drug."

"And did it look promising?"

"Yes, it did. Quite promising. Still does."

"In what way?"

"I've heard that several of the patients participating in the study have enjoyed considerable improvement during their clinical experience with this drug."

"Objection—this is hearsay!"

"Sustained."

"So *at her own request* you decided to try the new medication on Angela Calvecchi."

"Yes."

"And when the drug became available, did you speak to the parents about it?"

"Yes, of course."

"How did that come about?"

"I called them."

"And you told them about the new medication and all the rest?"

"Yes."

"Were they as enthusiastic as their daughter about this new treatment?"

"Not at first. But they said they would talk to Angela and call me back."

"And did they do that?"

"Yes. That same afternoon."

"And what did they tell you?"

"That they would like to go ahead with the treatment."

"And then what happened?"

"I turned them over to my receptionist to schedule an appointment for them to come in and discuss the details."

"And at that time—when they came for the appointment—did you explain the possible risks involved in taking this new medication?"

"Yes, I did."

"And were there risks in taking Mercipine that you knew about at the time?"

"There are risks involved with any experimental drug. That's why we do the clinical studies."

"To determine the extent and severity of these risks."

"That's correct. And for other reasons too, of course."

"What other reasons, for example?"

"Effectiveness, optimal dosages, possible long-term effects, and so forth."

"Doctor, was there any reason to believe that there were serious risks involved with the taking of this particular medication prior to the clinical studies?"

"None were known at the time."

"There had been no toxicity studies on animals, for example?"

"Of course. But as far as I know the results showed minimal toxicity, if any."

"No animals died in the toxicity studies."

"Not a one, as far as I know. The side effects were minimal, except at massive doses."

"How massive?"

"Hundreds of times the recommended dosages."

"And what about the preliminary human studies?"

"No serious problem there, either. Occasional flu-like symptoms."

"Any deaths?"

"Only one, I believe, but that was accidental."

"You mean the patient was given the wrong dosage?"

"No. He had a car accident."

"So even with a drug like Mercipine, where the risks are minimal, do you—"

"Objection—obviously the risks were not minimal in our clients' case."

"This is a semantic point, Mr. Allen, but I'll sustain the objection."

"Doctor, when Angela's parents came in to see you about this new treatment, did you tell them at that time about the possible risks associated with it, even though you personally believed these risks to be minimal?"

"Of course. Certainly."

"Did you tell them that these risks could be serious?"

"I did. But I also said that the risks associated with this particular drug appeared to be very low."

"Did you mention that one of the possible risks was death?"

"Yes, just as I do for any clinical study."

"And did they understand those risks?"

"Yes, I—"

"Objection! Witness couldn't possibly know what plaintiffs understood about the risks involved."

"Sustained."

"Dr. Mangan, did Mr. and Mrs. Calvecchi express any concerns about the risks involved with the treatment program?"

"They seemed concerned about the possible risks, but not overly concerned."

"So you gave them the medication for Angela to take?"

"Yes, after I had my nurse show them the release form and had them sign it."

"Release from what?"

"From liability on the part of the clinic if anything should go wrong during the trial."

"And did they sign such a form?"

"Yes."

"Is this a copy of that form?"

"... Yes, it is."

"We remind the court that this document was previously introduced as Defense Exhibit A."

"Thank you, counselor. The court is familiar with the document."

"Very well, your honor. Dr. Mangan, can you tell us now how soon the treatment for Angela Calvecchi was initiated, and how you followed up on the treatment?"

"My nurse gave them the drug that day along with explicit instructions, both oral and written, and sent them home with the vial. She also asked them to call me if Angela showed any side effects."

"What kind of side effects?"

"Oh, muscle pain, tiredness, nausea, diarrhea, dry mouth, that kind of thing. Those are typical reactions to taking a new drug."

"And do you know when Angela started taking the medication?"

"I believe she took the first capsule at dinnertime that evening."

"And what day was that?"

"A Friday."

"Did the parents report any problem with the treatment after it was begun?"

"My answering service received a call the following afternoon."

"For the record, sir, that was a Saturday?"

"Yes. Saturday afternoon. About three o'clock. The Calvecchis said that Angela was not feeling well and requested that I call them."

"And did you get that message?"

"Yes, I did. And I called them when I returned to my home that evening."

"And who did you talk to at that time?"

"I talked to Mr. Calvecchi."

"Did he tell you about Angela's symptoms?"

"Yes. There was some minor joint pain, a loss of appetite, and a general malaise."

"Did that concern you?"

"Of course it concerned me. At the same time, I told him that the symptoms were probably not serious and that Angela should continue with the medication."

"And that's what she did."

"As far as I know."

"Dr. Mangan, when did you learn of Angela Calvecchi's death?"

"The following Monday."

"And how did you learn of this unfortunate occurrence?"

"I received calls both from the hospital where she was taken and from the medical examiner."

"And that was the first time you were made aware that your patient had died."

"Yes."

"Doctor, did you do everything that could have been done for Angela Calvecchi in the last few hours of her life?"

"Mr. St. Clair, I don't think anyone could've done anything for her. Whatever happened to her was totally unpredictable, and there was nothing I or anyone else could have done to prevent it under the circumstances."

"The 'circumstances' being the taking of a new and experimental drug."

"Yes."

"Which always comes with a certain amount of risk involved."

"That's correct."

"A risk that the Calvecchis were made well aware of."

"I believe so, yes."

"Thank you, sir. Now, doctor, have you ever written prescriptions for medicinal compounds made by this company in the past?"

"Yes. Countless times."

"Then it's your opinion that the Mercer Corporation is a reputable pharmaceutical company?"

"Yes, of course. It's one of the best."

"Doctor, have you had any problems with prescriptions for drugs manufactured by the Mercer Pharmaceutical Corporation in the past, say, five years?"

"Not that I recall. There may have been some minor problems with allergic reactions, that sort of thing. But nothing serious."

"And despite the unfortunate death of Angela Calvecchi, would you hesitate to prescribe medications made by this company in the future?"

"Not at all."

"And you're satisfied that the treatment regimen was carried out properly in the case of this patient?"

"Yes. Absolutely."

"Thank you, doctor. No further questions at this time."

"Mr. Allen?"

"Thank you, your honor. Dr. Mangan, you say you prescribed Mercipine for little Angela Calvecchi because she asked you to do so, isn't that right?"

"Yes. She was a pretty determined little girl."

"Sir, are you accustomed to letting your patients decide which drugs you prescribe for them?"

"Objection!"

"Sustained. Jury will disregard the question. Counsel, please refrain from delving into the absurd."

"Yes, your honor. But you did say you gave Angela an experimental drug because she asked you to, did you not?"

"Not exactly. I told her about this new medication that showed promise in treating an intractable disease she thought she would have to live with for a very long time. But yes, when I told her about it, she jumped at the chance. It would have been pretty callous of me not to consider her request."

"Dr. Mangan, how many other thirteen-year-olds did you expose to Mercipine?"

"Objection!"

"Sustained."

"On how many other thirteen-year-olds, sir, did you initiate treatment of Type I diabetes with Mercipine?"

"None. But there were other adolescents in the total program, I believe."

"But Angela was the youngest?"

"Objection, your honor. Dr. Mangan doesn't have access to all the clinical trial records."

"Sustained."

"Very well, your honor. Sir, did the research organization administering the tests give you permission to test Mercipine on young Angela Calvecchi?"

"Well, not Angela specifically."

"But you were permitted to test the drug on thirteen-year-old patients?"

"That's correct. The protocol specified that thirteen would be the minimum age for the trial."

"And who determined this minimum age?"

"Why, the Mercer company, I suppose."

"Thank you, sir. Now, Dr. Mangan, besides Mercipine, are there any other 'promising' alternatives to this experimental drug?"

"I believe another pharmaceutical company has put out a similar drug recently."

"Was this drug available at the time you prescribed Mercipine for Angela Calvecchi?"

"I'm not sure on that."

"Well, we have an article from *The Journal of the American Medical Association* published three months before Mercipine was approved for clinical testing. Its title is, 'Two new drugs for the treatment of diabetes.' Are you familiar with this article?"

"I may have read it."

"Your honor, this is Plaintiff's Exhibit Four.

"Clerk will enter it into the record."

"Thank you, your honor. Dr. Mangan, with two drugs coming out at about the same time, how do you decide which is the best one for the patient's needs?"

"The pharmaceutical company usually sends out literature on the possible benefits of the drug in question."

"That's not all they send out, is it, sir?"

"I'm sorry?"

"Don't they usually send salespersons to hype their drugs?"

"Well, yes."

"And don't they also send quite a few doctors on vacation trips, golf outings, things like that?"

"Objection, your honor!"

"On what grounds, Mr. St. Clair?"

"Counsel insists on bringing irrelevant issues into this trial. Gifts from pharmaceutical companies to physicians are a common occurrence in the industry."

"Ordinarily I would agree, Mr. St. Clair. However, the attempts by this particular pharmaceutical company to get this particular physician to prescribe this particular drug is relevant here. Overruled."

"Thank you, your honor. In light of Judge Bates's ruling, sir, I'll rephrase the question: Did the Mercer Corporation send you on any vacations or outings prior to your prescribing Mercipine to young Angela Calvecchi?"

"There's nothing wrong with that! Every physician—"

"Where did they send you on your last excursion?"

"Objection!"

"I've already ruled on that, counselor. I'll allow the answer."

"The Bahamas. But it wasn't a vacation. It was a medical conference."

"The Bahamas. Nice place for a conference, isn't it? Golf. Scuba diving. And can you tell us how much the last outing paid for by the Mercer Corporation cost them?"

"I haven't the slightest idea."

"You mean you're free to go anywhere you want for as long as you want without any regard whatsoever for the expenses incurred?"

"Objection, your honor!"

"Let's not get back into that realm of the absurd, Mr. Allen."

"Sir, did the competing drug company—the one that produced the other new medication for the treatment of Type I diabetes—did they also send you to the Bahamas for golf and scuba diving and all the rest?"

"No."

"And do you know whether their drug has had a similar record with respect to fatalities and other incidents?"

"I can't answer that."

"Well, do you know which went into a clinical trial first?"

"I believe the Gentrexin was a little ahead of Mercipine."

"And yet you prescribed Mercipine for Angela Calvecchi."

"Yes."

"Why?"

"I trust the Mercer Corporation and have a good relationship with them."

"I'm sure you do. Now, regarding my earlier question about Angela being the youngest patient in the Mercipine study: I believe you testified that Mercer and company stipulated a minimum age of thirteen for patients taking part in the clinical trial, is that right?"

"Yes."

"And do you know how they arrived at that figure?"
"No. I suspect it had to do with the onset of puberty."
"Puberty? Do all girls go through puberty by the time they're thirteen?"
"Not all, no."
"Would you have given the drug to any prepubescent children who happened to be thirteen?"
"No."
"Doctor Mangan, are adolescents usually included in clinical studies?"
"Depends on the study."
"Can you elaborate on that?"
"Teenagers wouldn't be included in a study of Alzheimer's disease, for example. On the other hand, vaccines against childhood diseases are usually tested in children."
"Are you saying that most victims of diabetes are children?"
"Not at all. But many are, and it may prove more beneficial to initiate the treatment at the onset of the affliction, rather than later on."
"But it's rare to test a new drug in an adolescent?"
"I wouldn't go that far, no."
"Dr. Mangan, you testified that Angela's parents were warned about the possible side effects of the drug Mercipine, did you not?"
"Yes."
"What did you tell them?"
"I told them that with any new experimental—"
"Sir, I think you may have misunderstood the question. I'm not talking about experimental drugs in general, but Mercipine in particular."
"I told them there were risks involved in taking the drug, yes."
"Despite its being found safe in healthy human volunteers and in experimental animals?"
"Yes."
"Doctor, why would there be any risk in taking a drug that has been found safe in diabetic animals?"
"Because there is always the possibility that humans might react differently to a given pharmaceutical than would a mouse or guinea pig."
"In other words, doctor, the animal tests are essentially useless, isn't that true?"
"Not at all. A drug that causes liver or kidney damage in rats, for example, would probably do the same in humans."
"Well, would you say they are reliable indicators of human toxicity or not?"
"Most of the time, yes."
"But not in the case of Mercipine."
"It's too early to conclude that."

"It's not too early in the case of Angela Calvecchi, sir, wouldn't you agree?"

"Objection, your honor!"

"Sustained, Mr. Allen. Sustained."

"Dr. Mangan, did you tell Angela's parents there was a finite chance of death associated with taking this drug despite its safety record in animals?"

"Not in those exact words."

"What did you tell them, exactly?"

"I told them that the odds of a young, basically healthy patient like Angela being seriously harmed by this medication was very small. But that it was a possibility."

"A possibility like in being struck by lightning?"

"I may have said that. I don't remember."

"Sir, you gave Angela's parents a waiver to sign, isn't that right?"

"I instructed my nurse to do so, yes."

"Is this a copy of that document, which has been introduced by defense counsel as Exhibit A?"

"It appears to be, yes."

"And were the Calvecchis afforded a chance to read that waiver before they signed it, doctor?"

"Yes, of course."

"Have *you* read this document, doctor?"

"Yes, I have."

"Doctor, I've read this document, too. It took me twenty minutes and I'm still not sure I understand everything in there."

"They could've taken it to a lawyer."

"Do most patients or their parents do that?"

"No."

"Why not?"

"I suppose they trust their physicians to be honest with them and they want to get on with it. Or, in some cases, they don't want to know about the risks."

"And they didn't even get a copy of the thing. Isn't that what you said earlier?"

"No, I didn't say that."

"But, in fact, they didn't get a copy, isn't that true?"

"They were supposed to get one. I learned later that they left without it. It was an oversight on the part of my nurse."

"Has she been with you long, doctor?"

"Six years."

"Aren't you required by law to give the parents of a minor a copy of this document?"

"Yes, and we almost always do. Like I said, it was an oversight."

"Dr. Mangan, looking back on what happened to Angela Calvecchi, would you have prescribed Mercipine for her?"

"Objection, your honor! This is another of counsel's hypothetical—"

"Sustained."

"Then let me ask you this: other than young Angela Calvecchi, did you prescribe Mercipine to any other of your patients?"

"Objection."

"On what grounds?"

"Irrelevant, incompetent, and immaterial."

"Overruled."

"Thank you, your honor. Please answer the question, sir."

"No. I didn't."

"Why not?"

"Well, for one thing, I don't have all that many diabetic patients . . . ."

"Did it have anything to do with your uncertainty about the safety of the drug?"

"Objection. Counsel is badgering the witness."

"I'll hear the answer, counselor."

"I don't know the answer to that, Mr. Allen. I sometimes wait awhile before giving a new drug to a second patient in a clinical study."

"To see how it went the first time?"

"Yes."

"Thank you, sir. Your honor, I'm finished with this witness."

"Mr. St. Clair, any re-direct?"

"Only a few more questions, your honor."

"Proceed."

"Thank you, judge. Dr. Mangan, did you have a good relationship with your patient, Angela Calvecchi?"

"Very good, I'd say."

"Do you attribute that to any particular set of circumstances, doctor?"

"She was very smart, and she wanted to be a physician. Every time I saw her she had a lot of questions about everything she saw, everything I did, even about medical school and beyond. We had plenty to talk about."

"Would you say you got to know Angela pretty well?"

"I'd say so, yes."

"Despite the fact that she was a minor, do you feel, Doctor Mangan, that Angela understood the consequences of her participation in a clinical study of this type?"

"As I said earlier, Angela was a special patient. She was mature beyond her years. It was almost like talking to an adult. When she asked me to include her in the study—well, you had to be there, I suppose, to see the hope in those big, brown eyes. She was pleading for a chance. She wanted so much to get well. But it was more than that: she wanted to do it for others like herself who suffered from her affliction. By participating in this study, it was as if—as if she were already a physician. Her own physician. She was a remarkable child . . . ."

"And did she ever tell you that *she* understood the risks involved?"

"Objection!"

"Sustained."

"Thank you, sir. No further questions."

"Mr. Allen?"

"It seems clear from your testimony, Dr. Mangan, that if young Angela had lived, she would've gone on to become a great doctor. Is that your impression?"

"Yes, I believe she would have."

"No further questions, your honor."

"Court stands adjourned until two o'clock this afternoon."

*

"How did you know he didn't prescribe Mercipine to anyone else?"

"Just a hunch. He seems like a decent sort."

"Mrs. W liked the answer."

"I'm not sure that works in our favor or theirs. What about the rest of them?"

"Not much of a reaction either way."

"Maybe they're becoming saturated."

"I know. There's a lot here for them to take in. Maybe we ought to ease up a bit."

"Not until we see the whites of their eyes. Well, I've got something to do. See you at two."

"What—no invitation to lunch?"

"Nope."

"Sounds good to me!"

*

"Don't tell me—a dozen roses."

"That's right."

"Red or yellow?"

"Red."

"Aha! The romance with Ms. White is beginning to flourish!"

"No, they're not for her."

"Oh. So what's the address this time?"
"Do you have to be so smug about it?"
"Hey, I couldn't care less. You're keeping me in business!"

*

"Your honor, defense calls Dr. Ryan Kerr to the stand . . . ."
("Good God—how much did that suit set him back?")
("A thousand if he paid a dime.")
("More like twenty-five hundred, I'd say.")
" . . . Dr. Kerr, what is your official title at Mercer Pharmaceuticals?"
"Vice-president in charge of research and development."
"And are you an M.D. or a Ph.D.?"
"An M.D. with an M.B.A."
"A degree in business administration."
"That's right."
"Dr. Kerr, will you please tell us a little bit about how the Mercer Corporation is organized?"
"To begin with, there are three divisions at Mercer Pharmaceuticals. The first is the research wing, the second is the production facility, and the third is the business office. The function of the Research Division is to come up with new compounds which we hope will prove effective in various medical applications. Once we find a new drug that shows promise in the treatment of a particular disease, we test it for safety and effectiveness, as prescribed by government regulations, and pass it on to the Production Division. But first we have to convince the Financial Division that it's worth spending millions of dollars for development."
"What exactly do you mean by 'development'?"
"Devising a new drug is a lengthy procedure. It takes years. First, the biochemists must either design a new substance for some specific purpose, or isolate some naturally-occurring compound that looks to have some effect on pathogenic bacteria, cancer cells, or whatever. Then there are a series of animal tests designed to find out whether the new 'bullet'—we call them 'bullets'—is as effective as it was thought to be. Then—"
"Excuse me a moment, doctor. Let me just ask you this: Out of a thousand new substances your biologists and chemists come up with, how many are deemed promising enough to go into animal testing?"
"Oh, maybe fifty."
"And of that fifty, how many actually end up in clinical studies?"
"Four or five, if we're lucky."
"And out of *that* number, how many are approved by the FDA?"

"One or two, if any."

"So the development of new pharmaceutical compounds is not only time-consuming, but it's also a very expensive proposition, is it not?"

"Very."

"And what does it cost to bring a new drug from inception to market?"

"Anywhere from two hundred to five hundred million."

"Dr. Kerr, the Mercer Corporation, or anyone else, isn't likely to waste that kind of money on something that appears to be ineffective or unsafe, is it?"

"Objection."

"On what grounds?"

"Counsel is attempting to prejudice the jury. No matter what Mercer and company spends to develop a drug, it doesn't necessarily mean that the drug is safe, or that they never cut corners or make mistakes."

"I see your point, Mr. Allen, but I'll allow counsel to finish this line of questioning. I want to see where he's going."

"Thank you, your honor. In fact, Dr. Kerr, it would be a monumental waste of time, effort, and money to put an unpromising compound into clinical testing, let alone full-scale production, wouldn't it?"

"Yes, and besides that, the FDA wouldn't allow us to proceed with something that was ineffective or unsafe."

"Dr. Kerr, how long has Mercer and company been in business?"

"Over eighty years."

"And how many new pharmaceuticals has the Mercer Corporation produced in, say, the last fifty years?"

"Oh—twenty-five hundred or so."

"And out of that total, have there been any problems?"

"Yes, we've had a few recalls."

"Can you tell us how many?"

"Maybe twenty."

"And that's what—on a percentage basis?"

"Less than one per cent."

"That's a pretty good record, sir, wouldn't you say?"

"Mercer Pharmaceuticals takes great pride in the quality and effectiveness of its products."

"And how many people would you estimate are taking medications made by the Mercer Corporation at this moment?"

"In the U.S., or worldwide?"

"Let's start with the U.S."

"Probably a couple hundred million people."

"That's about two thirds of the total population."

"About, yes."

"Of course that would include non-prescription drugs."

"That's right—painkillers, digestion aids, and all the rest."

"And how many of those people are taking Mercer prescription drugs?"

"Still in the millions. Maybe fifteen to twenty million."

"And how many recalls have there been for prescription drugs in the past year?"

"None."

"None at all?"

"Not a one."

"What about two years?"

"One."

"Five years?"

"Maybe two or three more."

"Because they were unsafe?"

"Two of those weren't as effective as we had hoped they'd be. Another one or two had some unforeseen safety problems."

"Now, doctor, in your experience, when there have been problems with the clinical testing of a new drug, what's usually been the cause of the problem?"

"Well, patient tolerance is probably the biggest factor."

"Meaning that the side effects were greater than expected?"

"Exactly."

"And what other factors enter into this?"

"As I indicated before, effectiveness is another."

"Any other problems?"

"Well, the other major cause of clinical problems would be physician or hospital error."

"Meaning—"

"Physicians and nurses, and of course even pharmacists, sometimes pass out the wrong drug, or prescribe it for the wrong people, or prescribe the wrong dosage—things like that."

"Does that happen often?"

"More often than we'd like."

"So it's a significant problem?"

"Not a major problem, but a significant one, yes."

("My God, the little twerp's going to try to pass it off on the doctor!")

"So if a new pharmaceutical was tested on, say, a thousand people, and there were a dozen or so isolated cases of serious side effects in an otherwise successful trial, would you say it's likely or unlikely that physician error was the cause of the problem?"

("He's only doing his job, Candace. We'd do the same thing in his situation.")

"When you're working with individual cases, there can be individual idiosyncratic reactions to any drug. But given that scenario, I'd say physician error could well be involved."

("But Mangan's their own witness!")

"And this is a common occurrence in this kind of situation?"

("Yes, but he's not here now.")

"No, it's not common. It just happens from time to time. It might not explain all the negative incidents. But it could well explain a portion of them. Of course it's difficult to pinpoint which of the incidents can be attributed to which causes . . . ."

"But physician error is a possible explanation for any given 'incident,' is it not?"

"Of course. Definitely."

"Well, could this explanation account for the death of Angela Calvecchi in particular?"

"It could."

"Could you be more specific?"

"As I said earlier, there could have been some mixup or misunderstanding about the medication. For example, perhaps he shouldn't have told the parents to let Angela take that last dose on a nearly empty stomach. That's one possibility. Or he might not have clearly explained the risks involved in taking an experimental medication."

"Lots of room for possible error, is that what you're saying?"

"Exactly. And at this late date, it may never be possible to know exactly what happened."

"Thank you, sir. No further questions at this time."

"Thank you, Mr. St. Clair. Mr. Al—Sorry, Ms. White will be doing this cross, is that right?"

"No, your honor. I'll be examining the witness."

"My mistake. Please proceed."

"Thank you, your honor. Good afternoon, Dr. Kerr."

"Mm."

"Sir, you testified that it costs a lot of money for a company like Mercer Pharmaceuticals to develop a new drug for human use, did you not?"

"Yes, but that's not news. Everybody knows that."

"That's probably quite true, sir. But the Mercer Corporation is run by human beings, isn't that right? I mean, the CEO isn't an orang-utan or anything like that, is he?"

"Objection, your honor."

"Very droll, counsellor. What point are you trying to make here?"

"I'm coming to that."

"Well, come to it in a different way. Jury will disregard the question about orang-utans at Mercer Pharmaceuticals."

["Ha, ha, ha, ha, ha."]

"Very well, your honor. Dr. Kerr, Mercer Corporation is actually a subsidiary of a German-South African conglomerate known as Ochsenheim Droge Körperschaft, isn't that so?"

"Yes."

"And can you tell us the combined assets of this conglomerate of which the Mercer Corporation is a part?"

"Objection. Totally irrelevant, judge."

"You brought up the financial issue, Mr. St. Clair. Overruled."

"Dr. Kerr?"

"I think the last figure I saw was in the neighborhood of six hundred billion."

"That's a pretty big pharmaceutical company, isn't it, sir?"

"The biggest in the world, I believe."

"And you testified that it costs two hundred to five hundred million dollars to get a new drug on the market, isn't that right?"

"It's in that ballpark, yes."

"That's a lot of marks even for a wealthy corporation like Ochsenheim, isn't it?"

"Well, sure. That's why—"

"Dr. Kerr, would you agree that people who have invested a great deal of money in a project are loathe to give it up, even when evidence comes forth that—"

"Objection!"

"Okay, I see where it's going. Sustained. Jury will disregard."

"Sir, are you familiar with the Congressional mandate of 1997, which urges pharmaceutical companies, and the FDA, to get new drugs out more expeditiously?"

"Objection!"

"Again, sustained. Let's not get into the workings of the United States Congress, Mr. Allen, unless they have to do specifically with the drug in question."

"Yes, your honor. Dr. Kerr, has the Mercer Corporation ever been fined for putting out an unsafe or ineffective drug?"

"Objection, your honor! This line of questioning—"

"Gentlemen, please approach the bench. . . ."

("Mr. Allen, do you know something the court doesn't know?")

("Your honor, the Mercer Corporation has a history of non-compliance with FDA regulations, and such compliance is at the heart of defense's argument in this case.")

("Do you know anything about these violations, Mr. St. Clair?")

("Yes, your honor, we do. But they occurred seven or eight years ago. They are totally irrelevant to these proceedings.")

("Mr. Allen, do you have some evidence for more recent infractions by Mercer Corporation?")

("No, your honor. But Mercer and company was in the process of developing Mercipine at that time!")

("Mr. St. Clair?")

("Your honor, Mercipine was still in the research stage at that point in time. Mercer was never cited for the research they do. The violations of eight years ago were for their production methods and they involved other drugs.")

("I'm going to come down on the side of defense on this one, Mr. Allen. The past is not on trial here. I caution you not to bring this particular matter up in your examination of the witnesses. Now let's get on with this case, shall we?")

("Very well, your honor.")

("Thank you, judge.")

"Mr. Allen, please proceed."

"Dr. Kerr, you testified that a significant problem in the clinical testing of new drugs is 'physician error.' Is that right?"

"I said it was not necessarily a major problem but it could be a significant one, yes."

"Sir, do you have some evidence that Angela Calvecchi's physician, Dr. Richard Mangan, gave her the wrong drug, or the wrong dosage of the drug?"

"Well, no. But he may have been less than prudent in choosing a thirteen-year-old girl for the Mercipine trial."

"So your specifications limited the study to older children?"

"Well, no, but he was pushing the limits with that one."

"But that age was permitted by the protocol, was it not?"

"That's true, but there would have to be unusual circumstances for a physician to put a patient that young in the clinical trial."

"Well, did the protocol preclude his doing so?"

"Not in so many words. But it specified extra precautions in the case of adolescents."

"Such as . . . ?"

"The adolescent should have a well-developed case of diabetes which would likely become debilitating at some later date. Other than that, of course, the patient was required to be in good general health."

"Sir, do you have any evidence that Angela's health would have precluded her participation in the clinical trial?"

"No."

"Well, do you have some evidence that Angela would not have 'become debilitated at some later date'?"

"Well, no, not exactly."

"In other words, sir, Dr. Mangan proceeded according to the protocols established by your own company in administering Mercipine to little Angela Calvecchi, did he not?"

"I'm not saying he did anything wrong. I'm saying there is the *possibility* that he *might* have done something wrong in this particular case."

"In other words, Dr. Kerr, if there was some problem with this drug, the blame almost certainly lies with the Mercer Corporation, isn't that true?"

"Objection!"

"Sustained."

"Your honor, plaintiffs would like to submit the Mercipine protocol sheet as Plaintiffs' Exhibit 5."

"Any objection, Mr. St. Clair?"

"No, your honor."

"So ordered."

"And finally, sir, when was the last time you visited the animal testing facilities at Mercer and company?"

"Objection!"

"Sustained. Take a different route, counselor."

"Certainly, your honor. No further questions of this witness."

"Any re-direct, Mr. St. Clair?"

"Yes, your honor. Dr. Kerr, how long does it take a new drug to go from conception into the marketplace?"

"Ten to fifteen years, on average."

"And how long did it take Mercipine to make this journey?"

"Twelve years, give or take a month or two."

"Hardly a hurryup job, wouldn't you say so, sir?"

"I wouldn't argue with that."

"No further questions, your honor."

"Mr. Allen?"

"Again, sir, you testified that a typical drug costs two hundred to five hundred million dollars to market?"

"Yes, I've already testified twice to that."

"And how much did it cost to get Mercipine, specifically, into the clinical trial?"

"I'd have to check on that."

"Well, was it in that box?"

"It was a bit higher, I believe."

"A billion?"

"Probably not that much. I don't remember."

"A billion and a half?"

"Objection!"

"Sustained."

"An *enormous* investment to lose, wouldn't you say, sir?"

"Objection!"

"No further questions."

"Very well. In view of the hour, court stands adjourned until tomorrow morning at ten o'clock."

*

"Good afternoon, my friend. According to our previous arrangement, I believe the time is up on your joke moratorium."

"Oh, hello, 'Seinfeld.' All right—here's ten bucks. Don't tell me any jokes for another month."

"If you say so. But all work and no play . . ."

"Yeah. So I've heard."

*

"Marc! Hey, Marc!"

"Oh, hello, McBain. How are you?"

"Marc, I'd like you to meet a friend of mine."

"Hello."

"Hi! So you're Marcus Allen!"

"Maybe. Who are you?"

"Diedre Barker. Wow! This is my lucky day!"

"Probably not. Well, it was nice to meet you, Diedre. So long, McBain."

"I think you're great. I've been reading about the Mercer case in the papers. It's about time somebody got an animal rights case like this in court."

"Animal ri—No. This isn't a case about animal rights. It's in the courts because the Mercer Corporation may have violated certain FDA requirements. It's strictly a matter of law."

"Sure, and it's about time the laws were changed."

"You may be right. But—"

"Kids, I've got to run. So long, Diedre. Catch you later, Marc."

"Can I help? Can I do something for you?"

"Not—Hey. I was about to go out for some dinner. You want to talk about it?"

"Sure! But I don't want—"

"No imposition at all. I'd like to get your point of view on all this. Besides, I hate to eat alone."

"So do I!"

"Maybe afterwards you can come back to my apartment and meet my cat. She's an animal, and she definitely demands her rights!"

"I'd love to meet your cat!"

*

"Marc! This just came in by fax!"

"What the hell is it?"

"It's a document showing that Szybalski was asked to review the Dalrymple paper before it was published!"

"What 'document'? What are you talking about?"

"Look at it! It's a letter signed by Szybalski indicating that he reviewed the paper and, except a few minor suggestions, approved it for publication."

"How did you find out about this?"

"I didn't! It just came!"

"Well, what's the fax number at the top?"

"'Unidentified.'"

"It looks like we have an angel watching over us."

"Or maybe somebody at Mercer doesn't like what's been going on there."

"Partner, you look like the cat who— Do you know anything about this?"

"I didn't put her up to it, if that's what you mean. She's sort of an undercover agent working for an animal rights group."

"Who is?"

"Hey, I don't ask you about your social life!"

"All right, touché. Let's just hope the judge doesn't ask us where we got this thing . . . ."

*

"Mr. St. Clair?"

"Your honor, defense calls Dr. Menslew Szybalski to the stand."

" . . . Proceed."

"Thank you, judge. Sir, is the 'doctor' an M.D. or a Ph.D. degree?"

"It's actually two Ph.D.'s. One is in chemistry, and the other in bioengineering. I'm a scientist, I don't practice medicine."

"Dr. Szybalski, as head of Mercer Pharmaceuticals' Research Division, what is your role in the production of new medications for human use?"

"My job is to supervise the research that leads to that production. In other words, I'm responsible for our division coming up with new pharmaceutical compounds, from conception all the way through the testing phase."

"And in simple layman's terms, what does that involve?"

"Primarily, we synthesize all manner of derivatives of compounds that are already known to have some beneficial effect on humans. We also—"

"Can you please explain to the jury what a 'derivative' is?"

"It's just what it sounds like. You take a molecule and you make some small change in its structure. The second one is derived from the first. Sometimes that makes for a more effective drug. Or a safer one."

"Please go on."

"We also screen compounds obtained from various plant and microbial sources for their biological effects."

"How does that work, exactly?"

"Well, for example, we obtain thousands of plant extracts every year from all over the world, and we try to find if there are any useful compounds we can obtain from these plants."

"Go on."

"In some cases we synthesize totally new compounds that we think, based on their expected properties, might be effective in the treatment of certain human diseases."

And can you tell the court how the effectiveness of a given drug is determined?"

"Very simple. In the case of an antibiotic, for example, once the bullet has been isolated and characterized, we infect certain animal hosts with the infectious organism we want to destroy, then find out whether the antibiotic renders the animal free of the infection. All this after a lot of test tube and Petri dish studies to ascertain what types of organism are killed by the substance in question."

"And, in fact, doctor, it's much more complex than that, isn't it?"

"Much more. Once we determine that the compound works, we have to establish the optimal dose of the antibiotic, the best route of administration—whether it is best injected into the blood stream, or into a muscle or the peritoneal cavity, or given orally—how stable the antibiotic is in the animal, and what are the breakdown products and all that. And then we need to know whether the stuff kills all of the pathogen that's around or whether the bug comes back once the antibiotic is no longer present—those are the kinds of things that we need to find out. And of course whether the material is toxic to the host or not, and if it is, how toxic. Or whether it interacts in some negative fashion with other common drugs, and so on. And, if so, can it be modified to make it less toxic. All this takes a very long time."

"And regardless of whether you're developing an antibiotic or an anti-cancer agent or anything else, the procedure is essentially the same, is that correct?"

"There are differences in technique, but the idea is the same: how effective is the bullet and how toxic is it to the host."

"When you say 'host,' doctor, you mean either the animal or the human patient, isn't that right?"

"That's correct."

"Now in the case of the drug you call Mercipine, how was its effectiveness determined?"

"In the usual way. By checking blood and urine sugar values, primarily. As well as exercise stress tests and so on."

"Very well, sir. Now can you tell us how a drug's toxicity is determined?"

"In that regard, we have very little leeway. The FDA prescribes what has to be done to test a compound for toxicity."

"And does this involve animal testing?"

"Yes, of course. We are required to test for toxicity in one rodent species and one non-rodent species."

"Is any particular non-rodent species specified by the FDA?"

"No. That choice is left up to the scientists."

"And the numbers of animals used in the tests?"

"That depends on the drug. At all events, we don't use as many animals as we used to because our tests have become more sophisticated. We might use on the order of a hundred mice or rats, less in the case of dogs or other large animals."

"Now doctor, with regard to Mercipine in particular, were all the tests for effectiveness and toxicity carried out to the full letter of the law?"

"Of course. All our drugs are thoroughly tested for effectiveness and safety before they go on to clinical trials."

"And was Mercipine found to be effective in the pre-clinical tests?"

"Yes. Those studies were very promising."

"In what way was the drug found to be effective?"

"Out of a hundred mice, seventy percent were effectively normalized, and another twenty-five percent were benefited by the drug."

"What about those other five mice?"

"They showed no significant improvement. But a ninety-five percent success rate is an excellent indication of effectiveness by anyone's standards."

"And what about the safety studies?"

"Mercipine was tested on both rats and rabbits and found to be extremely safe in both cases."

"No toxicity at all to either species?"

"None at all. Only at the highest doses was any negative effect found with rabbits. None with rats."

"How high?"

"Massive doses. We are required by law to do this."

"How massive?"

"It would be like a human being eating a watermelon-size pill every day."

"Wouldn't be very easy to swallow, would it, doctor?"

"Ha, ha, ha! No. Not at all."

"And can you describe for the court the 'negative effect' found in rabbits?"

"Yes. There was some hair loss."

"No effect on any other organs?"

"Autopsies showed no effect on any of the animal tissues."

"And that includes the heart?"

"That includes the heart and all the other organs."

"And there were no deaths in that study."

"No. None."

"And the procedures that Mercer used in these tests were fully in accord with FDA requirements?"

"Yes, of course."

"And all the tests and all the documents to support those tests for safety and effectiveness were submitted to and approved by this agency of the federal government, is that right?"

"Yes."

"If it please the court, we submit these documents as Defense Exhibit D."

"Mr. Allen?"

"No objection, your honor."

"Clerk will enter the documents."

"So both Mercer Pharmaceuticals and the federal Food and Drug Administration concluded that this was a very safe and effective medication for the treatment of Type I diabetes, isn't that right, sir?"

"Yes. Absolutely."

"Thank you, doctor. No further questions, your honor."

"Mr. Allen?"

"Your honor, Ms. White will be examining this witness."

"Counsel likes to keep the court guessing. Proceed, Ms. White."

"Thank you, your honor. And good morning, sir."

"Good morning."

"Dr. Szybalski, in your opinion did Mercer Pharmaceuticals comply with the letter *and the spirit* of the FDA requirements for the testing of the drug Mercipine for use in human patients?"

"Of course. Undoubtedly."

"And are you familiar with the wording of the requirements for toxicity testing which must be complied with before a new experimental drug can go into clinical trials with human beings?"

"The exact wording?"

"Yes. What the FDA regulations are, specifically."

"More or less. I haven't memorized the whole thing. It's an enormous document."

"Well, can you tell the court what the FDA requires from a pharmaceutical company in order to determine whether a new drug is safe for human use?"

"I've already testified to that. The FDA requires determining the toxicity, if any, of any new compound in a rodent species and a nonrodent species."

"Plus autopsies on the animals and all that?"

"To determine organic and microscopic effects, yes."

"Your honor, at this time, plaintiffs would like to enter into the record Plaintiffs' Exhibit Six, the Federal Food, Drug and Cosmetic Act of 1997."

"Well it's about time someone introduced this thing. So ordered."

"Doctor, I'm going to hand you a copy of this exhibit, which, among many other things, lists the FDA requirements for such toxicity testing, and ask you to read the portion highlighted in red."

"Uh—'Before any clinical testing of a new drug is undertaken, the manufacturer or sponsor of the investigation shall submit reports showing that the safety and effectiveness of such drug is adequate to justify the proposed clinical study.'"

"Thank you. And this section, also highlighted in red, please."

"'The investigator shall submit all reports of basic information, certified by the applicant to be accurate reports, necessary to assess the safety of the drug for use in clinical investigation.'"

"Thank you. What interests me about this language, as I'm sure it does you, sir, are the parts that require the applicant, namely the drug company, to submit reports 'necessary to assess the safety of the drug for use in clinical investigation,' and also the one requiring 'reports showing that the safety and effectiveness of the drug is adequate to justify the proposed clinical study.' In other words, besides the technical requirement for the use of a rodent and a non-rodent species, the FDA requires the drug company to actually *demonstrate* that the drug is safe in humans prior to the clinical testing. Do you agree with that assessment?"

"Well, I—sure. Of course."

"In other words, sir, if you used the required kinds of animals, and didn't prove the drug was safe for human trials, you would not have complied with the FDA regulations, isn't that so?"

"Objection!"

"On what grounds?"

"Counsel is trying to confuse the witness. Dr. Szybalski is not a lawyer, and his function is not to interpret the language of the FDA requirements. The requirements are to use a rodent and a non-rodent species, and Mercer Pharmaceuticals complied to the letter with that provision."

"Overruled. Let's not oversimplify the issue, Mr. St. Clair."

"Dr. Szybalski?"

"That's not my interpretation of the regulations."

"Isn't it, sir? Don't the regulations stipulate the use of '*at least* one rodent and one non-rodent species?'"

"Yes, but only one rodent species is actually required."

"But you could do more if you wished? I mean the regulations do not *preclude* your using two or three species, do they?"

"Well, no."

"Then let me ask you another question: Suppose you had used rabbits and *two* rodent species to test the safety of Mercipine in the laboratory. And let's suppose further that the drug had no effect in the first rodent, let's say a rat, but was extremely toxic to the other, let's say a guinea pig. Would you ignore all the dead guinea pigs and report to the FDA that the drug was safe because you tested it on rats and rabbits?"

"Objection! All this is pure speculation!"

"Overruled."

"Dr. Szybalski?"

"No, of course not."

"And similarly, if you had tested the drug *only* on rats and not on guinea pigs as your rodent species, you would report to the FDA that you had a very safe drug for your clinical trial, even though it actually was not, isn't *that* true?"

"Well, I suppose so, but if there were some reason to suspect that guinea pigs would be sensitive to the drug, we would use those, too. Or instead of the rats."

"Dr. Szybalski, what animal species did you, in fact, use to assess the toxicity of Mercipine?"

"I already testified to that, but I'll say it again: we used rats and rabbits."

"No guinea pigs? Or cats?"

"No."

"And was the use of rabbits for the toxicity study *your* decision?"

"Well, not personally. The laboratory chief, Dr. Chang, made that decision."

"Dr. Szybalski, I show you now what I believe to be the appropriate forms specifying the use of rats and rabbits for the toxicity testing of Mercipine. Are these those forms?"

"Yes. Signed by Dr. Chang. Right here, see?"

"Thank you. And on the next page, we see that the order was countersigned by Dr. Menslew Szybalski. Is that your signature, sir?"

"Well, yes, but—"

"Your honor, we would like to introduce this form as Plaintiffs' Exhibit Seven."

"Defense counsel?"

"Your honor, defense sees no relevance—"

"Court sees the relevance, counselor, unless you're suggesting that the document and the signatures thereon are forged."

"No, your honor."

"Clerk will enter the document as Plaintiffs' Exhibit—uh—what is it . . . ?"

"Seven, your honor."

"Plaintiffs' Exhibit Seven. Please proceed."

"Thank you, judge. Sir, are you aware of a series of papers coming from the laboratory of Dr. Joseph Dalrymple at the Waring Institute in Philadelphia?"

"Dalrymple . . . Dalrymple . . . Yes, in general."

"And could you summarize their finding for the court?"

"Well, they reported a couple of years ago that cats and—uh—amphibians, I believe, are better indicators than rats of the negative effects of certain drugs on the heart."

"And what about guinea pigs, Dr. Szybalski?"

"They may have mentioned guinea pigs. I don't remember."

"And were you aware of these papers at the time of your decision to use rats as your rodent species for the testing of Mercipine for its possible effects on the heart and other organs?"

"No. I was not. They came out after we had already done those tests and reported the results to the FDA."

"And when was that?"

"Um, let's see . . . October of '98, I think."

"Dr. Szybalski, I now show you the first paper coming out of Dr. Dalrymple's laboratory. Your honor, this will be Plaintiffs' Exhibit Eight."

"Very well. Clerk will enter."

"Objection, your honor—this is the same report you rejected yesterday!"

"There was no relevance yesterday, Mr. St. Clair. In the present context, there is."

"Thank you, judge. Sir, does this paper look familiar to you?"

"It looks like a scientific publication, yes."

"And can you tell the court when this paper was published?"

"It was published in the *Lancet* in December of 1998."

"So you were, in fact, aware of this paper when the rat experiments were set up at Mercer."

"No. I told you: Those were already finished by December of '98!"

"Dr. Szybalski, who decides which papers are accepted for publication in the medical journals?"

"Your honor—"

"Overruled."

"The editor of the journal, I suppose."

"All on his own?"

"No, he sends out papers to be reviewed by other members of the scientific community."

"Sir, do you ever review scientific papers that are under consideration for publication?"

"Not very often. That's usually done by academic scientists."

"Dr. Szybalski, did you ever review a paper by Dr. Dalrymple?"

"Perhaps. I'm not sure."

"Let me refresh you memory. I have a cover letter signed by you and dated June 29, 1998. Your honor, we'd like to enter this document as Plaintiffs' Exhibit Nine."

"So ordered."

"Where did you get that??"

"Dr. Szybalski, do you recognize your signature on this letter?"

"Well—uh—yes, it's mine. I had forgotten all about this. But the paper was not reviewed by me. It was reviewed by another scientist at Mercer under my name."

"I see. Sir, is this practice condoned by the scientific community?"

"Objection, your honor! Dr. Szybalski is not on trial here!"

"Sustained. Get to the point, counselor."

"Sir, was the person who actually refereed that paper a member of your group?"

"I believe he was, yes."

"And who was that person, do you remember?"

"I believe it was my associate, Dr. Chang."

"Ah, the hardworking Dr. Chang. And did he discuss the review with you at all?"

"We may have discussed it. I don't remember."

"Dr. Szybalski, if you *had* read that paper, the one you signed off on, would you have used rats and rabbits for these tests rather than the recommended cats or guinea pigs?"

"Objection! Counsel is yet again asking for endless speculation on the part of the witnesses!"

"Sustained."

"Dr. Szybalski, given the negative effects so far reported for Mercipine—"

"Objection!"

"Sustained."

"Your honor, plaintiffs have no further questions of the witness at this time."

"Mr. St. Clair? Any re-direct?"

"We sure do, your honor. Dr. Szybalski, at the time the toxicity tests were done, rats and rabbits were the accepted animals for testing compounds that affect blood sugar levels, isn't that right?"

"Absolutely."

"And even if you had known about these other recommendations, they weren't confirmed or generally accepted at the time, isn't that also true?"

"Yes."

"And, in any case, the FDA accepted the toxicity studies, did it not?"

"Yes, of course."

"And therefore Mercer Pharmaceuticals complied with the requirements imposed by law in these tests, correct?"

"As far as I'm concerned, that's quite correct."

"Thank you, sir. No further questions."

"Ms. White?"

"Dr. Szybalski, was there ever any discussion at Mercer and company to go back and repeat the toxicity studies using cats or guinea pigs?"

"Objection, objection, objection!"

"On what grounds, Mr. St. Clair?"

"Several. First, it's the worse kind of speculation, the kind based on hindsight. Second, it's irrelevant given FDA approval of the drug for the clinical trial."

"Ms. White, do you have any evidence to support this speculation?"

"No, your honor. But—"

"I'm going to sustain this one, counselor."

"No further questions, your honor."

"Court stands in recess until two o'clock this afternoon."

*

"Well done, partner! I may let you do all the interrogating from now on."

"Thanks, Marc."

"Mrs. W. loved it! She even chuckled once when you trapped Szybalski on the dates. She doesn't seem to like him much."

"Who does? Did you know he's on his fifth wife?"

"I feel sorry for her. He's cold as a witch's—Well, never mind. How are you feeling after all that work?"

"Fine. Why?"
"No reason. I was wondering . . . ."
"Wondering what?"
"Maybe we can just be friends?"
" . . . . Sure. Why not?"
"Good! How about some lunch, friend?"
"Thanks, Marc, but my cat's sick. I've got to take him to the vet."
"You've got a cat?"
"Yes. Why?"
"So do I!"
"So do a lot of people."
"Maybe your cat would like to meet my cat."
"He might, but I'm taking him in to be put down."
"Oh. I'm sorry. He must be pretty old, then?"
"No. Only six. He developed a tumor on his liver."
"I'm sorry to hear that."
"Thank you. I've got to go. See you at two . . . ."
"Would you like me to go with you?"
"Thanks, but you need to be here in case I get stuck in traffic."
"Maybe *you'd* like to meet my cat sometime."
"I don't think so. He'd probably remind me too much of Winston."
"He's a she."
"Sorry, she. See you later, partner."
"Should I save you a sandwich or something?"
"No, thanks. I'll be okay. I've got to run. See you later!"
"Maybe you'd like to meet my father? *My mother? MY BROTHER* . . . ?"

*

"Mr. St. Clair, please call your next witness."
"Your honor, defense calls Dr. Marcia O'Rourke to the stand."
" . . . I do."
"State your full name and occupation for the court, please."
"Marcia Melissa O'Rourke, M.D. Associate Director of Minskoff and O'Rourke."
"Dr. O'Rourke, you're a medical doctor?"
"Yes, I am."
"And how long have you been Associate Director of Minskoff and O'Rourke?"
"Five years."
"Doctor, would you tell us please what sort of work your company does?"

"Yes. We're a corporate research organization. Commonly known as a CRO. Our primary function is to supervise the clinical testing of new drugs produced by American pharmaceutical companies."

"And how many clinical testing protocols has your company supervised since you took the helm?"

"We're approaching the hundred mark."

"And a drug called Mercipine is on that list?"

"Yes, that's right."

"Dr. O'Rourke, exactly what does Minskoff and O'Rourke do when a new pharmaceutical compound like Mercipine comes down the pike?"

"It's our job to farm out the clinical tests to a list of physicians who are either family practitioners or who specialize in some aspect of medicine that the new drug addresses itself to."

"So you administer what is known in the industry as 'clinical trials,' is that correct?"

"That's correct."

"And what do clinical trials involve?"

"Just what the name implies. Before going on the market, a new pharmaceutical must be tested for any harmful effects it might have in human beings. In phase one, low doses are given to ten or twelve healthy volunteers. If that works out okay, another hundred or so volunteers are given increased doses and for a longer period of time. In stage three, the drug is administered to a thousand patients, some of whom may be in the later stages of the illness against which the drug is targeted."

"Any heart irregularities found in stages one or two?"

"No. No significant abnormalities were found."

"And are all these 'phases' regulated by the government?"

"Oh, yes. We come under FDA regulations just as does the company that produces the drug in the first place. We simply carry out the next step in the overall process."

"Why don't the drug companies administer the clinical tests themselves?"

"Some do. Most don't because they're not specialists in this aspect of the procedures. There's an enormous amount of paperwork involved. Most pharmaceutical companies find it less expensive to farm out the administration of the clinical trials than to do it themselves. This leaves them free to focus on what they do best—produce more and better drugs."

"Are there any other options to the administration of a clinical trial? Other than the company producing the medication, or a CRO, I mean?"

"Often a new compound is tested in a university environment, usually at a large medical center where there are many patients at all stages of an affliction to choose from."

"And what's the advantage of a corporate research organization over a large medical center?"

"Efficiency. Clinical testing is our only business."

"And exactly how are the clinical trials set up?"

"Well, for more general medical problems, such as testing a new medication for the flu—something like that—we invite doctors in family practice in all parts of the country to participate."

"And besides family practitioners, you also have lists of specialists in various fields of medicine, isn't that right?"

"Yes."

"And how does a specialist get on one of your lists?"

"Well, he should be not only a licensed practitioner, but one who is an expert in one area of medicine or another."

"And how did Dr. Mangan get on the list?"

"Dr. Mangan is a pediatrician, and a very good one. I believe he has a several diabetes patients in his practice, or the pediatric clinic he is associated with does. The protocols were sent to all the practicing physicians in that clinic."

"And how do you determine which patients are to participate in a clinical trial?"

"We don't. That is left entirely to the discretion of the physicians who choose to take part in the study."

"And do these physicians report directly to you on the progress of these studies, or do they send the information to the FDA?"

"To us. We act as a sort of liaison between the participating physicians and the FDA, as well as between the physician and the pharmaceutical company."

"They report to you and *you* report to the FDA."

"That's correct, yes."

"Why don't the participating physicians report their results directly to the FDA?"

"It's more efficient all around for a CRO, or a university, to manage a clinical trial and to catalog the results before they are forwarded to the regulatory agency."

"The 'regulatory agency' being the Food and Drug Administration."

"That's right."

"Now, Dr. O'Rourke, is there any requirement for a physician to report any problems arising from the use of an experimental pharmaceutical compound? For example, if someone in the program dies, does the doctor have to report this to you immediately?"

"He or she has thirty days to notify us of such an event."

"And in the case of the compound known as Mercipine, did Dr. Mangan notify you of the death of Angela Calvecchi within the thirty-day time frame as required?"

"Yes, he did."

"And, so far, how many patients were treated with Mercipine and how many deaths have been reported to you?"

"The protocols called for the phase three testing of this drug on a thousand patients suffering from Type I diabetes. We ended up with nine hundred seventy-nine. Out of that number, there have been nine deaths reported."

"Is that an unusually high number of deaths resulting from the clinical testing of an experimental drug?"

"Not at all. It's often somewhat higher."

"Why is that, doctor?"

"Because many of the patients who take part in an experimental program are people in the latest stages of the disease, and the new drug is their last hope. Many would have died regardless of the treatment they received."

"And were any patients in the terminal stages of the disease in the Mercipine trial?"

"Several, yes."

"Doctor O'Rourke, do all your data suggest to you that Mercipine is a safe substance when compared to other experimental medications?"

"I would say so, yes."

"And what about the effectiveness of the drug?"

"The early results suggest improvement in a number of cases. But it's too early to reach a definitive conclusion. The trials are still ongoing."

"And finally, doctor, did Minskoff and O'Rourke file all the necessary reports on a timely basis to the Food and Drug Administration?"

"Yes, of course."

"And have there been any complaints about these reports by the FDA?"

"No, none at all."

"In other words, your organization, the doctor, and the Mercer Corporation all complied explicitly with FDA requirements in this matter, correct?"

"Yes. That's correct."

"Thank you. No further questions at this time."

"All right, Mr. St. Clair. Mr. Allen, do you anticipate a lengthy cross-exam?"

"Fairly lengthy, your honor, but not ridiculously so."

"I'm happy to hear that, counselor. Let's see if we can finish with this witness today."

"I'll try, your honor. "Doctor O'Rourke, I'm a little puzzled by some of your earlier testimony, and I wonder if you could straighten me out on a few things."

"I'll try."

"Good. To begin with, could you tell me whether the 'O'Rourke' of 'Minskoff and O'Rourke' refers to you?"

"Your honor, this isn't relevant."

"Mr. Allen, do you have something concrete in mind here?"

"I'm getting at the direct involvement of Dr. O'Rourke with the Mercipine trial, your honor."

"Overruled for the moment."

"Thank you. Shall I repeat the question, doctor?"

"That won't be necessary. The company was founded by my uncle, Jeffrey O'Rourke, along with Arthur Minskoff. But I have been assuming more of the responsibility of the business as my uncle Jeff moves closer to retirement."

"So you're not one of the partners in this enterprise."

"No. Not yet."

"What is your title and position, exactly?"

"I'm Associate Director in charge of operations."

"And what does that entail?"

"Just like it sounds. My job is to supervise day-to-day operations."

"Meaning that you supervise everyone else in the company?"

"Everyone involved in the collecting and reporting of scientific data, yes."

"What does that *exclude*?"

"Things like accounting, housekeeping, personnel."

"And were you involved with 'collecting and reporting of the scientific data' for the drug Mercipine, specifically?"

"Indirectly, yes."

"Meaning you supervised those employees who were actually doing the paperwork, is that right?"

"Yes."

"So you had nothing to do with which physicians were chosen for the study, or with their reports?"

"Not directly."

"In fact, Dr. O'Rourke, you've never even read the reports submitted by those physicians, have you?"

" . . . . Not all of them, no."

"Well, how many have you read?"

"Objection!"

"Overruled."

"Please answer the question."

"One or two."

"Dr. O'Rourke, were you ever reprimanded by the FDA for failing to get your reports in on time?"

"Objection! Irrelevant and immaterial!"

"Overruled."

"Were you ever reprimanded by the FDA, ma'am?"

"Only once, in 1995."

"And did that involve a drug that was found to be unsafe during its clinical trial?"

"Yes, but there were extenuating circumstances."

"What were they?"

"I was pregnant."

"Are you saying that your personal life came before the lives of the people in the clinical trial?"

"I object to this line of questioning!"

"I think you've made your point counselor."

"I hope so, your honor. Dr. O'Rourke, what was your position in medical school?"

"Excuse me?"

"Were you first in your graduating class? Second? Third?"

"Not that high, no."

"Well, were you last?"

"Objection!"

"Overruled."

"No."

"Do you remember what your rank was in your graduating class?"

"I was seventy-ninth."

"In a class of how many?"

"I don't remember."

"Well, was it a hundred? A thousand?"

"Your honor, if the witness doesn't remember . . ."

"We could obtain this information if necessary, judge."

"That won't be necessary. I believe it was eighty."

"Thank you, Dr. O'Rourke. And is your low standing in your class the reason you chose not to practice medicine but to go into the family business?"

"Objection, your honor! This is *totally* irrelevant to these proceedings! Dr. O'Rourke's professional motivations have nothing to do with this trial!"

"Sustained. Mr. Allen, I think you've beaten this horse enough."

"Very well, your honor. Now doctor, you testified that the specialists who are chosen for a given study are on some kind of 'list,' is that right?"

"Yes, we have lists of specialists."

"And do you ever check the credentials of these specialists, or determine how successful a physician they are, anything like that?"

"No, we don't, and neither does any other CRO. The state does the licensing of physicians, not us."

"So anyone with a medical degree is fair game as a director of an experimental program with human beings?"

"Only if their specialty corresponds with the disease in question."

"And is Angela's doctor, Doctor Mangan, a specialist in the treatment of diabetes?"

"Dr. Mangan is a pediatrician. He specializes in childhood diseases."

"And Type I diabetes is a disease of childhood?"

"Yes. But of course it occurs later in life as well."

"But your CRO decided to allow at least a part of the clinical testing of Mercipine to be carried out in children."

"A few adolescents were allowed into the program, yes."

"And was one of those children Angela Calvecchi?"

"I believe so."

"And you testified that her death was promptly reported to your company by Dr. Mangan, isn't that right?"

"Yes."

"Was it the first such death reported?"

"Yes, it was."

"And when a death like Angela's is reported, do you get a copy of the autopsy report?"

"Yes, we do."

"And what did the autopsy report on young Angela Calvecchi tell you the cause of death was?"

"A heart arrythmia."

"And the second?"

"Same thing. A heart arrythmia."

"And the third?"

"Also an arrythmia."

"Now, Dr. O'Rourke, I believe you testified that there have been nine deaths reported so far in the Mercipine trial, is that right?"

"Yes."

"But other witnesses have reported a figure of seven."

"There have been two more deaths in the last month or so."

"So now the total stands at nine?"

"That's right."

"Well, do you know the cause of death in these latest casualties?"

"Objection!"

"Overruled."

"One was due to heart failure resulting from an arrythmia. The other was from natural causes."

"Natural?"

"Yes. The victim died of a heart attack."

"So out of the nine deaths reported so far, how many resulted from an impaired heart rhythm?"

"Seven."

"Seven of the nine victims died from the same cause, isn't that right?"

"Apparently."

"And that cause was heart failure brought about by an irregular heartbeat, isn't that true?"

"The reports suggest that to be the case, yes."

"Well, do they suggest some other cause?"

"No."

"And Angela Calvecchi died from this same side effect, isn't *that* true?"

"Perhaps, but it hasn't been established that these deaths resulted from the drug treatment."

"You're suggesting it could be pure coincidence?"

"No, of course not. But—"

"Or that the deaths *caused* the irregular heartbeats?"

"Objection!"

"Sustained."

"Dr. O'Rourke, when the fatality reports started coming in, did you recommend to Mercer and company or to the FDA that the clinical trial be stopped?"

"No."

"Why not?"

"That's not our job! Our job is to report the figures back to the pharmaceutical company and on to the FDA! That's *their* decision!"

"And you did that?"

"Yes!!"

"Thank you. No further questions . . . ."

"Perhaps the witness would like a glass of water?"

"I'm fine! I'm fine!"

"Very well. Please proceed, Mr. St. Clair."

"Doctor, we can all sympathize with you for undergoing a b-b-browbeating by counsel for plaintiffs. I just have one or two additional questions for you. First, all requirements of the Food and Drug Administration were followed to the letter in the case of Mercipine, isn't that so?"

"Yes. To the letter."

"And second, all reports made to you by *all* the physicians involved in the clinical trial of this medication were properly filed within the required time periods, isn't *that* true?"

"Yes."

"And finally, all of *your* reports to the FDA concerning the testing of this experimental pharmaceutical were properly filed and within the required time frame, correct?"

"Yes. That's absolutely correct."

"Thank you. No further questions."

"Witness may step down. Court stands adjourned until ten o'clock tomorrow morning."

*

"Hi, Dad."

"Well, look who's here: the prodigal son! Sit down! Sit down!"

"I can only stay for a minute. Just came by to see how you're doing."

"Sure, I understand. You don't want to be here when I kick the bucket."

"Dammit to hell, Dad, you're not kicking anything. Will you stop that?"

"Well, if the disease don't kill me, the drugs will."

"C'mon, Dad, it's not that bad, is it?"

"Not if you consider chronic nausea, mindboggling constipation, total lack of appetite, and a permanent sore mouth to be 'not that bad.'"

"Sometimes things have to get worse before they can get better."

"There's hope for you yet. It's always good for a lawyer to be well-stocked with clichés. Actually, between me and my attorney son, they tell me these new drugs are doing the job. Lousy, stinking things that they are."

"That's what Mom said! But I thought that might just be wishful thinking. That's great!"

"I'll believe it when I see it."

"You've already seen it, Dad!"

"Time will tell. It could turn around at any time. Did you know that most of the cocktail they're giving me is made by Mercer and company?"

"So I've heard. Are you trying to prejudice my case?"

"Not at all. Only presenting the facts, counselor. How's it going, anyway?"

"He stuttered."

"How many times?"

"Once or twice."

"Not enough."

"How many does it take?"

"Five or six. Then you know he's got a thorn in his foot and he can't get it out."

"We've already ordered a fresh supply of thorns."

"I hope they're barbed. How's your girlfriend doing?"

"What girlfriend?"

"Your partner in crime."
"Candace? Nothing happening there."
"You've given up altogether?"
"Not exactly. It's more complicated than that . . . ."
"Isn't it always?"
"This is different."
"How?"
"Trust me, Dad, you don't want to hear it."
"I'm a lawyer. I don't trust anybody."
"All right, you asked for it. She's dying."
"She's *what*?"
"You heard me, Dad."
"What's the matter with her?"
"I don't even know."
"How did you find out?"
"Lew told me."
"I'm sorry, son. I truly am."
"Thanks, Dad."
"Do you think that's why she's been keeping away from you?"
"Not exactly. I think she genuinely dislikes me."
"Maybe she's onto something I've missed. I'd like to meet her sometime."
"Thanks a *lot*, Dad. But she probably wouldn't like you, either."
"No, I suppose not."

"I've got to run. I'm glad you're doing so well. I'll give you a call in a few days. The Mercer thing is winding down. Maybe you and I could go over to Mom's for dinner sometime after that, if you feel like it."

"Let's see if I'm still alive then."

*

"Mr. St. Clair? Please proceed."
"Defense calls Dr. Walter Grossman to the stand . . . ."
"I do."
"Dr. Grossman, good morning."
"Good morning."
"Sir, you're employed by the U.S. Food and Drug Administration, is that right?"
"Yes, that's right."
"Please tell the court how long you've been with that agency."
"Twenty-seven years."
"And your title?"

"Assistant Director."

"During your tenure with the FDA, doctor, did you ever meet a Dr. Robert Small?"

"Not personally, no."

"Professionally?"

"I'm familiar with his work, yes."

"And what can you tell us about his abrupt termination?"

"I've heard—"

"Objection. This smells like hearsay, your honor."

"Sustained."

"Doctor, have you ever been fired by the FDA?"

"Objection, your honor!"

"Sustained. Let's save the levity for the news media, shall we, Mr. St. Clair?"

"Very well, your honor."

("Was that a smile on Mrs. W's face? Or stomach gas?")

("Who knows?")

"Now, Dr. Grossman, several of the previous witnesses have already given testimony as to the role of the Food and Drug Administration in regulating the production, testing, and marketing of pharmaceutical products. I'd just like to ask you this: is the FDA the final arbiter in all these matters, or is there someone above you who approves or disapproves your decisions?"

"Well, of course we ultimately report to Congress. But to answer your question, the buck on all aspects of pharmaceutical production in the United States stops with us. And foods and cosmetics, too, of course, but I realize the latter are not at issue in this trial."

"And it's by Congressional authority that the FDA operates?"

"Yes, that's right. We are granted authority and are funded by Congress."

"So do your regulations have the full authority and power of the law?"

"Absolutely. We establish the regulations and we enforce them."

"And if a company follows your regulations to the letter, and receives your approval to bring a new medication into a clinical trial, their responsibility to the law is satisfied, is it not?"

"Unless there is some evidence of falsification of data, or incomplete or delayed reporting of new information, something like that, yes."

"And in the case of the compound known as Mercipine, produced by the Mercer Pharmaceutical Corporation, all those regulations and laws were precisely followed, were they not?"

"Yes, they were."

"So if, for example, a physician gave the wrong amount of the drug or gave it to the wrong patient, or did anything else that was not according to the protocol set up by the scientists at the Mercer Corporation, then Mercer is not to blame for such a mistake, isn't *that* so?"

"That's quite true. There are other procedures in place to deal with malpractice and all that."

"And similarly, if a patient dies, for whatever the reason, Mercer Pharmaceuticals cannot be held accountable, isn't that also true?"

"Again, unless there is falsification or some other illegal activity of that type, yes, that's also true. Assuming that the patient or his guardian were clearly warned of the possible risks involved, of course."

"Thank you. Doctor Grossman, the FDA requires that all experimental medications be tested for toxicity before they can be administered to human beings, correct?"

"Yes, certainly."

"And can you describe these requirements for the court?"

"The safety of any new drug is as important as its effectiveness. For this reason, all experimental compounds are put through a rigorous program of animal tests to insure that they are not toxic, or are minimally toxic, in the animals tested."

("Is he a robot, or what?")

("No, he's a bureaucrat.")

"Dr. Grossman, why not just test new products directly on humans? At very low doses, say?"

"Too risky. Some chemical compounds are so toxic that they might kill or severely sicken a test subject even at extremely low doses. And even if they weren't toxic at low doses, they might be so at higher levels."

"And how can you be sure that the animals used for the tests reflect what might happen in human subjects?"

"You've probably heard the old saying, "A rat is a dog is a man." We all have essentially the same organ systems and basically the same cellular functions. Something like arsenic, for example, will kill anything, if the dose is high enough. And if something is as toxic as arsenic, we wouldn't want to begin human clinical trials with it, would we? Now, of course there are some chemicals that aren't toxic in rats or dogs, even though they are in humans. But that's an unusual situation, and animal tests are still the most reliable ones we have."

"Well, are there alternatives to animal tests for chemical toxicity?"

"Yes and no. There are some artificial tissues and organs available, and you can do computer simulations and all that, but the fact is that these alternatives are in themselves experimental, and expensive, and are often unreliable. By and large, they are not accepted by the scientific community at the present time, although they may be at some time in the future."

"So as far as the 'scientific community' is concerned—"

"STOP ANIMAL TESTING *NOW!*"
("What the—")
"STOP ANIMAL TESTING *NOW!* STOP ANIMAL—"
"ORDER! ORDER IN THE COURT!"
"—TESTING *NOW!* STOP ANIMAL TESTING—"
"BAILIFF, REMOVE THESE PEOPLE FROM THE COURTROOM!"
"—*NOW!* STOP ANIMAL TESTING—"
"ALL RIGHT . . . THAT'S IT . . . EVERYONE OUT! CHARLIE, GRAB THAT GUY! C'MON, FOLKS, MARCH RIGHT BACK OUT TO WHERE YOU CAME FROM!"
"—*NOW!* . . ."
"That's right, just keep moving and nobody's gonna get hurt. That's right . . . ."
("Marcus, did you have anything to do with this?")
("Of course not! Unless—")
("Unless what?")
("Unless Diedre—")
("Who's Diedre?")
("Never mind. Nobody.")
("Marcus, what the hell are you up to?")
("Nothing! I swear!")
"Lock that door! Who let them in here?"
"I don't know, judge."
"Well, don't let it happen again. Jury will disregard this outburst. Court will take a ten-minute recess."

*

"Partner, who is this 'Diedre'?"
"I told you, you don't know her. Oh, hello, Elmira. Tony."
"This is wonderful, don't you think?"
"What, those demonstrations? No, Elmira, I don't think they did us a whole lot of good."
"But all those people! It must mean that a lot of people think we're right! That animal testing isn't any good, so Mercer shouldn't be putting—"
"No, Tony. That's not the point. What matters is what effect they have on the judge and jury. A lot of people are turned off by things like this. They may think we put the demonstrators up to it, something like that."
"But we didn't . . . . Did we?"
"No, but the jurors don't know that. Did you see their reaction? Some of them looked pretty disgusted."

"Or scared."

"Even so, maybe it will get them to thinking about Mercer's procedures."

"Point is, it makes Mercer look like a victim. Of all the radicals in town. It's more likely that St. Clair is behind it all. Trying to embarrass us."

"Can he do that?"

"He can, and maybe he did. All we know is that it wasn't done by us."

"Oh. We were hoping it was."

*

"Mr. St. Clair, are you ready to proceed with your witness?"

("Whoever was behind those demonstrations, our friend Eddie is enjoying it immensely!")

"Yes, your honor."

("Look at that grin! And his face is redder than ever!")

"Proceed."

("Maybe it *was* him." He's a very smart lawyer.")

("Maybe he outsmarted himself this time.")

"Thank you, your honor. Sir, I was about to ask you whether the scientific community as a whole considers animal testing of new pharmaceutical compounds to be the ultimate evidence for drug safety."

"Yes, of course. There's a long tradition of animal research and testing in pharmaceutical houses. It's an integral part of the whole process."

"And finally, doctor, did Mercer Pharmaceuticals use the proper animal systems in their toxicity tests for Mercipine?"

"Yes, they fulfilled all the animal requirements to the letter."

"And so the clinical trial of Mercipine had the full approval of the federal Food and Drug Administration."

"That's right."

"And have you seen anything in the reports of the clinical tests to negate that approval?"

"No, I haven't."

"Thank you, sir. No further questions at this time."

"Mr. Allen?"

("Okay, partner. Your turn.")

("Me?")

("Go kick some ass.")

("But I'm not prepared for this wit—")

("I think you are.")

("Thank you, Marc!")

"Your honor, my colleague, Ms. White, will conduct the cross-examination of this witness."

"Very well. It appears to be your turn, Ms. White."

"Thank you, your honor. Dr. Grossman, you testified that animal testing is required by the FDA because the scientific community doesn't accept alternatives, is that correct?"

"That's correct. There are some scientists who think that the use of animals as models for human diseases is outmoded and not as productive as some of the alternatives. But most don't agree with that assessment."

"But you are aware, are you not, that there have been several recent reports in the scientific literature criticizing the use of animals as human models and calling for a modernization of the testing programs?"

"As I said, there are some scientists who hold that view."

"In fact, there are quite a few, aren't there? In fact, it's a pretty controversial subject at the moment, wouldn't you agree?"

"Objection, your honor. This case is about Mercer Pharmaceuticals being in compliance with the law, not whether current laws are controversial."

"Objection sustained."

"Sir, how long have pharmaceutical companies been using animals to test drugs for their effectiveness and toxicity?"

"Objection!"

"I'm going to overrule on this one, Mr. St. Clair. You asked virtually the same question."

"Dr. Grossman?"

"I testified already that animal testing enjoys a long tradition of success in this area."

"But it's also had its problems over the years, hasn't it?"

"Yes. And so would any other methodology."

"Dr. Grossman, are you familiar with the name Joseph Dalrymple?"

"Yes, I believe he's a biochemist at the Waring Institute."

"And are you familiar with his work?"

"Objection!"

"On what grounds, Mr. St. Clair?"

"Same ones, your honor. Counsel is trying to raise the issue of the effectiveness of animals testing, which we've shown over and over and over to be irrelevant to these proceedings."

"Is that what this is leading to, Ms. White?"

"No, your honor. We're attempting to show that defendant failed to comply with FDA regulations when they used the *wrong* animals in their tests, thereby compromising the safety reports for Mercipine."

"I'm going to allow you to proceed down that narrow path again, counselor, but don't stray too far off it, please."

"Thank you, your honor. Now doctor, I ask you again: Are you familiar with the published work of Dr. Joseph Dalrymple?"

"Some of it, yes."

"In that case, I'm going to ask you to read a paragraph from the FDA regulations, plaintiffs' Exhibit Six. The part highlighted in red."

"Sure. Uh—'Before any clinical testing of a new drug is undertaken, the manufacturer or sponsor of the investigation shall submit reports showing that the safety and effectiveness of such drug is adequate to justify the proposed clinical study.'"

"Thank you. Sir, would you agree that if the wrong animals are used for toxicity testing, then the corresponding reports assuring the safety of a new drug would not be valid?"

"Not necessarily."

"Why not?"

"Well, there may be a better animal than the one used to assess a drug's safety, but the one that was used might still be adequate."

"Dr. Grossman, is the FDA in the habit of accepting results on safety testing of new drugs in cases where better results could be obtained using other kinds of animals?"

"Objection!"

"Overruled."

"Sir?"

"No, it is not. Such a hypothetical case as you have raised would be extremely rare."

"Then it's safe to assume that if there *was* a case in which a better animal model was available, then the drug company would *not* have shown that 'the safety and effectiveness of such drug is adequate to justify the proposed clinical study,' isn't that true?"

"Objection!"

"Sustained. Let's not get *too* hypothetical, Ms. White."

"Very well, your honor. Let's get back to Dalrymple for a moment. Dr. Grossman, at the time Mercer submitted its safety reports on Mercipine, did the FDA know of Dr. Dalrymple's published paper on the use of cats and guinea pigs as superior to rats and rabbits in determining the safety of certain drugs that can affect heart function?"

"To be honest, I don't know. I'd have to look into the records."

"Well, if Mercer and company knew of these studies at the time they submitted their reports, wouldn't that mean the reports would be invalid?"

"Not necessarily. I don't believe Mercipine was one of the drugs used in the Dalrymple studies."

"But other biphenylmercaptans were used?"

"I believe so, yes."

"And if these studies were known to the Mercer Corporation, shouldn't they have at least tried Mercipine on cats and guinea pigs before submitting their safety reports to the FDA?"

"Your honor . . ."

"I'm going to allow this, Mr. St. Clair."

"Dr. Grossman?"

"Well, this is all hindsight again. We'd have to look very closely at the timing of the reports and the research involved, and exactly how these animals might respond to the drug. But we can't ask a pharmaceutical company to re-test their products every time a paper comes out in the scientific literature."

"But you do require the company to show that the drug is safe for human use as determined by animal testing, isn't that right?"

"Yes, of course."

"Then you would agree, wouldn't you, that in order to fulfill the FDA requirement that Mercer's safety reports were 'adequate to justify the proposed clinical study,' the Mercer people should at least have tried the drug on cats and guinea pigs?"

"I would agree at this point that if they knew about the Dalrymple work at the time, they probably should have used different test animals, yes. But there's no evidence that they knew about these studies when they submitted their reports."

"And if they had done so, and found that Mercipine did, in fact, affect heart function in cats or guinea pigs, the FDA would never have approved this drug for human use, isn't *that* so?"

"Probably not, but as I said, this is all hindsight."

"Thank you very much. No further questions, your honor."

"Mr. St. Clair?"

"Doctor, did the Food and Drug Administration approve the use of Mercipine for human clinical trials or did it not?"

"Yes, we did."

"And in your opinion, the Mercer Pharmaceutical Corporation c-c-complied with every governmental regulation and requirement in the production and testing of this m-m—this medicinal compound?"

"Based on what we knew at the time, yes."

"Thank you, sir. Your honor, defense rests."

"Thank you, Mr. St. Clair. Are you ready to proceed with closing arguments?"

"We are."

"Mr. Allen?"

"No, your honor. We'd like to recall one of the defense witnesses."

"Which one?"

"Dr. Menclew Szybalski."

"Court stands adjourned until this afternoon at two o'clock. I'll see counsel in chambers."

"All rise . . . ."

*

"I never should have worn these new shoes today. Ah—that's better. Marcus, Jr., why do you want to recall defense witness Szybalski?"

"We have reason to believe that Mercer and company has recently repeated the Mercipine safety tests on guinea pigs instead of rabbits."

"What's your point?"

"It means there's a tacit assumption on their part that the original safety tests may have been faulty, Judge Bates."

"Mr. St. Clair, do you object to Mr. Allen's recalling the witness?"

"Of course I do! He had ample time to do that when the doctor was on the stand."

"Mr. Allen, how recent is your information?"

"*Very* recent."

"You didn't have that knowledge when Dr. Szybalski was on the stand?"

"No, your honor."

"All that's going to do, Norma, is to show that Mercer is being more than prudent with the safety studies. It has nothing to do with the law in this case. This is turning into a pissing contest!"

"Well, is counsel for plaintiffs right on this? Has Mercer repeated the safety tests?"

"I don't know, Norma, and that's the God's truth."

"I think I'll let Marcus, Jr. dig his own grave on this. Your request is granted, counselor."

"Thank you, your honor."

"Eddie, can you have the good doctor back here by two o'clock?"

"I'll sure as hell try, your honor."

"Gentlemen, I'll be up front with you. You've both presented strong cases and, in my experience with juries, they could go either way on this one. So I thought I'd offer you both one final chance at reaching a settlement. I think it would get one of you off the hook without too much loss by the other. What say you?"

"Judge Bates, I'll be up front, too. Marcus here has presented a better case than I expected, but—"

"Thanks a lot, Eddie. That's the best lefthanded compliment I've ever had."

"But my client isn't about to cave in on this one. And *my* reading of the jury tells me that they've been paying attention and seem like a reasonable bunch. We'll take our chances on this one."

"Marcus, Jr., do you think you could come down a little on your request?"

"Personally, Judge Bates, I'd be willing to settle for less, and so would my clients. But the Calvecchis won't take any kind of settlement that doesn't involve removal of Mercipine from the market. I think I could get them to settle for the million and a half Eddie has offered, and even a non-disclosure clause, but only if Mercer agrees to end the clinical testing."

"Eddie? Does that sound reasonable?"

"For a possible miracle drug? No way, Norma."

"Going once . . . Going twice . . . All right. And after Szybalski, you're both prepared for closing arguments?"

"Yes, judge."

"We are, your honor."

"Very well. And good luck to each of you."

*

"You told her you had evidence that Szybalski *et al.* had repeated the safety tests on cats and guinea pigs?"

"Yep."

"Who told you that, partner? Was it this 'Diedre'?"

"Nope. I lied."

"You lied?"

"Well, in legal terms, I was bluffing."

"And she went for it?"

"I think she's thinking along the same lines as we are. That if Mercer *didn't* repeat those tests, they damn well should."

"What if Szybalski says he didn't repeat them?"

"Then he's going to look very bad. Terrible, in fact."

"I'm beginning to believe you're a smarter lawyer than I thought."

"I couldn't have done it without you, Candace. Do you think you'd be up to—I mean, do you want to interrogate Szybalski again?"

"Sure. Of course."

"You have the makings of a great lawyer, yourself, partner. Maybe you should present the closing arguments as well."

"No, Marc. This is your show. Besides, Mrs. W seems to like you for some reason. I can't imagine why."

"That reminds me: my father would like to meet you."

"Your father? Why?"

"I've been telling him about your work on this case."
"And?"
"I don't know. I guess he just likes lawyers."
"Well, there's no accounting for taste."
"He likes clichés, too!"
"I *would* like to meet him sometime. Maybe after all of this is over."
"That's good enough for me!"
"Who said you were invited?"

*

"Mr. Allen?"
"No, your honor. It's Ms. White again."
"(Sigh)—Ms. White, you may recall the witness."
"Thank you, your honor. Plaintiffs recall Dr. Menclew Szybalski."
"Court reminds the witness that he is still under oath."
"I know that, judge."
"Dr. Szybalski, I just have one question for you: in light of the reports by Dalrymple *et al.* suggesting that cats and guinea pigs would be better indicators of the toxicity of biphenylmercaptans than rats and rabbits are, has the Research Division at Mercer and company repeated those tests with Mercipine in these animals since the clinical trial was initiated?"
"Objection, your honor. That information has no bearing on this case."
"Thank you, counselor. The court would be interested in hearing the answer."
"Dr. Szybalski?"
"Well . . . Yes, we've recently repeated some of those tests."
"And what were the results, sir?"
"They were inconclusive."
"Inconclusive? How so?"
"There were some problems in guinea pigs, but only one died, and that was an aberration."
"An aberration?"
"Yes. Apparently it died from an infection."
"A bacterial infection?"
"Yes. But this was unrelated to the testing. It had cut itself on a wire sticking out of its cage."
"And no one noticed this?"
"No one noticed the problem until it was too late."
"Does that happen often at Mercer Pharmaceuticals?"
"Not often."

"And this was one out of how many?"

"Twenty."

"And Mercipine caused no serious side effects at all in the other nineteen?"

"There were some skin problems, but no effect on the heart."

"Any other problems?"

"Some loss of kidney and liver function. But Mercipine has not been found to have this effect in humans. So—"

"Sir, these are serious problems, wouldn't you agree?"

"Not necessarily, no."

"What about cats?"

"Cats?"

"You know, sir, those little felines with whiskers? Meow? Did you repeat the toxicity tests on cats?"

"Those tests are in progress."

"Anything to report so far?"

"Out of twenty, two have died. But that doesn't mean much."

"It does if you're one of those two cats!"

"My point is: it doesn't mean that the same thing would happen in human beings!"

"Are you saying that animal tests are invalid models for humans?"

"No! I mean—"

"Dr. Szybalski, you will concede, will you not, that these recent results render the drug suspect for use in humans?"

"Objection, your honor! Witness 'concedes' no such thing."

"Sustained."

"Dr. Szybalski, if you had done these tests in the beginning, would you have recommended the drug for human use?"

"Objection! Counsel insists on engaging in their f-favorite pastime: pure, unadulterated, s-s-speculation."

"And everyone in this courtroom knows this to be a valid speculation! No further questions, your honor."

"Mr. St. Clair?"

"Dr. Szybalski, your revisiting the safety tests was not required by the FDA was it?"

"No."

"Then why did you do it?"

"Because the Mercer Corporation is very concerned about the safety of its products. And we will continue to investigate the safety of Mercipine and every other drug we produce. Regardless of the outcome."

"Thank you, doctor. No further questions."

"Any final questions, Ms. White?"

"Sir, have you reported these recent findings with cats and guinea pigs to the FDA?"

"No."

"Why not?"

"Because they haven't been completed."

"And how long do you estimate it would take to complete them?"

"Several more months, at least."

"Several more months . . . Thank you, Dr. Szybalski. You've been very helpful."

"The witness is excused. Court stands adjourned until ten o'clock tomorrow morning, at which time attorneys will present their closing statements."

*

"Well, I'd better get back to the office and sketch out my closing arguments. I don't suppose you want to kick it around with me over din—I mean——"

"Sorry, got other plans."

"I figured."

"But I'll be home later on. Give me a call if you want to discuss anything."

"Sure. And thanks for all your help."

"You're welcome. Maybe we could work together on another case sometime."

"I truly hope so, counselor."

*

"Hello, Marc. Well, it's up to the jury now, eh?"

"Not quite. What the hell is going on out here, McBain?"

"It's the animal rights people. They've been here ever since they were thrown out of court."

"There weren't *that* many of them."

"Well, a lot of people have stopped to see what all the commotion's about."

"So it seems. By the way, what do you know about that demonstration back there in the courtroom?"

"You saw it for yourself."

"That's not what I mean. I'm asking you point blank whether you had anything to do with it."

"*Moi*, Marcus?"

"That's what I said. *Toi*. I smell a rat's ass somewhere."

"I swear, Marc, I had no knowledge of that demonstration."

"Really? And what about your friend Diedre?"

"You'd have to ask *her*."

"She works for Mercer, doesn't she? She's the one who sent that fax to Candace. Am I right?"

"How should I know?"

"Because she's your insider at the Mercer Corporation, isn't she?"

"Not exactly. I met her there when I came to interview Dr. Chang and some of the other people."

"And why did they let you in in the first place?"

"I told you: they thought I was giving your side a lot of unfair publicity."

"You passed on some information about the Calvecchis, and maybe about Candace and me, didn't you?"

"I had to gain their confidence, Marc. But I didn't divulge anything that would hurt your case. As a matter of fact, I'm on your side in this. That's off the record, of course."

"McBain, were you here when the jury came out?"

"As a matter of fact, I was. Some of them hung around for a while, too."

"Really? What was their reaction?"

"Hard to say. They seemed puzzled, more than anything."

"You realize, don't you, that this might give St. Clair grounds for an appeal."

"You mean you're afraid you're going to win?"

"I didn't say that."

"Anyway, it might work in *your* favor . . . ."

"Maybe. Unless someone suggests that we had something to do with this."

"Did you?"

"No."

"Then what are you worried about?"

"That someone will *think* we had something to do with it."

"Maybe you should consult a lawyer about that."

"Some other time. Got work to do."

"You guys work much too hard."

"Not really. Sometimes we take Christmas off."

*

"Hello, Mario."

"Morning, Marcus, Jr. What are you doing here? You were here last week."

"Just came in for a little trim."

"Ah. You must have closing arguments today."

"Yeah, it's the Mercer case."

"Oh, the little girl. Too bad about her."

"You've been reading about it?"

"Sure! It was in the newspaper again today."

"I know. I saw it."

"Who's going to win?"

"I don't know, Mario. We've done the best we can. Anyway, we'll know pretty soon."

"Good luck on it, Marc."

"Thanks."

"How's Marcus, Sr.?"

"He's doing fine. At the moment, the cancer's completely disappeared. By the way, he thanks you for the picture of your grandson."

"Tell him the kid turned out all right."

"I'll do that."

"Tell me something, Mario. You read about the case. How would you vote if you were on the jury?"

"Well, I didn't hear all of the arguments or anything."

"Okay, but based on what you *do* know, which side would you come down on?"

"Well, I wouldn't want all the medical research stopped just because somebody died taking a new drug like that, even if it was a little girl. I think that was just bad luck."

"But what if Mercer used the wrong procedures, which somehow got approved by the FDA anyway?"

"I don't know, Marc. I'd say those doctors know a lot more about it than I do. They go to school a long time and all that. I'd probably give them the benefit of the doubt."

"I'm sorry I asked."

*

" . . . Please proceed, Mr. St. Clair."

"Thank you, your honor. Ladies and gentlemen of the jury, this trial is about the regulations affecting the production of new pharmaceutical compounds in this country, and whether all of those regulations were complied with in the case of a drug called Mercipine. And that's *all* it's about. You've heard the arguments for both sides of this case. Defense couldn't agree more with plaintiff's contention that the American people should be protected from exposure to dangerous substances regardless of how beneficial they may be to some. And they are. We all are, by a governmental agency, the United States Food and Drug Administration. That's why a company like the Mercer Pharmaceuticals Corporation pours hundreds of millions of dollars into the production and testing of any new medication for both effectiveness and safety. Anything less would be not only a dereliction of duty to the American people, but very costly to the company in the long rug. Mercer Pharmaceuticals does not take this responsibility lightly, I assure you.

"But in order to make progress in any human endeavor, there are always going to be risks involved. For every drug on the market today, and there are many thousands, a few people have been harmed in some way, and yes, some have even died, before its safety and reliability were firmly established. That's why we have clinical trials in the first place: to test the safety and effectiveness of these new compounds, many of them life-saving, before they can be mass-produced for use by the general population.

"For example, some of you may have been treated with penicillin, or one of its derivatives, at some point in your lives. This antibiotic has been a godsend for humankind. But in the beginning there were many deaths associated with the use of this medication. Patients didn't get enough to do them any good, or too much, or at the wrong times. And there were a number of allergic reactions and all the rest. It was a long time before the safest and most effective doses were found, and these are the kinds of questions that can only be answered by clinical testing. Many brave souls have given their lives for the benefit of countless others during this initial testing phase in the development of penicillin and any number of other new pharmaceutical products.

"But this isn't enough. People are not guinea pigs. They must be notified of the risks, they must understand those risks, and the decision must be up to them. In the case of a patient who is also a minor, of course, it is a decision for the parents to make. That's why there's always a release form that must be signed by the child's parent or guardian, attesting to the fact that they understand the risks involved in testing any new drug, no matter how small these risks may be. And Angela Calvecchi's father himself testified that they were warned of these risks, and knew the risks, and that they signed this document testifying to their knowledge and understanding of those risks.

"And I want to remind you all—and I can't emphasize this strongly enough—that there is no incontrovertible scientific evidence that Mercipine had anything to do with Angela Calvecchi's death, or the death of any of the other patients in the clinical study. Dr. Epstein, the coroner, and plaintiffs' own witness in this case, was unable to state what dose would be necessary to cause death, or even a headache, in these patients. I remind you that if you have a serious doubt that Mercipine caused deadly harm to Miss Calvecchi, then you must find that her death might well have been a result of other, perhaps unknown, factors, and the rest of this lawsuit becomes moot.

"So that leaves the important question of whether the Mercer Corporation violated any laws in putting its promising new medication, Mercipine, on the market for the treatment of Type I diabetes, a disease that, up to now, was incurable and, at the least, often caused serious disabilities later in life, and sometimes even death. And that's what this case really boils down to, isn't it? Whether any laws were violated. That's what this case is all about . . . ."

("What's he looking at?")

("Nothing. He's just pausing for effect.")

"Our respected colleagues, the attorneys for the plaintiffs, have tried to confuse this issue by bringing in a number of extraneous matters which are not in any way material to this case. For example, they have tried to suggest to you that Angela Calvecchi's treatment should have been stopped when she began to feel some minor ill effects, symptoms which are commonly experienced with any prescribed medicine on the market today. But they presented no evidence whatsoever that these minor symptoms were in any way related to her death. And even if they had, and they did not, it would be irrelevant to these proceedings because the Mercer Corporation complied with all the legal requirements in initiating and carrying out the necessary clinical trial for their new and promising pharmaceutical compound, Mercipine.

"And they have tried to convince you that animal tests for drug toxicity are tricky and perhaps even invalid in determining whether a particular pharmaceutical is safe for human use. But even if this were true, and it is not, it would be irrelevant to these proceedings because the Mercer Corporation complied with all the legal requirements in determining safety and effectiveness prior to initiating the necessary clinical trial for Mercipine. And none of these demonstrations you've all been witnessing inside and outside this courtroom yesterday and today, regardless of who's behind them, or who had something to gain from them, are going to change that."

("What the hell's he talking about?")

("Stay cool, partner, he's just cleared the way for an appeal!")

"Moreover, plaintiffs have tried to convince you that the federal Food and Drug Administration's requirements may be faulty or outdated. But even if that were true, and it is not, it would be irrelevant to these proceedings because the Mercer Corporation complied with all the current legal requirements established by this agency of the federal government in initiating the clinical trial for their promising new pharmaceutical compound, which might yet prove to be a godsend to diabetes sufferers."

("Sure it will.")

("Shhh.")

"And they've tried to suggest that the corporate research organization, or CRO, did a poor job of administering the clinical trial. But even if that were true, and it is not, this, too, would be irrelevant to these proceedings because the Mercer Corporation fulfilled all of *their* requirements for the clinical testing of their new and promising medication, thus fulfilling all their obligations as required by law.

"And, finally, they have tried to convince you that even though the Mercer Corporation may have complied with the letter of the law in releasing Mercipine for clinical testing, they did not comply with the 'spirit' of the law underlying these FDA regulations. And here they finally got to something relevant to these proceedings, and the only question you, the jury in this case, should be concerned with: were any laws violated, either in letter or spirit, by the Mercer Corporation in producing their new pharmaceutical to fight diabetes? I submit to you, ladies and gentlemen, that my clients not only complied with both the letter and the spirit of the law, but they did everything considered reasonable and proper, and in accordance with pharmaceutical industry standards and those of the scientific community in general, in their testing of Mercipine for safety and effectiveness. We've had witness after witness testify to this fact, witnesses who speak for the entire industry and for the United States government, and therefore, as your representatives in this matter—you, the jury—and all Americans everywhere.

"So I ask you to consider a bigger picture here. Even after hearing all the evidence in this case, there may be one or two of you who will say to yourselves, 'But this girl died. Somebody ought to pay for it.' To that I can only say, the death of Angela Calvecchi is a great tragedy, and our hearts go out to her and her family. But I beg you: don't throw out the baby with the bathwater. Don't condemn the company that produced a promising new compound for the small number of unfortunate deaths that occurred during the clinical testing procedures. If you were to do that, you would be taking a senseless and unprecedented step toward stifling medical research everywhere, and for all time. The death of Angela Calvecchi is most certainly a terrible tragedy, but it's no one's fault. Let's not shut down medical research because of one untimely, unpreventable incident which could not have been foreseen by anyone. By anyone . . . .

"The only question you, the jury, need consider here is whether the Mercer Corporation violated any of the FDA's regulations in producing the drug known as Mercipine. That's the *only* question you should be dealing with when you begin your deliberations in this case. And the answer to that question is crystal clear. Thank you very much, ladies and gentlemen."

"Thank you, Mr. St. Clair. Court stands in recess until eleven o'clock, at which time we will hear plaintiff's closing arguments."

*

"Tony, Elmira, do you have anything you want me to include in the closing arguments that you didn't have a chance to say before?"

"Tell them to remember the Nazi's experiments on human beings during World War II."

"I see your point, Elmira, but I think that bringing the Nazis into it at this point may be a little counterproductive. Candace, do you have anything to add?"

"No. I trust you."

"You two make such a wonderful couple. I hope after all this is over . . ."

"Sometimes I think it will never be over, Elmira."

*

"All rise . . . ."

"Are plaintiffs prepared to present closing arguments?"

"We are."

"Who's going to do it?"

"I am, your honor."

"Please proceed, Mr. Allen."

"Thank you. Ladies and gentlemen of the jury, this case now comes down to you. It is for you to decide whether Mr. and Mrs. Anthony Calvecchi should be compensated for the irreplaceable loss of their daughter Angela, who died unexpectedly after taking an experimental drug called Mercipine, a drug produced by the Mercer Pharmaceutical Corporation.

"You've already heard abundant testimony to the fact that Angela was a precocious young lady, a thirteen-year-old girl with an extremely bright future, a child who wanted with all her heart to become a doctor. Defense's own expert witness, Dr. Richard Mangan, her pediatrician, has testified to that fact. I'll leave it to you to decide whether Angela would have become an outstanding physician and researcher, or perhaps a hopeless drug addict, as attorneys for the defense have suggested.

"But ladies and gentlemen, plaintiffs have lost a little girl, and when it comes down to the reality of it all, it doesn't matter whether this bright young girl would have become surgeon-general or a cabaret singer, a princess or a bum. At thirteen, her future was still ahead of her, and she was more precious than jewels to her bereaved parents, as is any child to any parent. They had a right to expect better things of a company they trusted, the company that produced the drug she was taking the night she tragically died.

"Throughout these proceedings we have attempted to show, through the expert testimony of the county coroner and others, that Angela Calvecchi died as a result of taking an experimental drug called Mercipine. Defense calls this finding 'pure speculation,' and suggests that you should have 'a serious doubt' that this drug was, in fact, responsible for her untimely death. Again, we must leave it up to you, the jury, to decide whether the preponderance of evidence supports the coroner's finding, or whether the death of this young girl and at least six of the other eight people who took this drug was pure coincidence, or was, in fact, a direct result of the experimental treatment. And if you look at all the scientific evidence, and the testimony of experts like Dr. Epstein, the coroner in this case, and the other witnesses, I'm confident that you, like Mr. and Mrs. Calvecchi, will agree that there is not a shred of doubt about what killed their daughter Angela.

"But given that Mercipine is the clear culprit here, is it true that those are just the 'breaks of the game,' as Mr. St. Clair would have you believe? That there is a certain amount of risk in the clinical testing of any new, experimental drug, and that any deaths resulting from the testing of such a drug are just unavoidable blips in the data? Perhaps. And is it possible that the Mercer Corporation is the perfect drug company, incapable of mistakes in its procedures and protocols? Yes, that's possible, too. But we all know that drug companies, even gigantic ones, are made up of human beings, and human beings are capable of error. Of making mistakes. Of making terrible mistakes in judgement, no matter how many degrees they have or how benign their motivations.

"And is it possible that Mercer and company complied to the letter—crossed all their t's and dotted all their i's, as the defense has so elegantly put it—with the FDA requirements which are meant to ensure that new drugs placed on the market are safe for the general public? It's possible, yes. But the *fact* is, they did not. The *fact* is, the Mercer Corporation submitted incomplete data to the Food and Drug Administration assuring this agency that Mercipine was a safe drug for Angela and others to take, an error that another of defense's witnesses, the assistant director of the FDA, Dr. Grossman, admits would be grounds for rejecting Mercer's application for a clinical trial. The *fact* is, Mercer and company knew, or should have known, that the animal tests they used *could not* have led to a proper assessment of the safety of this drug. Why? Because the *wrong animals* were used for these tests. And therefore the results this giant corporation submitted to the FDA did not comply with the government's requirement to provide 'results necessary to assess the safety of the drug for use in clinical investigations.'

"Now, defense has argued that the FDA does not specify which animals should be used in tests to determine the safety of new drugs as long as 'one rodent and one non-rodent species' are used. Defense has tried to convince you that therefore Mercer complied with every regulation and requirement set up by the government, and so they should be free of responsibility in the death of

Angela Calvecchi and at least six others up to this point. And maybe you'll buy this argument. But before you buy it, I ask you to remember that human lives are at stake here, and that the responsibility for producing a safe drug is a large one, and that safety is the responsibility of the drug company, and not that of patients like young Angela Calvecchi or her parents. In order to comply with *the Food and Drug Administration's own requirements*, it's not enough to dot all the i's and cross all the t's. It is also an FDA requirement to provide the very best evidence that can be obtained to support the claims of the drug company that a new compound is absolutely safe for human use. *By their own admission*, Mercer and company did not do this. Additional experiments subsequent to their initial safety investigations showed that if Mercipine had originally been tested in cats or guinea pigs, the company might never not have put this unsafe drug into clinical testing, not to mention later production and marketing.

"Defense would have you believe that all this is irrelevant. That this is merely a case of 20/20 hindsight, even though the head of that division, Dr. Szybalski, *knew, or should have known*, which animals might have proven more indicative of the danger inherent in the use of their new drug in human beings. And the only hindsight here is in seeing very clearly that a terrible mistake was made, one that the Mercer Corporation appears to be blind to.

"Ladies and gentlemen of the jury, we leave it to you to decide whether the Mercer Corporation answered all the FDA requirements and fulfilled their obligation to Angela Calvecchi and to all the rest of us. We leave it to you to decide whether Mercer Pharmaceuticals could have done more to ensure the safety of Mercipine before it was allowed into the clinical trial. We leave it to you to decide whether the Mercer Corporation cut corners in order to get their expensive, though potentially very lucrative, new drug on the market as soon as possible, without being absolutely certain that it was safe for use in human beings.

"And there's one final consideration. And it's an important consideration. Don't be fooled by defense counsel's contention that a finding in favor of Mr. and Mrs. Calvecchi would permanently harm, or even shut down, the medical establishment. Of course it won't! It will merely slap the wrist of one giant corporation for an egregious mistake, and perhaps encourage it to be a little more careful before placing poorly-tested drugs into clinical testing for the next Angela Calvecchi to swallow. By finding for plaintiffs you would, in fact, be doing a great service not only to everyone who depends upon their medications for their well-being, or even their survival, but, in the long run, to the medical community itself, which is harmed just as much as are we by faulty practices and procedures over which they have little or no control.

"Ladies and gentlemen, you are the jury. In a very real sense you are also the judges in this case. Plaintiffs ask you to do no more, and certainly no less, than to judge this case on its merits, and if you do that, Mr. and Mrs. Calvecchi are confident that you find Mercer and company liable in the death of their brilliant young daughter, Angela. For them, and for all of us, I thank you."

"Thank you, Mr. Allen. Members of the jury, this concludes the attorneys' presentations. We'll break for lunch and when we reconvene I will give you some instructions to guide your deliberations in the case of Calvecchi v. the Mercer Pharmaceutical Corporation. Court stands adjourned until two o'clock this afternoon."

*

"I looked right into Mrs. W's eyes and I think she nodded slightly and winked back at me!"

"Well, that's one vote! Hi, Elmira. Tony."

"Marc, Candace, can we take you to lunch? To thank you for everything you've done for us?"

"Well, Tony, we haven't really done anything yet. Whoever loses the case will undoubtedly want to appeal the decision. We've still got a long way to go, and it will probably take a long time before it's finally resolved. And there's no guarantee we'll come out on top, even if it goes all the way to the Supreme Court. Besides, I've got some phone calls I've got to make before we reconvene. But to answer your question, I'd love to go to lunch with you. How about if I meet you all somewhere in about fifteen minutes?"

"This is what happens to lawyers, folks: once they get going, it's hard to shut them up."

"How about 'The Blue Teacup?'"

"That sounds good, Elmira. Order something for me—I'll see you there in ten or fifteen minutes."

"Don't count on it, folks."

*

"Mom? Hi, it's me.... Marc, Mom! Hey, I found a message from Tim last night on my answering machine, but I couldn't make it out. Something about coming over to see me or Dad about something today. Is he around?... Okay, tell him I'll call him tonight or tomorrow, will you?... Now, don't start, Mom.... I know, I know. 'Bye—.... Yes, I know. 'Bye, Mom."

*

"Ladies and gentlemen of the jury, you've heard the case of Calvecchi v. the Mercer Pharmaceutical Corporation as presented by attorneys for the plaintiffs and for the defense. You've heard a great deal of testimony from the principals involved, as well as from expert witnesses in the areas of drug production, testing, and clinical trials of new pharmaceutical compounds, or 'drugs.' For the purposes of this hearing I caution you to remember that there is no stigma attached to the word 'drug,' which is synonymous here with 'medication' or 'pharmaceutical compound.' All those terms refer to the same thing."

("Thanks a *lot*, judge.")

"The Mercer Corporation is a legitimate drug manufacturing company. No one here disputes that. What is at issue in these proceedings is whether this corporation violated its obligation to produce, to the best of its ability, and in accordance with the laws of the land, a safe and effective product when it released a new diabetes medication called Mercipine for use in a clinical trial situation. In short, whether the company complied with the requirements established by the federal Food and Drug Administration in producing and testing this pharmaceutical compound."

("Thanks *again*.")

"I caution you also that this governmental agency, also called the FDA, is not on trial here. In other words, you are not to concern yourselves with whether their rules and regulations are adequate or inadequate to ensure the safety of Mercipine, or any other drug, but whether Mercer, in fact, followed these regulations and fully complied with the requirements laid down by this agency.

"Some of the witnesses were asked to read a portion of those regulations. At this time I'd like to re-read the part that applies to this case: 'The investigator shall submit all reports of basic information, certified by the applicant to be accurate reports, necessary to assess the safety of the drug for use in clinical investigation.'

"The question for this jury to decide is whether Mercer Pharmaceuticals complied with those requirements, in accordance with the law. No one questions whether the Mercer Corporation, and the corporate research organization that administered the clinical trial, submitted accurate and timely reports. The question before you is this: did Mercer's reports provide all the basic information 'necessary to assess the safety of the drug' before putting it into its clinical trial?"

("Now you're talking, judge!")

"Evidence was presented by the plaintiffs that there might have been better subjects for testing the safety of the compound called Mercipine than those used by the Mercer Corporation. Defense argues that this is irrelevant and, in any case, those tests are as yet incomplete. It is for you, ladies and gentlemen of the jury, to decide whether the Mercer Pharmaceutical Corporation knew, or should have known, that the animals they used for these tests were perhaps not adequate for the task."

("Yes!")

"However, I caution you that it is not your duty as civil jurors in this case to rewrite the laws of the land. That is the duty of the legislative branch of the government, not the juries or the courts. Your duty is to determine whether current laws have been violated in this instance. Nothing more and nothing less.

"And if, after reviewing the FDA regulations, and in considering all the evidence presented in this court, you feel that the Mercer Corporation complied with these governmental rules and regulations, even if you believe some of these regulations to be outdated or faulty, you must find in favor of the defendant. If, on the other hand, you believe that the company did not expressly comply with the letter of these regulations in some material way, you should find in favor of the plaintiffs.

"In a few minutes I will excuse you to begin your deliberations in this case. Exactly how you conduct these deliberations is a matter for you to decide among yourselves. If you have any questions at all about what you've heard during the many hours of testimony, you may write those questions on a slip of paper and hand them to the jury officer, who will forward them to the court for a reply. Or if there is anything that would prevent you from reaching a fair and just conclusion in this case, you should bring this to the attention of the court as well.

"Now about the disruption we had yesterday. I caution you to make no judgement whatsoever about who was responsible for that unfortunate demonstration. It is irrelevant to these proceedings and must have no bearing whatever on your deliberations or your verdict in any way, shape, or form.

"And one final word: The burden of proof in this case rests solely with the plaintiffs. In order to find for plaintiffs you must conclude that there is a reasonable degree of certainty that the drug known as Mercipine caused the death of plaintiffs' daughter, and that the Mercer Corporation knew, or should have known, that they were not following the safety requirements set down by the Food and Drug Administration in the production of this new medication. On the other hand, if you feel there is a reasonable doubt either that the drug was instrumental in causing the death of Angela Calvecchi, or that the Mercer Corporation was negligent in assuring its safety, then you must find for the defendant in this case.

"I remind you also that if you believe that counsel for plaintiffs have made their case, you do not need to reach a unanimous verdict. Two of you may cast a dissenting vote. However, if three or more of you cast a vote against the plaintiffs, your verdict will go in favor of the defendant.

"Whatever your decision, until a verdict is reached I urge you to keep an open mind and to listen carefully to all the discussions that will take place among you as your deliberations progress. That's why we *have* a jury system. Some of you may have heard or understood things that others have missed or heard differently. So listen carefully to one another's point of view. But when all the deliberations are over and it's time to reach a verdict, I expect you to vote your conscience and your understanding of the law in this case regardless of how others may vote.

"Good luck with your deliberations. You've been an attentive jury, and the court thanks you for that and for doing your civic duty in a conscientious manner."

("And thank *you*, your honor.")

The Verdict

"Hi, old fuzzer, how you doin'? Huh? How are you doing? Guess what? We finished the case today! You know what that means, don't you? Yep. I'm going to call out for a pizza and just stay home with you tonight. We'll watch TV together or something. Okay? Yeah, I thought you'd be pleased. So! Want your dinner, Fuzz? Oh, you *do* want your dinner. I thought you might! All right—oh, oh. Just a minute, old girl. Just a minute . . . . Hello? . . . Oh, hi Dad, how are— . . . Oh, no . . . oh, God . . . . What happened? Where was he? . . . Oh, God. Is Mom all right? . . . Yes, I can imagine. I can't believe it . . . . he's where? . . . Yes, I know where St. Luke's is. Is Mom there now? . . . Okay, Dad, I'll see you there in half an hour."

"Oh, Fuzzy . . ."

"Rrrrrrrrrrrrrrrrrrr."

*

"Next? Oh, hi, Mr. Allen. Red or yellow?"

"Everything. I need to fill a hospital room with flowers. Roses, carnations, everything you've got."

"Are they for your dad?"

"No. My little brother."

"Oh, I'm sorry, Mr. Allen. What happened?"

"He was riding his bike over to see Dad yesterday afternoon, and got hit by a truck."

"Oh, God. Is he okay?"

"Not okay, no. He's in a coma."

"I'm so sorry! I mean—Is he going to—"

"We don't know yet."

217

"Look, I'll tell you what. You just leave it up to me, will you? You won't be disappointed."

"Thanks. I think I'll do that. Just put it on my bill."

"No charge, Mr. Allen."

"Oh, c'mon—"

"Please. It may be my one chance to make up for all the business you've given me, and for everything your dad did, too. Please—let me do this."

"Well . . ."

"I insist!"

"All right. And thanks."

"No. Thank *you*. But do me one favor."

"What's that?"

"Don't tell your dad I'm doing this. That's the way he would do it, if it were him. And I hope your brother recovers real soon from all this."

"Right now they're not sure he's ever going to come out of the coma. But I guess they're doing everything they can."

"I'll send him a big bunch of roses every single day while he's in the hospital. All colors!"

"Thank you, uh—"

"Roger."

*

"Hi, Mom."

"*Now* you show up."

"Mom, I don't know what to say. I just wish—"

"Don't say anything. Just leave."

"Aw, Mom . . . ."

"Please."

*

"Oh, Marc, I'm so sorry."

"Thank you, Candace."

"How's your mother doing?"

"Not too well."

"I'm sorry. And your dad?"

"He's doing okay, considering. Of course he'll never forgive himself. Now he says he's sorry he didn't die."

"I hope that changes. It's not his fault your brother was riding his bike over to see him."

"Yeah. Everybody says it's nobody's fault. But it's *somebody's* fault! Mine as much as anyone's."

"Marc, it was an accident."

"Yeah, but maybe it wouldn't have happened if I had made one little phone call."

"Or maybe it would have."

"Maybe. Well, I'm going over to the hospital. I'll see you later at the office."

"Oh-oh. The jury's about to come in. Do you want to wait around for that, or do you want me to call you?"

"I'll wait to see if there's a verdict."

"I've got some good news and some bad news for you if you feel like talking about it."

"I would be happy to hear some good news, believe me."

"I just saw McBain, the reporter? He says there have been another couple of deaths attributed to Mercipine."

"That's the good news?"

"No, that's the bad news. The good news is, Mercer has stopped the clinical trial."

"Well, I guess that's a victory of sorts."

"But that's not all! A House subcommittee is going to hold hearings on the FDA regulations. Starting next month."

"Is that just a coincidence, or what?"

"McBain thinks it's all the letters people have written to their Congressmen. Angela Calvecchi's death just won't go away in the media."

"Well, maybe some good will come of all this even if we lose the case."

"There's the bailiff. Let's go in."

*

"Mister foreman, have you reached a verdict?"

"Yes, your honor, we have."

"And was the verdict unanimous?"

"No, your honor. There were two dissenting votes."

"And what is the verdict of the majority?"

"Your honor, we find in favor of the defense, the Mercer Corporation."

"Thank you, sir, and thanks to all the other jurors for doing their civic duty in a fair and impartial manner. The court also thanks the attorneys for both sides for their decorous behavior during this hearing. This concludes the case of Calvecchi v. Mercer Pharmaceuticals. No damages will be awarded to plaintiffs. Court stands adjourned."

"Well, that's that. I'm sorry, Marc."

"Not your fault, partner. You did a good job. I'm glad the Calvecchis weren't here to see this. Will you call them?"

"Of course. But—"

"Candace, I've got to go. But before I do, I have to know something. Maybe this is a bad time, but—"

"What is it, Marc?"

"How long do you have?"

"What do you mean?"

"Do I have to spell it out? How much time do you have left on Earth?"

"What a strange question. *I* can't answer that."

"Please don't be coy with me. Lew told me you were dying."

"Uncle Lew told you that?"

"Lew is your *uncle*?"

"He's my mother's brother. Didn't you know that?"

"No, I didn't."

"He told you I was dying?"

"Yes."

"Why?"

"That's what *I'd* like to know."

"When did he say this?"

"The morning after you had dinner with him."

"Oh. Now I remember. I told him that you were being—uh—persistent."

"So?"

"Well, he knows I've had some problems. I guess he was trying to protect me."

"So you're not dying?"

"Not right away, I hope. There was a time when I wouldn't have cared. But now, thanks to you and the Mercer case, I'm—well, let's just say I'm glad Lew wasn't telling the truth."

"I have mixed feelings about that."

"What's *that* supposed to mean??"

"I'm glad you're going to be around for a while. But I'm mad as hell at Lew."

"Why? For lying to you?"

"Of course!"

"What can I tell you? He's a lawyer!"

"I've got to go."

"May I come with you?"

"To the hospital?"

"Yes. Maybe I can help in some way."

"I sure hope so."

*

"Tony? How are you? . . . Fine, I guess. I was about to call you and go over the options on the appeal. But I just got a message from Eddie St. Clair—remember him? . . . That's right. Well, he wants me to come over tomorrow morning and discuss something with him. I just thought you ought to know . . . . I don't know. He didn't say. Maybe he's going to try to talk us out of an appeal or the class-action lawsuit. I just wanted to let you know, and to find out whether you still want to go ahead with the appeal . . . . Good. Good. I couldn't agree more. Anyway, I'll be seeing him in the morning and I'll let you know later what he has on his mind . . . . Thanks, Tony, and thanks for coming to the hospital to see Tim . . . . Well, I appreciate it, and so did Mom and Dad . . . . Oh, all right, sure . . . . Hi, Elmira . . . . Yes, it was tragic. He was thirteen . . . . No, it's not fair, is it? . . . Thank you, Elmira. She's doing okay, considering the circumstances. I'll tell her you asked . . . . Thank you . . . . We'll do that . . . . Okay . . . . Hi again, Tony. Yes, we did find out. We got Mr. Zedick and Mr. Steiner . . . . No, we lost her . . . . Yeah, I know. Thanks, Tony . . . . I will. Speak to you soon . . . ."

*

"Hi, Mr. Allen!"
"Hello, Goose—how are you?"
"Fine and dandy! The usual?"
"No, let's do something different this time. An apple danish and a cup of that cinnamon coffee!"
"You got 'er, Mr. Allen! I'm awful sorry about your brother!"
"Thanks, Goose. So am I."
"Yes, sir! How's your dad taking it?"
"Not too well."
"You tell him how sorry I am, will you, Mr. Allen?"
"I'll do that."
"How's your dad doing? You know—with the other thing?"
"I think he's going to be okay. They've stopped the chemotherapy—there's no sign of the cancer at all!"
"That's great, Mr. Allen! You tell him I said hello, will you?"
"Tell him yourself. He's coming back to work part-time on Monday."
[HONK! HOOOOOOOOONK!]
"He is? That's great! I hope he stops over to say hello sometime!"
"I'm sure he will, Goose!"
"I've still got some fat-free! A lot of people seem to want it!"

"He'll appreciate that."

"Well, you take care, Mr. Allen! Good to see you again!"

"Thanks, Goose. You, too!"

"I'm sorry that case turned out the way it did!"

"Me, too, Goose. But it's not over yet!"

"That's the way to talk, Mr. Allen! That's exactly what your dad would say!"

"Thanks, Goose. I consider that a compliment."

"It was meant to be!"

"Got to run."

"He'd say *that*, too!"

*

"Hello, Eddie."

"Howdy, Marcus. Ms. White. How are y'all?"

"Fine as froghair, Eddie. God, this *is* an enormous cave of an office, isn't it?"

"Big enough for me, anyhow. Look at those clouds—it's gonna rain like a cow a-pissin'."

"Is that what you called us over here to discuss?"

"Now don't be so impatient, Marc, Jr. I'm coming to that. But first, I sure was sorry to hear about your little brother."

"Thanks, Eddie."

"Your mom doin' okay?"

"I guess so. Dad and I are having dinner with her tonight. I think they may be getting back together."

"Well, maybe something good will come of all this."

"I suppose that's one way of looking at it."

"And I hear your pappy is coming back to the firm. That so?"

"Yep. On a part-time basis, of course."

"Good. Good. You keep him out of mischief, you hear?"

"I'll try."

"Okay, then. I called you over to find out if you're still planning to go ahead and appeal in the case of Calvecchi/Mercer."

"Yes, we are."

"I thought you might. And I thought it might be time to put an end to this here thing and discuss a possible settlement."

"We're listening."

"What do you say to a nice, round, five million?"

"I was thinking more in terms of the original seven point five."

"Five big 'uns should help you to recoup your losses, son. Get your senior pardners off'n your back."

"Actually, Bill and Lew are quite pleased with our work on the case, Ed. Thanks to the favorable publicity, we've got some hefty new clients already lined up."

"So I heard, son, so I heard. All righty then, what do you say to a compromise? Say—oh—six big ones?"

"Sorry, Eddie. Candace, shall we go?"

"All this because of those damned animal rights people. Okay, so I lost my head. Where are all of them comin' from? My own d-daughter is a goddamn b-b-b-bunnyhugger, can you believe it? All right, God d-damn it! You can have your s-s-seven, but we keep the non-d-d-d—non-disclosure clause."

"Let's go, partner. I've got a couple of appoint—"

"Okay! Okay! You little sh-sh-sh-shit, I knew you when you were still p-pissin' your fuckin' p-p-pants. I'll draw up the goddamn p-papers. You'll have 'em in the morning. And tell your old d-d-d-d-your old man that he'll never die as long as you're s-s-still alive."

"Thanks, Ed. He'll be very glad to hear that."

*

"Any loose change, sir? Oh, it's you. You've still got a couple of weeks left on that ten, haven't you?"

"Changed my mind. I need a good laugh. Tell me a joke."

"You asked for it. Well, Tiger Woods was playing golf with this lawyer, see, and . . ."

The Preliminaries

"Mr. Nolan?"

"That's right."

"C'mon in. How are you?"

"Okay, I guess."

"That's good. Coffee or something?"

"No, thanks."

"Now, what can I do for you?"

"My wife and about fifteen other people were gunned down by some crazy bastard with an assault rifle."

"I heard about that. I'm very sorry."

"Thank you. So am I."

"So you want to sue the gun manufacturer?"

"No. I want to go after the guy who did it. I want to sue him for having a gun to do this with."

"Well, in the first place, that's a criminal matter. Unless—"

"I want to sue him in civil court. No one should be carrying guns around in their car, assault rifles or anything else."

"If you're talking about better gun control laws, you should call your Congressman."

"I'm not talking about gun control laws. I'm talking about doing away with guns altogether."

"That's a very difficult proposition. You're talking about a possible violation of the man's second amendment rights, even if he killed people with those rights."

"That's what I want to do. To test the second amendment."

"No one has ever formally done that, as far as I know."

"Then it's about time someone did, isn't it?"

"Well, I'll have to talk about it with my wife, who's my partner here. And my dad, who helps us part-time. But it might be very costly."

"How costly?"

"Well, *if* we decide to take the case, we could do it either on a fee basis or a percentage arrangement."

"What's your fee?"

"Two seventy-five an hour."

"I'll take the percentage arrangement . . . ."

Acknowledgments

I am extremely grateful to Stephan H. Peskin, Esq., member of the New York, Pennsylvania, and District of Columbia bars, for his generous advice on a vast number of legal matters; to Philip Mossman, M.D., for excellent advice on a variety of medical issues; and to Dr. Ray Greek, co-author of *Specious Science* (Continuum, New York, 2002), for valuable information regarding animal testing of new drugs for human use.

visit the author at www.genebrewer.com

Afterword

If you believe, as I do, that the lives of human beings, as well as billions of experimental animals, are more important than maintaining an outdated and scientifically indefensible drug testing system, please write fax, call, or e-mail your senators and congressional representative and ask them to initiate hearings on the testing of new drugs for safety and effectiveness.

> Write to: Hon. _____
> United States Senate
> Washington, DC 20510
>
> Hon. _____
> U.S. House of Representatives
> Washington, DC 20515

Or call: 202-224-3121

Obtain congressional fax numbers at 800-688-9889, and e-mail addresses at congress@hr.house.gov

Write to the president and vice-president at:

> The White House
> 1600 Pennsylvania Ave.
> Washington, DC 20500
> or e-mail:
> president@whitehouse.gov
> or
> vice.president@whitehouse.gov

Your call or letter should mention the loss of valuable new medications that have been discarded because of their negative effects on non-human animals, as well as the tragic history of the many unsafe drugs that have been placed on the market after animal testing. You might also point out the enormous waste of taxpayer dollars resulting from the use of faulty science in the development of new pharmaceuticals for human use.

Gene Brewer
April, 2006